CH

Also by Ellen Hopkins

RUMBLE

Ellen Hopkins

Margaret K. McElderry Books

NEW YORK LONDON TORONTO SYDNEY NEW DELHI

MARGARET K. McELDERRY BOOKS • An imprint of Simon & Schuster Children's Publishing Division • 1230 Avenue of the Americas, New York, New York 10020 • This book is a work of fiction. Any references to historical events, real people, or real places are used fictitiously. Other names, characters, places, and events are products of the author's imagination, and any resemblance to actual events or places or persons, living or dead, is entirely coincidental. • Text copyright © 2014 by Ellen Hopkins • Jacket illustration copyright © 2014 by Sammy Yuen Jr. • All rights reserved, including the right of reproduction in whole or in part in any form. • MARGARET K. McELDERRY BOOKS is a trademark of Simon & Schuster, Inc. • For information about special discounts for bulk purchases, please contact Simon & Schuster Special Sales at 1-866-506-1949 or business@simonandschuster.com. • The Simon & Schuster Speakers Bureau can bring authors to your live event. For more information or to book an event, contact the Simon & Schuster Speakers Bureau at 1-866-248-3049 or visit our website at www.simonspeakers.com. • Interior design by Mike Rosamilia • Jacket design by Sammy Yuen Jr. • Book edited by Emma D. Dryden • The text for this book is set in Chaparral Pro and Trade Gothic Condensed No. 18. • Manufactured in the United States of America • 10 9 8 7 6 5 4 3 2 1 • Library of Congress Cataloging-in-Publication Data • Hopkins, Ellen. • Rumble / Ellen Hopkins. • p. cm. • Summary: Eighteen-year-old Matt's atheism is tested when, after a horrific accident of his own making that plunges him into a dark, quiet place, he hears a voice that calls everything he has ever disbelieved into question. • ISBN 978-1-4424-8284-5 (hardcover) • ISBN 978-1-4424-8286-9 (eBook) • [1. Novels in verse. 2. Atheism—Fiction. 3. Family problems—Fiction. 4. Dating (Social customs)—Fiction. 5. High schools—Fiction. 6. Schools—Fiction. 7. Grief—Fiction.] I. Title. • PZ7.5.H67Rum 2014 • [Fic]—dc23 • 2013037681

FIRST
EDITION

This book is dedicated to the far-too-many young people
who ended their lives because they couldn't see beyond the pain
of the present to the joy waiting for them in the future.
Also to those who loved them then, and still love them now.

Acknowledgments

As always, I must thank my family for putting up with my author quirkiness, absences, and sequestrations; my posse for supporting me in times of doubt; my editor, Emma Dryden, for her insight, talent, and friendship; my agent, Laura Rennert, for fielding questions and concerns, sometimes at odd times of the day; and my team at Simon & Schuster, who, start to finish, help me create the very best books possible and put them into my readers' hands.

With special thanks to those who were willing to share their thoughts about God, science, belief, nonbelief, and possibilities—most memorably, Susan Patron and Topher King, whose insights were especially valuable.

In the Narrow Pewter Space

Between the gray of consciousness
and the obsidian where dreams
ebb and flow, there is a wishbone
window. And trapped in its glass,
a single silver shard of enlightenment.

It is this mystics search for. The truth
of the Holy Grail. It is this believers
pray for. The spark, alpha and omega.
It is this the gilded claim to hold
in the cups of their hands. But what

of those who plunge into slumber,
who snap from sleep's embrace?
What of those who measure their
tomorrows with finite numbers, cross
them off their calendars one by

one? Some say death is a doorway,
belief the key. Others claim you only
have to stumble across the threshold
to glimpse a hundred billion universes
in the blink of single silver shard.

Have Faith

That's what people keep telling me.
Faith that things will get better. Faith
that bad things happen for a reason.
Implicit in that ridiculous statement
is the hand of some extraterrestrial
magician. Some all-powerful creator,

which, if his faithful want to be totally
frank about it, would also make him/her/it
an omnipotent destroyer. Because if
some God carefully sows each seed
of life, he is also flint for the relentless
sun beating down upon his crops until

they wither into dust. Zygotes to ashes
or some other poignant phrase. And why
would any of that make someone feel
better about snuffing out? The end
result is the same. You get a few
years on this sad, devolving planet.

If you're lucky, you experience love,
someone or two or three to gentle
your time, fill the hollow spaces.
If you're really fortunate, the good
outweighs the bad. In my eighteen years
all I've seen is shit tipping the scales.

Case in Point

I've been abruptly summoned to
the front of the classroom at the urgent
request of my English teacher, the oh-so-
disturbed, Savannah-belle-wannabe
Ms. Hannity, emphasis on the Mizz.
She pretends sympathy, for what,
I've no clue, and like she gives half

> a damn about anything but clinging,
> ironfisted, to her job. *Mr. Turnahhhh.*
> Fake "South" taints her voice and
> her eyes—no doubt she'd describe
> them as "cornflower"—are wide
> with mock concern. *Would you*
> *please come he-ah for a minute?*

I think she thinks she's whispering,
but twenty-seven pairs of eyes home
in on me. I straight-on laser every one
until they drop like dead fly duos.
"Yes, ma'am?" The feigned respect
isn't lost on her, and she doesn't bother

> to lower her voice. *Mistah Carpentah*
> *wishes a word with you. Please see*
> *him now. And the rest of y'all, get back*
> *to work. This doesn't concern you.*

Why, Then

Did she make it exactly everyone's
concern? The ends of my fingers tingle
and my jaw keeps working itself
forward. Backward. Forward. I force
it sideways and audibly, painfully, it pops.

For some messed-up reason she smiles
at that. I really want to slap that stinking
grin off her face. But then I'd get expelled,
and that would humiliate my father,
everyone's favorite science teacher, not to

mention the coach of the best basketball
team this school has seen in a dozen years.
Then Mom would bitch at him for not kicking
my ass and at me for turning him into such a wuss,
until I had no choice but to flee from our miserable

termite-ridden shack. And I'd have to live in
my fume-sucking truck, eating pilfered ramen,
drinking Mosby Creek water until I got the runs
so bad I'd wind up in the ER, hoping Dad
hadn't had time to dump me from his insurance.

And, despite all that, Mizz nose-up-my-ass
Hannity would still be a rip-roaring bitch.

As I Wind Up

That extended interior monologue,
I notice everyone is once again staring at me,
waiting for some overt exterior reaction.

Expecting, I'm sure, one of my infamous
blowups. More fun to keep 'em guessing.
"Can you tell me why he wants to see me?

Have I done something I'm not aware of?"
I'm pulling off As in every class. Maintaining
the pretense that all is well, despite everything

          being completely messed up. It would be nice
          to have some idea of what I'm walking into.
          But Hannity gives nothing away. *Just go.*

Don't flip her off. Don't flip her off. Don't . . .
I flip her off mentally, sharp turn on one heel,
head toward the door. Laser. Laser. Laser.

Pairs of dead flies drop as I pass, anger obviously
obvious in the death beam of my eyes. What now?
All I want is to be left alone. All I want

is to cruise in radar-free space. Scratch that.
What I really want is to disappear. Except,
if this in-your-face place is all I'll ever

get to experience, I'm not quite finished
here. "Live large, go out with a huge bang,"
that's my motto. Too bad so many minuscule

moments make up the biggest part of every
day. Moments like these. A familiar curtain
of fury threatens to drop and smother me.

I push it away with a smile, hope no one
takes a candid photo right now, because
I'm as certain as I can be that I resemble

some serial killer. Tall. Good-looking.
The boy next door, with near-zero affect.
Totally fine by me. Keep 'em guessing.

I swear, I can hear the collective breath-
holding, all those goddamn flies hovering
silently at my back. I plaster a grin. Spin.

"Boo!" Audible gasps. Yes! Okay, screw it.
I flip off the lot of them, dig down deep
for something resembling courage, and skip

from the room, a not-close-to-good-enough
tribute to my little brother, Luke, deceased
now one hundred sixty-eight days. Exactly.

A Tribute

So why do I stop just beyond
the door, assess the scene . . .
what am I waiting for? A sign?
The hallway is vacant. Silent.
No one to bear witness to . . .
what? Some ill-conceived
testimony? "Fuck you, Luke."

Another pointless statement,
echoing. Echoing. Echoing
down the corridor. Luke. Luke.
Luke. You selfish little prick.
My eyes burn. No, damn it!

If the vultures see me cry,
they'll swoop in, try to finish
me off. And I'm just so tired
of fighting, they might actually
manage it this time. Screw that.
They already got my brother.
It will be a cold day in hell
before I give up, give in, allow
them to claim another victory.

I'm Not Quite

To Mr. Carpenter's office when the bell
rings. Okay, technically it's a blare, not
a bell. Some new-wave administrator
decided to replace the old *buuurrrriing*

with a blast of music so we don't feel
so much like we're in school, despite
the off-white cement walls and even
offer-white linoleum, lined with

not-quite-khaki lockers. Doors slam
open and out spills noise. Lots of it.
Laughter and curses and screeches
echoing down the corridor. I scan

the crowd, as I always do, hoping
for even just a glimpse of her. There,
on the far side of the counselors' offices.
She's hard to miss, my amazing girl—

a whole head taller than her pack
of loser friends, with perfect slender curves
and thick ropes of honey-colored hair.
"Hayden!" I yell, though it's impossible

to hear in this obnoxious swell. Yet
she turns, and when those suede chocolate
eyes settle on me, her diamond smile lifts
my mood. She gestures for me to come there.

I shake my head, tip it in the direction
of the counseling offices. Even from here,
I can see the way concern crinkles her eyes
at the edges. I shrug a silent, "No worries."

That's one thing I love about Hayden—how
we can communicate without words. It's not
the only thing I love about her, or even close
to the most important. But it's really special,

sort of like Heath bar sprinkles over the vanilla
cream cheese frosting on top of the very rich
red velvet cupcake. Ultra extra deliciousness.
Sometimes it's hard to believe she's mine.

But knowing that—trusting it—helps
me tilt my chin upward, straighten
my shoulders, and put one foot in front
of the other, toward Mr. Carpenter's lair.

As Is Usual

Whenever you're called, posthaste,
to the counselor's office, it becomes
a game of *Hurry Up and Wait.* I sit
on a hard plastic chair, pretty much
the color of a rotting pumpkin, just
outside the inner sanctum. Not a whole

lot to do but try and discern words
in the muffled exchange behind
the closed fiberglass door. This
school is barely ten years old and
the builders had some new tricks
up their sleeves—things that might

thwart punches, kicks, and other
assaults that damage painted wood.
Eventually, the door clicks open,
and Alexa Clarke emerges, thin
tracks of mascara trailing down her
cheeks. Guess it didn't go so well.

Hayden and Alexa used to be best
friends, until Alexa veered off
the straight and narrow, or whatever.
Personally, I have no problem with
detours. "Hey, Lex." I grin. "Thanks
for warming Carpenter up for me."

The Defiance

So obvious only seconds ago melts
from her eyes, and she manages a smile.

> *Warm. Yeah, right. But it's all good.*
> *He's only on you 'cause he cares.*

"I'll remember that." I've barely spit
the words from my mouth when

> Mr. Carpenter's hulking form appears
> in the doorway. *Come on in, Mr. Turner.*

"So formal? I thought we were on
a first-name basis." I pretend hurt,

> and he pretends to be hard of hearing.
> *Please go on back to class, Miss Clarke.*

Alexa and I do a mutual eye roll
thing and as she leaves I call, "Always

important to understand motives.
Thanks for letting me know he cares."

Without turning around, she flips a hand
up over her shoulder. To slaughter I will go.

Hi-Ho-the-Merry-O

That's what I'm humming as I take
the seat on the far side of Carpenter's
desk. He looks at me like I've lost
my mind, or lost it even worse than
he figured I'd lost it, or whatever.

I could ask what's up, I guess. But this
is his party. It's up to him to kick it off.

> *I suppose you're wondering why*
> *you're here.* He looks at me like

I really should know. But I seriously
don't. "Uh, yeah. I mean, I hear I have
a twin, and people see him smoking
sometimes. Personally, cancer scares
the crap out of me, and—"

> His head rocks side to side. *Don't mess*
> *with me, Mr. Turner. This isn't funny.*

Damn. He really looks concerned.
"Mr. Carpenter, my grades are jake,
I'm not abusing drugs, I don't beat
my girlfriend. I have absolutely no
idea why I'm here. Please enlighten me."

The Weight of His Sigh

Could crush an elephant.
I mean, really, what could
I have done to rate that?

He moves a folder from atop
a stack of papers, pushes a thin
sheaf across his desk. Oh. Duh.

> *Ms. Hannity thought maybe this*
> *was worthy of some discussion.*

It's my senior essay: *Take*
Your God and Shove It.
I thought the title was a nice

play on words. "I'm sorry, but
what, exactly, is the problem?
Looks like she gave me an A."

> *It's not the grade, obviously. But*
> *the content raises a red flag or two.*

My first reaction is a wholly
inappropriate snort, courtesy
of the picture that popped up

in my head—paragraph two,
page four, hit the last word and
"Taps" plays as a scarlet banner

lifts off the page. But as that vision
fades, and I consider why I wrote
what I did, every crumb of humor

disappears, smashed into powder
by a huge fist of anger. Adrenaline
thumps in the veins at my temples.

I summon every ounce of will.
Detonating will accomplish
exactly nothing. "I'm afraid

you'll have to be a little more
specific, Mr. [*Carpentah*] uh,
Carpenter. What worries you?"

He clears his throat. *Let's start
with your thesis statement. . . .*

Which Would Be

There is no God, no benevolent ruler of the earth, no omnipotent Grand Poobah of countless universes. Because if there was, there would be no warring or genocide in his name; those created "in his image" would be born enlightened, no genuflecting or tithing required; and my little brother would still be fishing or playing basketball instead of fertilizing cemetery vegetation. And since there is no God, this nonentity has no place in government or education and certainly not in constitutional law. The separation of church and state must remain sacrosanct.

No bonus points for using the word
sacrosanct? "I'm sorry, but was I not
clear enough? Or was it the 'Grand Poobah'
thing? Because if that's offensive,
I don't mind changing it. Although—"

That's enough. You know, Matthew,
some people might find your biting
sarcasm humorous. But I have to
wonder what lies beneath it. Tell me.
Just what are you trying to hide?

Fucking Great

The last thing I need is more therapy
courtesy of some armchair shrink.
"Surely the school district isn't paying
you to attempt psychoanalysis?"
I summon my best pretend smile.

> His shoulders stiffen like drying
> concrete. *Ahem. See . . . uh . . .*
> *Ms. Hannity thinks I should*
> *mention our concerns to your par—*

"You mean Mizzzzz Hannity, right?"
I interrupt. A change of subject
matter is probably wise. "You know,
if you've got nothing more important
to worry about than my essay,

maybe you don't have enough to do.
So, here's what I think. You should
petition the Lane County School
District to verify the authenticity
of Ms. Hannity's birth certificate."

> Consternated. That's the only way
> to describe the look on his face.
> *Wha—wha—what do you mean?*

"Well, it's obviously fictitious,
don't you think? Jeez, man, my brother
talked me into watching *Gone
with the Wind* once and Mizz Hannity
is sooooo not Scarlett O'Hara."

His jaw literally drops, exposing
a mouth full of fillings. Old silver
mercury-laden ones. When I stare,
he snaps his mouth closed. *Shut up.
I mean it. This is really not funny.*

"Okay. Look, I'm sorry. Didn't
mean to offend you, let alone
question the veracity of Ms. Hannity's
Southernness. I just think this is all
much ado about nothing, to quote

the Bard. An essay should express
an opinion, correct? My opinion is that
it's inappropriate to allow religion—any
religion—to influence the laws that
govern this country. That's a valid

viewpoint, right? And even if it's not
somehow, it's mine, and I'm allowed
to hold it, not to mention argue it."

He Tries Another Tack

I watch as his whole demeanor softens,
like gelatin on a hot plate. *Matthew,
the truth is, I'm worried about you.
I'm not sure you've really processed
Luke's death. It's been almost six months.
Don't you think it's time to move on?*

That fist of pissed again, only this time
it smashes me square in the face.
"Dude, I *have* fucking moved on.
I don't call him to dinner anymore.
I don't think I hear him coming in
the back door. I hardly ever dream

about how he looked when . . .
when I found him. But if you mean
I should accept what happened,
you're out of your mind!" Winded,
I catch a breath, realize I've been
yelling, lower my voice. "I never will."

Mr. Carpenter studies my face, and
what he finds there—truth, that's all
he can possibly see—seems to make
him sad. *I'm sorry you feel that way,
Matthew. But what happened to Luke
wasn't God's fault. Why blame him?*

For a Counselor

This guy is awfully dense. "I'm not sure
how you draw the conclusion that I blame
God when I clearly state I'm one hundred
percent certain no such creature exists."

> *I don't understand.* His eyes hold
> genuine confusion. Maybe even shock.

"I'm an atheist. You know, a nonbeliever.
Considering Lane County demographics,
you must have run into another one before.
I can't be the only sane person in this school."

> He yanks himself together. *That may
> be. But the others don't brag about it.*

Blah, blah, blah. The game grows old.
"All I did was state my opinion. Do you
actually see that as bragging? Because
seriously, Mr. Carpenter, I don't."

> *But there's more.* He loses steam.
> *It's . . . it's the tone of your writing.*

The tone? Angry? Yeah, but more.
Bitter? Closer, but not quite. Acerbic?
Almost. Caustic. That's it. Still.
"Everything's fine. Totally fine."

It's a Total Lie

Not sure there's been a single day of my life
when everything was totally fine. And now?

The best I can say is once in a while I'm not
somersaulting in chaos. I sink into my well-

practiced bullshit-the-shrink tone of voice.
"Look, Mr. Carpenter. It *has* been a rough

few months. Losing Luke *did* throw me
off balance for a while, but day by day

it gets a little better. I appreciate your concern.
Ms. Hannity's, too, and I understand where

it comes from. The truth is, you're right.
I will never forgive the people who are

ultimately responsible for Luke's demise.
But I don't really see why I have to."

> *Maintaining your sanity?* He gives a tiny
> smile. *Anyway, be very careful of the blame*
>
> *game. It can get you into all kinds of trouble.*
> *And it's always possible that you're wrong.*

Doesn't Matter

If I'm wrong or right (not that I'm wrong).
All I want is out of here, so I agree, keeping
a perfectly straight face. "I know. And thanks."

Unbelievably, he lets me leave without another
comment, not even another warning to play a less
provocative game. He's not stupid, and neither

am I. We both understand what's at stake,
and it's more than my sanity. It's my freedom.
Lockup's the only thing that frightens me.

The one insistent whisper of fear has kept
my temper mostly in check these past few months.
More than once, I thought about taking a dead-

of-night slow cruise through certain neighborhoods,
drawing a long bead on designated silhouettes
shadowing their bedroom windows. One squeeze

of my Glock's trigger, and *BLAM!* Eye-for-an-eye justice,
just like their Good Book calls for. But then that
niggling little voice would ask me to consider life

walled in by concrete and metal bars. That would
do me in, and I'm not quite ready to check on out
of here yet. I've got some living to do. Hard living.

First Things First

And right now, top of the list is simply to make
it through this day, which bumps right up against
a nice extended weekend. Time off the rat race
to celebrate the life—and death, I suppose—
of a charismatic black leader. Carpenter gives
me a pass back to class, but I'm not in a huge
hurry to use it. I only took physics for Dad.

I suppose some of it is fascinating enough,
but what would I ever use string theory for?
I time it so I'm mostly in my chair when
the lunch bell rings. Perfect. It's a dreary,
soggy day, de rigueur for the Willamette
Valley in January. Sometimes I bring lunch
and eat outside. But not in winter. Juniors
and seniors are allowed to leave at lunch,

and I usually jet as soon as I can round up
Hayden. But today I can't seem to locate her.
She's not at her locker. Not exiting the gym,
hair wet from a post-PE shower. I try attendance
office, just in case. She's not here, but a flyer
in the window reminds me where she must be
right now. YOUTH MINISTRY MEETING,
11:55 A.M. FRIDAY IN THE LIBRARY.

Guess I'm Eating Solo

Angers shimmers

> red hot
> white hot
> silvery hot.

Not because
I can't stand

> eating alone
> thinking alone
> immersing myself in alone.

But because
she knows I hate

> her church
> her youth group
> her condescension

when she goes
all fucking missionary
on me. Not talking nouns,
talking adjectives

> moralistic
> preachy-whiny
> holier-than-thou.

Okay, I Know

That's not exactly fair.
That she's truly worried
for my immortal soul.
That, in itself, is rather
endearing. And so is
the fact that she loves
me at all. Little enough

of that in my life. So if
she wants to believe
the source of our love
(and, indeed, all love)
is some all-powerful
wizard with wings or
whatever, hey, what's
the point of arguing?

As long as she lets me
sleep in late on Sundays
while she wastes time
in church. As long as
she lets me kiss her how
I like, warm and steaming
and barely breathing and . . .

A Sudden Uncomfortable Tug

Just south of my belt buckle reminds
me that a locker-heavy hallway is so not

the place to think about such things.
Glad I wore Jockeys today. Still, I feel

like everyone is staring at my groinage.
I glance up at the clock on the wall. Damn

it. Lunch is half over. If I leave now, I'll be
late to American Culture, a class I actually like.

Skip lunch? My gut growls in answer.
The deli cart beckons, and I'm halfway

there when someone taps my shoulder.
Okay, more like semi-punches it. I spin,

ready to defend myself if I must. But it's
just Marshall. "What the fuck, dude?"

> His goofy smile reveals way too many
> teeth in need of straightening. *Hey, man.*
>
> *Don't get all defensive. Just wondered
> if you're going to Freak's party. My car died.*

"Again? Jesus, why don't you bury
the goddamn thing already?" He winces

slightly. "What? Did I offend you
somehow? You don't think that car

should be junked?" He just shrugs and
now the clock says I've got less than ten

minutes until the bell. They're probably
packing up the cart, but I start walking

that way. Maybe I'll get lucky. "Come
on. I need food. Anyway, let me talk

to Hayden about the party. I planned on
going, but I should probably check in

with her before I agree to play chauffeur.
I'll text you." He makes a one-eighty,

> heads the other way, and I'm pretty
> sure I hear him mutter, *Pussywhipped.*

A soft haze of anger lifts, mushrooms
when I reach the empty deli cart. Shit!

Great

All I can think about now is how hollow
my belly feels. In Culture, Mr. Wells
gives a great lecture about how modern
American eras can be defined by their music.
Normally, I'd be totally engaged. Instead
I keep thinking about foods that start with
p. Why *p*? I seriously have no idea.

Pastrami.
Pancakes.
Plums.
Pinto beans.
Pretzels
Provolone.
Prosciutto.

And a slight variation—Pesto on sPaghetti.
Great. Now I've got that going on.

sPinach.
sPam.
sPaetzle.
sPring rolls.
sProuts.
sPumoni.
sPumante.

Yeah, I realize spumante isn't a food,
but it seemed like a reasonable segue.
It's how my brain works when I go obsessive
and, yes, I understand that's exactly what it is.
If I let myself wander into compulsiveness,
too, I'll have to go back and alphabetize.
Hmmm. No, better not. Mr. Wells

is already giving me a quizzical look.
Quizzical. Cool word. I like *q* words.

Quiche.
Quinoa.
Quince.
eQuus.

Okay, I wouldn't actually eat horse,
but a giant cheeseburger would sure
go down well right now. . . .

> *Matt? Am I boring you or what?*
> *I spent a lot of time preparing this talk,*
> *and I thought it was pretty good.*

The Tips of My Ears

Feel like someone just blowtorched
them. "Sorry, Mr. Wells. My mind
must be somewhere else right now."

> *Obviously. Do you think you can return*
> *it to this location, at least until the bell*
> *rings?* He's smiling, anyway. Good thing

he and I have a decent teacher-student
relationship. "I'll do my best." I do, and
actually get caught up in the whole

Vietnam/Bob Dylan/Buffalo Springfield
thing. Not to mention Richard Nixon
and J. Edgar Hoover vs. John Lennon.

Damn. If I had any ambition, I think
I'd try to be a cult hero. Are there college
courses for that? Can you get a degree

in cult heroship? Never mind. Pretty
sure that wouldn't satisfy my parents.
Not that what I'm planning to do after

graduation will. Oh my God. There goes
my brain again, wandering elsewhere.
I think I've got a serious case of ADHD.

Toward the End

Of class we have (by design, I'm sure)
circled back to the late 1960s and MLK
Jr. Beyond Vietnam protests, the civil
rights movement was also making
headlines. Snickers in the back of the room
underline the fact that not everyone here
is what you might call enlightened.

> *So what kind of music defines that?*
> sneers ever-the-dick Doug Wendt.
> *Hip-hop? Rap? Gospel? Or maybe*
> *back then it was spirituals?*

> Mr. Wells quiets the ludicrous back-row
> giggling with a single look. *In a way, yes.*
> *Spirituals informed the music that would*
> *come to be called "the blues." Sort of like*
> *how Moses's exodus story informed MLK's*
> *"Promised Land" speech. He'd figuratively*
> *climbed to the mountaintop, viewed the place*
> *where his people belonged, and believed*
> *God wanted them to get there. . . .*

"Yeah. And how did that work out
for him?" The question slips past my lips
without my even thinking about it.

And So Does

Mr. Wells's answer. *He knew he wouldn't
reach it, Matt. He knew with absolute certainty
that his death was more than possible. It was
probable. But he didn't back down, didn't
back away from his plea for nonviolent
protest. Without his unshakable faith in God,
and the creator's determination that all men
truly are created equal, Dr. King might very
well have retreated to the safety of his pulpit.*

"And he'd probably be alive today,
sitting in a rocking chair somewhere,
enjoying his grandchildren. If there really
was a God, one who wanted Martin Luther
King Jr. to lead his people toward equal
rights, why would that God allow him to die
before the task was accomplished? It makes
no sense. His people continued to suffer,
and he was just dead. Martyrdom is stupid."

That came out stronger than I meant
it to, but I'm not going to take it back.
Wells frowns. *I'm sorry you feel that
way, and I'm pretty sure most of Dr. King's
followers would disagree with you. His voice
gave them strength and shone a spotlight
on their cause, one the world couldn't ignore.*

Sheep

I make the mistake
of saying it out loud.
"Sheep." And, of course,

that jerkwad Wendt has
to expound, *Yeah. Black
sheep.* And the room erupts.

Idiot.

Right on.

Dick.

Shut up.

Word.

Oh my God.

Until, finally, Mr. Wells
yells, *Enough! Settle down.
Look, we're about finished
here. Enjoy your weekend.*

As everyone gathers their
stuff, he adds, *Hey, Matt.
Can I see you for a minute?*

Shit. Shit. Shit. What now?

I'd Try the Ol'

"I'll be late to my next class" excuse,
except for a couple of things. One,
the bell didn't even ring yet, and two,
I've got a study hall prior to Wood Shop.
In a way, I'm surprised they let me
around saws. "What is it, Mr. Wells?"

>   *I saw your God essay. . . .*

Jesus. Teachers actually *share* these
things? "My English essay? Really?"

>   *Come on, Matt. We both know there*
>   *were some, uh, concerns. But I wanted*
>   *you to know that while I don't agree*
>   *with everything you wrote, your thoughts*
>   *on religion are remarkable. I'm impressed.*

I have to smile. "Glad someone's
impressed. Thanks, Mr. Wells."

>   *You might consider taking comparative*
>   *religion in college. I think you'd find*
>   *it fascinating, especially since you already*
>   *have an obvious interest in the subject.*

Maintain, Matt, Maintain

I try, really I do, but a big burst of laughter
kind of explodes from my mouth. "Interest?
Not really. Dearth of interest is more accurate.
Anyway, I'm not exactly sure I'm going to
college." Damn. That slipped out, too. He
and Dad are friends, and I haven't confessed
my lack of ambition to my parents yet.

> His grin dissolves. *Wow. That surprises
> me, and it would be a spectacularly amazing
> waste of talent, in my opinion. You're one of
> the brightest young men I know. I hope
> you reconsider. You've got a lot to offer.*

Backpaddle. Quick! "I haven't decided
for sure yet. I mean, I'm already accepted
at UOregon." I never considered anywhere
else, and only applied there because Dad
insisted. Mom figures I'm a lost cause,
anyway. If she even remembers I'm alive.
"Well, thanks for your concern, and I'll
definitely think about that religion class."

> He looks downright sad, like he knows
> I'm flat BSing him. *I hope you do, Matt.
> One thing I hate is watching a special kid
> fall through the cracks. Have a great weekend.*

Dismissed

Booyah! I can finally get something to eat.
But not before I track down Hayden. The halls
are jammed, everyone buzzing about the long
weekend ahead. I thread through the throng,
heading for my locker. There. There's my girl,
waiting for me. Only thing is, she's not alone.
Standing beside her is Jocelyn Stanton. One look
at her and irritation shimmers, but before it can

> fan into anger, Hayden flashes perfect
> pearl-white teeth and I kind of melt. I reach
> for her, and she slips into my arms like
> satin. *Hi, baby.* Her soft, full lips seek
> mine, and this kiss, like every kiss, is all
> I could ever ask for. Well, maybe not all,
> but it's more than enough for right now.

We unlock our mouths, but I keep her close,
inhaling the orange-ginger scent of her hair.
"Missed you at lunch." I think a second, add,
"Actually, I missed lunch, too. But I missed
you more." Behind us, Jocelyn tsks impatience,
lifting a froth of annoyance. "What's her problem?"
Before she says a word, I know I'll hate her answer.

Didn't Realize

I had ESP, but apparently I've acquired
it somewhere along the way. Hayden

> gives me a quick kiss to mute the blow.
> *She has to drive her little brother home.*

My turn for impatience. "And . . . just
what does that have to do with you?"

> *I'm going, too. After we drop him off,*
> *we're going to change before the game.*

"You mean the basketball game?
I didn't know we'd decided to go."

I especially didn't know we'd decided
to go as a threesome, but I don't say so.

> *Well, I, uh . . . kind of figured I'd go,*
> *with or without you. It's a big game—*

"I know, Hayden, I mean, my dad being
the coach and all. But Freak's having a party

and I thought that would be a lot more fun.
I tried to find you at lunch to discuss it, but . . ."

The unfinished sentence dissolves in silence,
the accusation watery but easy enough

       to discern. *I told you about the meeting,*
       Matthew. Not my fault you didn't remember.

The shrew in her voice is a reaction to hurt,
of course. But I'm hurt, too. And more than

a little pissed off. "Don't call me Matthew."
Only Mom and my teachers do. "You're right.

I did forget, and I'm sorry. But why would you
make plans with Jocelyn without asking me

first? I wouldn't do that to you!" Petulant,
that's how I sound, like a pissed little boy.

       Come on, Matt. Placating, that's how she sounds.
       What's one night? We have three whole days

       to spend together. Anyway, you're welcome
       to come. Your dad would like you to be there.

Right. Like he'd even notice. "Never mind.
You go to the game with your girlfriend."

If I Wanted

To be really nasty, I could add,
"And I'll go to the party with mine."
But that would be such an incredible
lie she'd no doubt laugh at me.
She knows I'd never mess up
what we have, even if I do feel
coldcocked by her indifference
to my distress. I tuck my tail,
mostly wishing I had the cojones
to snarl instead. "If you change
your mind, call. If not, guess
I've got a date with Marshall."

Behind Hayden, Jocelyn taps
idiotically long fingernails against
too-plump thighs, and her eyes roll
toward the ceiling. All things
considered, I have a hard time
understanding why Hayden
and she are still friends, and
if I wasn't mostly a gentleman,
I'd be tempted to shake her. If
I thought it would do any good,
I might resort to a small shoulder
jab, but pretty sure that would
only make Hayden dig in deeper.

I give my girl one last pleading
glance, start to walk away. But
I change my mind, mostly to
impress Jocelyn (in a negative
way). I reach for Hayden, pull
her into my arms, kiss her with
every ounce of love I hold inside.
At first, she is stiff, aware we have
an audience, but she softens quickly,
slipping the tip of her spearmint
tongue between my lips. My own
tongue lifts in eager greeting.

And now the two dance like
a snake charmer and cobra—
a quick, sinuous pirhouetting.
My heart drums, staccato, and
I can feel hers stutter against
my chest. With my eyes closed,
I could get carried away, but I
keep them open, watching
Jocelyn tsk and mutter beneath
her breath, totally tweaked at
this waste of her time and,
I suspect, not a little jealous.

Now Come Catcalls

From random guys walking by,
so reluctantly I pull away. Hayden
smiles and I kiss my way up her neck

to whisper in her ear, "You're pretty
hot for a Christian girl. Sure you won't
come to the party? We could do something
biblical. Build an ark, or sacrifice a lamb."

> She wants to be offended, but can't quite
> bring herself to, and laughs instead.
> *You are completely incorrigible, you know*
>
> *that? Not to mention sacrilegious and*
> *most likely damned. I will pray for you,*
> *and if God doesn't strike you down between*
> *now and then, I'll call you tomorrow morning.*

Great sense of humor for a Christian
girl. While she's still laughing, I go
ahead and risk ruining her lighthearted

mood by asking Jocelyn, "How's that
prick brother of yours? I hear his stats
aren't exactly overwhelming. Tell him
I said to break a leg. Literally."

Both Girls Sputter

And that's fine with me. Hayden
needs to realize that her friendship

with Jocelyn makes me crazy, and
the idea of her driving anywhere

with that bitch's brother just about
puts me over the edge. "Enjoy the game."

I watch them walk stiffly to Jocelyn's
way-too-sensible Prius. Not so sensibly,

they stand in the drizzle, waiting for
Cal Stanton, who occupies the top spot

on my "People Who Should Just Go
Ahead and Die Now" list. Not that

I'd dare admit I keep such a roster
in my head. If my therapist discovered

all those sessions we've shared haven't
netted much in the way of my forgiving

the people on my hypothetical hit list,
she'd be downright concerned.

But My Lips Are Sealed

I make a dash through the rain
to my unsensible, but completely amazing
2013 Ford F-150, "Blue Flame" over gray.
It was an eighteenth-birthday gift
from my grandparents. The Portland
techies, not the Creswell Baptists.

Unfortunately, it's the latter who live
closest to us, where they can keep
an eye on their daughter—my mother,
and their biggest disappointment. Well,
except for Luke. But the Portlanders,
hey, turns out they're pretty cool.
(Hard to believe, considering they gave

birth to my dad.) I thought so even
before they gifted me with an awesome
ride "to celebrate my arriving."
I wasn't exactly sure where I'd arrived.
All I knew was from that day on, I was
going to arrive everywhere in style.

Best of All

This baby is loaded.
5.0 liter engine.
Supercab design.
4 x 4 drivetrain.
Satellite radio.

Bluetooth built into
the steering wheel for
hands-free calls while
I drive. I use it now
to let Marshall know

I'll pick him up around
nine. Freak's parties tend
to go really late. Get there
too early, and you risk
a DUI on the way home

or one hella hangover
the next day. Too bad
drinking comes with
so damn many intrinsic
reasons not to do it.

Hasn't Stopped Me Yet

And it won't stop me tonight, especially
without Hayden's disapproving looks
to slow me down. But I'll definitely
keep in mind I want to spend time
with her tomorrow, hangover-free.
At least I don't have to shower now.
Who cares what I'll smell like?

As I turn onto our street, I can see down
the block to our driveway, where Dad's
car is parked. Odd. Why would he be here
now, with the JV game only a couple of
hours away? Usually he just stays at school.
Maybe he forgot something this morning.
I park in my usual spot against the curb.

Rain drizzles down the windshield, and
I watch it for a few minutes before going
inside. Rarely does the Turner family deviate
from the norm, and some small whisper
of foreboding stirs. But no, that's stupid.
If someone had died, I would've gotten
a call. The thing about technology is,

surprises of a major sort are few and far
between. I stow the unease, go inside.

Where It Becomes Clear

In a half breath that I was correct in
my assumption that something is skewed
toward "holy crap." I can hear Mom and
Dad talking in the kitchen. Talking. They
never do that. And it's me they're discussing.

>Mom: *What are you going to do about him?*

>Dad: *What am I going to do? This is a joint
>problem, Pam. Joint, meaning the two
>of us, not that there's much "us" left.*

Ah, shit. What did I do now? Or, more
accurately, what did I do that they found
out about? Not to mention, care about.
I consider a quick exit, but whatever this
is won't disappear in the next few hours.

Especially not if Dad loses one of the "big
games" tonight—basketball or blame.
Anyway, what's the worst they can try
to do to me? Ground me? Right. It's party
night, and I won't be denied. So I'll go

kiss a little ass, whatever their problem
might be. I whistle as I sashay toward
the nonproblem and its nonconsequence.

They're at the Table

Backs to the door. When they hear me
coming, they spread a little before turning
in my direction, and I can see a small stack
of paper on the weathered wood. "What's up?"

> Dad's face colors pink, as if I've busted
> him doing something wrong. *What's up
> with* you, *Matt? I think that's the question.*

"You'll have to be a little more specific,
Dad, I . . ." He picks up the sheaf with two
fingers, gingerly, as if it might be hot. "Oh."
It's a photocopy of my essay, at least that's

what the top page looks like. "Don't tell
me. Mr. Carpenter and Ms. Hannity think
I'm considering mayhem and thought you
should know before I went off. Right?"

> *Something like that.* He drops the papers
> back on the table, then pierces my eyes
> with his stare. *Are you considering mayhem?*

I glance at a couple of pages, remembering
what I'd written on them. "It's just a freaking
essay. Not a manifesto for murder. Jeez, Dad—"

Shut up! screeches Mom. *Don't take*
the Lord's name in vain on top of the rest.
What is wrong with you, Matthew?

"Uh, Mom? 'Jeez' isn't short for Jesus.
It's really a rather innocuous expression,
in fact. Don't worry. God isn't offended."

I could say more. I could remind her that
she never said one word about God or church
or faith or religion to me until the day Luke died.
That her overbearing Baptist upbringing backfired

and, according to stories I've heard Dad tell
after a few too many, she was about as far
from a pure, little Christian girl as they came
when she was my age. I could insist that makes

her the worst kind of hypocrite—the kind
who takes, uses, and abuses until life bites her
in the ass. Then, rather than try to fix the damage
she's caused, she dumps it all into God's lap,

begging *him* for forgiveness. I could go
even further and ask her to please explain
what's the point of deity worship, anyway?
No matter how low she genuflects or how

high she lifts all those prayers, she faces
an arduous climb up Misery Mountain.
Maybe, just maybe, if she could reach
the top she'd find the tiniest glimpse

of happiness, somewhere in the far
distance. But those peaks are steep
and treacherous, and all she does is keep
slipping backward toward the morass

below. And the real truth is, even if
she scaled the cliffs, stood tall atop
the summit, Luke wouldn't be there,
and neither would any chance to rekindle

whatever love she and Dad ever had.
Both have vanished forever. But what's
the point of saying any of that? Even if
she listened, she wouldn't get it. So I'll

go back to playing defense. "I'll try to watch
my mouth, okay? As for the essay, I was just
blowing off steam. With words. Not my fists.
Not an assault weapon. Just words."

Let's look at religious genocide. We could in theory go all the way back to Noah, of ark fame, whose God was so angry at human sin that he chose to wipe out every living thing except for Noah's family, and two of each species on earth. Nice creator you've got there. The Old Testament is, in fact, rife with Jehovah-driven genocide. But since it's fiction anyway, let's move on.

Under early popes, we find the Crusades. Christians killing Christians who weren't acceptable Christians— those pesky Protestants. Jews. Muslims. Nonbelievers. And what to do about the pagans? Behead them. Impale them. Chop them up. All in the name of a forgiving God.

Keep marching forward. Centuries of witch hunts. Burn those bitches at the stake. The Spanish Inquisition. Extermination of Native North and South Americans. Torture them, rape them, enslave them. Or just outright murder them. "God's will," their Christian killers said. The will of a peaceful God.

You might think religion would get more civilized, approaching the twentieth century. But no. We've all heard about the Nazi population cleansing. But few realize that Catholic priests and Muslim clerics were, at the same time, willing accomplices to the extermination of eight hundred thousand Yugoslav citizens—orthodox Serbians, Jews, and Roma, many torched alive in kilns. The ovens of a loving God.

Buddhist monks in Vietnam. The Tutsis in Rwanda. Bosnian Muslims. The list of those killed with the aid of so-called Christians goes on and on. Figure in the flipside—Muslims killing Christians in Indonesia and the Sudan, Khmer Rouge and Soviet Communist wipe-outs, the Turk massacre of Armenian Christians, not to mention the whole war-without-end in the Middle East—and what you come up with is one seriously bloodthirsty God, not a loving creator who urges forgiveness and peace.

No, mass destruction has nothing to do with God. It's all about human lust for sex, for wealth, for power. Easier to lay culpability at the feet of some conjured being than admit such gluttony. Much easier to allow your priest or rabbi or imam to direct your inner murderer toward an agenda. Easiest of all to hide behind your cassock or thobe and order your flock to the killing fields where you can oversee the slaughter.

To blame such zealous hatred for your fellow man on an invention of the imagination is a display of cowardice. Were I to take someone out because of his religious posturing, I would assume full responsibility. Hell, I'd take ownership of the deed. . . .

My Eyes Stop There

Okay, I guess maybe that might
cause a little concern, especially
in this day and age of mass-shooting
scares. And I do own a gun. A lovely,

if totally deadly, Glock. But I only
use it for target practice, and despite
anything I wrote in that essay, or
the odd whim (they always pass by),

I'd never draw a bead on a human
target. Anyway, can't these people
(who really should know me better)
tell I was just taking a firm stand?

"Really, you guys. I have absolutely
no plans to go off on anyone, not
even the assholes who might deserve
it." Mom hmphs, but doesn't comment.

Dad looks so relieved I can almost
believe he was actually worried
about me. But I know he's just
in a hurry to get back to school

and his warm-ups. *That's good to hear.*
You know I don't care about the God
stuff. But the rest . . . He waits for me
to agree, and I do with a nod. But before

        I can say anything, Mom flips out.
        Well, I care about the God stuff.
        Can't you act like a man for once,
        Wyatt, and tell your son to stop acting

        all crazy and such? If you won't, I will.
        No one feels sorry for you, Matthew.
        So quit, would you? Stop looking
        for sympathy. This time a big, sharp

stick of anger spears me right in
the eye, drawing water. "I never
asked you to feel sorry for me,
nor would I expect the tiniest

particle of sympathy from you,
Mother. Let alone affection. I mean,
why look for any now? Not like
you've ever been generous with love."

I Turn Away

Before she can have the satisfaction
of seeing me cry. Damn, damn, damn!

I am a pussy. I start toward my room, call
over my shoulder, "Good luck tonight, Dad."

I think he replies, but whatever he says
gets swallowed up in Mom's meaningless

tirade. She just goes on and on and on,
and what is she so upset about anyway?

There's so much I wish I had the strength to say.
Like: Hey, Mom, be sure to take a Prozac

before calling your preacher to bitch about me.
Like: Hey, Mom, I miss my little brother, too.

But what he did wasn't my fault. And neither
was your screwing Dad latex-free and getting

pregnant with *moi*, so why the fuck do you
keep blaming *me* for ruining your life?

I Kick Off My Shoes

Consider leaving them there, in the middle
of the floor, one upside down, the other
sideways. But disorder irritates my mother
and downright pisses off Dad, especially after
a couple of drinks. I've been raised better,
that's what he'd say. Which explains why
my bed is made, my tidy desk is dust-free,
my clothes folded and in the proper drawers.

I put my shoes in the closet, toes against
the wall, beside three other pairs of pricey
athletic shoes and one pair of heavy boots.
When I have my own place, will I be able
to leave them askew in the middle of the room,
or will my upbringing forever deny that?
Could I ever plop down on an underwear-
and sock-strewn sofa, settle into a nap?

The thing is, all this external order can't quite
make up for the internal turmoil that is central
to my parents' lives, and so to mine. It's one
reason I need Hayden, who is my daily small
dose of tranquillity. I need her more than ever
with Luke gone. I send her a text, tell her
I love her. Ask her to forgive me for being
such a hothead. I don't expect a quick answer.

Beyond the Door

The house has fallen silent.
Dad has returned to school
and the one thing he cares
about. Mom is gone, too.
Showing property this time
of day? She didn't bother
to say, but the static energy
tells me she isn't here.

For some reason, I'm drawn
to Luke's room. Everything
is the same as it always was—
pin-clean, like mine, only
painted mauve (his favorite
color) instead of slate gray.
His absence presses down,
tangible weight on my chest.

I lie on his bed, sink
into a bath of eiderdown, turn
my face toward the window,
curtained gray with drips of
rain. "How could you, Luke?"
I whisper. "How could you
leave me alone with them?"
There's a clock on the wall
shaped like a train. It ticks

audibly, and now it tells me
it's the top of the hour with
a low whistle. Four o'clock.
Luke did love trains. When
we were kids, we'd often ride
our bikes along the tracks,
talking about where we'd go
once we got big enough.

We rode bikes everywhere,
especially in the summer
when the treetops nodded
at the urging of tepid breezes.
I close my eyes and find one
of our favorite spots on Mosby
Creek, in the shade of an old
covered bridge. We'd jump
into a still, cool pocket of river,

always wearing old sneakers
because of the goobers who
thought it was funny to trash
beer bottles against the rocks.
Then out we'd climb, teeth
chattering and goose bumps
raising into regular little hills.
And we'd laugh and laugh.

But Always

After the laughter came deep conversation,
at least as deep as it got for preadolescent
boys, meaning sometimes suprisingly so.

One Sunday we had escaped the house after
a visit from our Creswell grandparents. Dad
had gotten into it with them, hot and heavy,

over not making us go to church. He'd told
them in no uncertain terms that he would not
be coerced into indoctrinating his kids with

mythology designed to steal their pitiable
allowance pennies. I remember those words
specifically because I determined to ask him

for a raise in the near future. The only people
in the world Mom won't confront are her parents,
and that was the case that day. The argument

was well out of hand when Luke and I exchanged
a "let's get the hey out of here" look and sneaked
out the back door. We pedaled hard, just in case

someone had noticed, and when we finally skidded
to a stop in our usual place, were completely winded
and dripping sweat. "Let's dive!" I said, and we did.

That Day

After the laughter subsided, we lay,
side by side, on a soft stretch of sand,
caring not at all that our backs
would be plastered with it.

>   *Do you think there's such a thing*
>   *as God?* Luke was probably eight,

which would have made me eleven.
"Nope. Why? Do you?"

>   *I don't know,* he admitted. *But lots*
>   *of the kids at school do. They get*
>   *mad when I say I don't think so.*

"People get mad over all kinds
of stupid things, Lukester. Don't
pay any attention to them. They
don't know one way or another."

>   *Yeah, but sometimes I wonder.*
>   *Dad says creation all comes down*
>   *to science, but he's a science teacher,*
>   *so what else would he say? When I*
>   *think on it, I'm not so sure how it*
>   *can all be completely random.*

Luke always was a little too smart
for his own good. "How what can
be completely random, dude?"

> You know. Everything. The universe.
> This planet. Life on this planet. How
> did it begin? What made it evolve?
> Why are people the smartest animals?

"Who says they are?" I tried to joke,
but he seemed totally perplexed.
I thought it over for a few.
"Know what I think? It all
comes down to aliens."

I was, at the time,
into reading
Isaac Asimov
and Ray Bradbury.

> *Aliens?* Luke read a lot,
> but sci-fi for eight-year-old
> readers tends to lack
> sophistication. *You think
> God is an alien?*

My First Reaction

Was a giant cough of laughter.
But then he looked so hurt, I figured
why not just make up a bunch of crap.
God was fiction, aliens, too. Why
couldn't they be fiction together?

"What if aliens from the planet
Alphatrypton scanned the universe
for the perfect place to settle down
and create a new generation
of Alphatryptonites? And what if

their gigantic telescopes homed in on
the Blue Planet, which had excellent
water and decent weather, at least
compared to the encroaching ice
age on Alphatrypton?" His eyes lit up,

and he started nodding his head, and
then he added to the tale. *Yeah. And
what if they were magic? And when
they got here, they mated with monkeys
and then that made human beings?*

Aliens Mated with Monkeys?

He had a better imagination than I, that
was for sure. But what the hell? I went
right along with it. "So maybe we're not
earthlings at all. Maybe we're ten
thousandth generation Alphatryptonites.
And maybe we have magic powers,
too, only our genes have forgotten them."

He was quiet for a few. Then he said,
But you know what, though? What if
aliens came from more than one planet?
And some of those guys sucked. Like, they
were mean and stupid. And when they mated
with monkeys, the people who came from
them ended up being mean and stupid, too.

"That would explain a lot. Like, Mina
Boxer's probably a ten thousandth generation
mean and stupid alien." Mina's our neighbor.
She wasn't Luke's worst bully, but she was
his first, almost like she recognized things
before the rest of us did. "But here's the thing.
You and me? We're Alphatryptonites. And we
have to try really hard to find our magic. Deal?"

Luke Agreed

But he didn't stick around
        long enough to find his.
                A train wails a mournful
dirge. Train? I twitch awake.
        The clock on Luke's wall
                whistles again. Six o'clock.
It's dark in the room, only
        the small night-light on
                by the door to remind me
of the way out. Of this room.
        Of sleep-induced memory.
                Sorrow bleeds into the joy
of reliving that day. And, as
        always, anger taints it all.
                I flip on the light switch
so I can see to straighten
        the covers on Luke's bed.
                "Wouldn't want you to come
back for a visit and think
        I've lost respect for you,
                little man." Great. Talking
to ghosts now. Out loud, even.
        As I reach for his pillow, I can't
                help but notice an evil waft
of stink emitted by my armpits.
        Kind of disgusting. Guess I'd
                better take a shower after all.

Stench-Free

Hair combed and clothes hanging
mostly straight, I check my phone
for messages, find what I'm hoping

> for: *DON'T WORRY. YOUR HEAD'S*
> *PRETTY FROSTY MOST OF THE TIME.*
> *LOVE YOU. SEE YOU TOMORROW.*

It's almost eight by the time I leave.
I'll catch a burger before I pick up
Marshall. When I open the front door,

the smell of lit tobacco wallops my nose.
Canopied by the porch awning, Mom leans
against the side of the house, drink in one

hand, cigarette in the other, watching
the drizzle. Dad hates when she smokes,
which is why she does it outside. Don't

> think he cares much about the gin, in
> or out. Mom glances sideways at me.
> *Where you goin'?* Not her first drink,

or maybe she did, in fact, use it to
chase a Xanax. "Gonna grab a bite,
then see if I can track Hayden down."

She Takes a Deep Drag

Exhales slowly. Yellow smoke
clouds the damp evening air.

You're being careful, right?

I grin. "Caution is my middle name."
But, wait. "What do you mean, careful?"
She can't be talking the condom talk.

You know. With that girl. When you . . .

"Now, hold on. Hayden and I aren't
doing *that*. Go—" Her eyes go wide
and I drop the *d*, modify, "Gosh,
Mom, why would you think so?"

*Don't lie to me, Matthew. All boys
your age are doing* that. *It's nature.*

"Not lying to you. I love Hayden
with all my heart. But, nature or no,
condoms or no, we are not having sex."

The furrows between her eyes tell
me she doesn't believe it. Before
this conversation can devolve, I'm out
of here. "You should go in. It's cold."

Those Six Words

Slide out of my mouth,
soft as meringue. I think
we both choke on them
a little. I keep my eyes
straight ahead, even after

> Mom calls, *You smell good.*
> *But Matthew, please be careful.*

Okay, we'll call that a draw.
I can't believe she's so
positive I'm boinking
Hayden. Of course Mom
doesn't know my girl

very well. In fact, she
doesn't know her at all.
I avoid mixing downers
(like Mom) with uppers
(like Hayden). What's

the point of dropping
low right before working
yourself up? I suppose
that's what I do, dating
Hayden. Work myself up.

One thing abstinence
education doesn't teach you
is how hard it is to maintain
an intimate relationship
that doesn't include actual sex.

Frustrating, that's what it is.
But I love Hayden so much
I have no choice but to respect
the boundaries she puts in place.
Problem is, the lines she draws

aren't always real straight.
Gut complaining, I head on
over to Carl's Jr. No lunch,
so what the hell? I order
the Memphis BBQ Six Dollar

Burger, with Pulled Pork (two
p words in one) and onion
strings, add guacamole for
vegetable matter. Plus fried
zucchini. I'm in the mood for *z*.

Eight Thousand

Greasy calories later, I'm ready to party.
I pull up in front of Marshall's and he sprints

to the truck, jumps up inside, bounces on
the seat. "Chill, dude. What's with you?"

> *Nothing!* One word and it's obvious he's lit.
> *I borrowed a couple of my sister's diet pills.*
>
> *Lainie's coming tonight and I wanna
> be sure I can, you know . . . no problem.*

"Lainie Brogan? First of all, in what
possible universe would Lainie want to

'you know' a little squeak like you? And
second, do you have regular dick problems?"

I'm keeping both eyes fixed on the road,
but I'm pretty sure he just clenched his fists.

> Bet he's about to pop a brain vein! *My dick's
> A-OK, thanks. Adipex just keeps it up longer.*

"Longer than six hours, call your doctor.
But personally, I don't want to know."

Freak Lives In

A big dilapidated mobile home,
way out of town on ten acres of trees.
They form two crooked lines on each
side of the gravel driveway. At the end,
where road meets trailer, vehicles
litter the unpaved parking area. Mud,
that's what it is. Squishy red slop.

It slurps at my shoes as I follow Marshall
to the door, noticing for the millionth
time in my life the incredible scent of wet
cedar. How do people live in the city,
where all you inhale is exhaust and piss
and subterranean steam? Of course, it
doesn't smell a whole lot better inside,

where it's booze over BO over a vague
fart stench, all fogged with a blend of
smokes—tobacco, weed, something else.
Eau d'party! Now to figure out just how
much "eau" I'm up for. I'll start with a beer.
I toss a five-spot into the "Keg Donation
Can," on top of maybe six single dollars.

Considering probably twenty people
are slurping suds out of red plastic cups,
I'm thinking Freak's going to come up
a little short. Since he earns his keg cash
selling dope, no one's too worried
about kicking in, but I like to pay my way.
Don't want to be beholden to anyone,

except maybe Hayden, who would be
horrified at the red mud getting tracked
everywhere. She and my parents would
see eye to eye on that, at least. Personally,
I'm kind of enjoying all the "shoe painting"
going on. It's so not-neat it gives me shivers.
My eyes are welded to the floor, so when

someone taps my shoulder, my arm
jumps, tossing something-I'm-guessing-
is-Pabst into the air and over my shoulder.
*Hey! Not much into wearing beer! Try to
keep it in the cup, okay?* But then she laughs,
and before I can turn to face her, I know
it's Alexa. We've laughed together before.

She Follows Me

Over to the keg, where I rectify the spill,
refilling her cup, too. Someone has turned
on music, if you can call Slayer music.
More like a growl with a beat and some bass.

Whatever. All I know is it's really loud.
"I'm going in the other room where my ears
can take a vacation." It comes out invitation-
like and Alexa takes me up on it.

We manuever carefully through a tangle
of partying people and it's a challenge
to make it to the back room—once a bedroom,
but now set up like a den, with crippled chairs

and a seedy sofa where, unbelievably,
Marshall is tongue-to-tongue with Lainie
Brogan. Guess she was swayed by the promise
of an everlasting boner. I'll never look at her

the same way again. There's one open seat,
and Alexa sinks into it. I opt for the arm,
pray it holds. It's either converse with her
or keep staring at Marshall, who has coaxed

Lainie onto his lap. Oh, hell, no. They're
not going to get it on right there, are they?
"Holy crow. What got into her?" I ask,
and Alexa knows exactly what

I'm referring to. *Vince broke up
with her yesterday. She's just trying to
make him jealous.* Sure enough, on the far
side of the doorway stands my ex-good

buddy Vince Rosario, looking unnervingly
like the Incredible Hulk. He's even a pale
shade of green. "Damn. Hope Vince
hasn't changed his mind. He could snap

Marshall in two without even trying."
Instead, he watches the sordid scene
for a couple of seconds, turns, and walks
away. Pretty sure Marshall never knew

he was there. I'm also pretty sure Alexa
was right. Lainie knew. She's smirking
around her semi-exposed tongue. "Man,
some girls are downright disgusting."

Alexa laughs. *Ain't it the truth?
And most guys like them that way.*

True Enough

Except, "Not me. Personally, I prefer
class ladies to crass women." There seem

> to be mostly the latter here tonight.
> *And we class ladies appreciate that.*

Alexa's smile seems more predatory
than classy, but I keep that to myself

and change the subject. "So why were
you in Carpenter's office today?

Curricula-tory problems?" She cocks
her head, perplexed. "Sorry, lame joke."

> *Oh.* Now she looks consternated, but
> tells her story anyway. *Believe it or not,*
>
> *Carpenter called me in because of a post*
> *on my Facebook page. I called Karla Decker*
>
> *a whack and said I wished someone would*
> *cut off her head so she'd finally shut up.*
>
> *I guess someone saw it and sent it to Karla,*
> *who told her mom, who reported me for*

making threats against her daughter.
Jeez, man, I didn't say I was bringing

my chain saw over, you know? I guess
zero tolerance isn't enough with all

the gun violence in the news. Now they
feel the need to investigate any little burp

that might be a sign of stomach cancer.
How about you? Did you burp or what?

"More like a major silent-but-deadly fart."
I tell her about my supposed infraction.

It takes a while, including a cup refill,
but I get to the end, omitting the "amen"

at home. Alexa listens without comment,
other than a nod or vocalized *Yeah.* I want

her to say, "That's so fucked up." I want
her to say, "Why in the hell would they be

worried about a freaking essay dismissing
God?" Instead, she goes to straight to Luke.

Well, Luke, Plus

The first thing she says is:
> *I kind of hope there is a heaven.*
> *Wouldn't it make you feel better*
> *to know Luke isn't really dead,*
> *and that he's watching over you?*

To which I reply:

"Considering I was the one who
always had to supervise Luke,
I think he'd do a piss-poor job of
watching over me. Next question."

Slightly stung, she continues:
> *I'm not big on church or religion,*
> *but I want there to be something*
> *more. Wouldn't it be cool if we*
> *could come back, get another chance?*

I've considered that, actually.

"I don't think it's possible, so I've
decided to up the ante on the cards
I've been dealt. I don't need another
chance if I kick ass in the present tense."

Speaking of Kicking Ass

There seems to be a little row in the other
room. Everyone here crowds that way,
anxious to see what's up. That action
pries Lainie and Marshall apart, and when
someone yells, *Get him, Vince,* I start
thinking maybe it's time for Marshall
to leave, just in case this is a matter

of misplaced rage. "Hey, Lainie. You
didn't know Vince would be here, right?
I mean, you wouldn't set up my buddy,
would you?" If there's one thing I hate,
it's games, especially the kind that get
my naive friends into trouble. Lainie's eyes

       narrow, and she gives me a vile smirk.
       Why don't you shut the fuck up, ass licker?
       What I do is none of your business.

"Nice mouth. Careful you don't catch
something ugly hiding in there, Marshall."
With a chorus of groans, the group in the hall
swells backward into the room, and there's
a loud thump just beyond them. "Time to
go, I believe. Marshall?" Against all that
is logical, the dimwad shakes his head.

Nah. I've got plans for little Lainie girl.
You go ahead without me. You'll get me
home, won't you, Lainie? Totally unfazed
by the commotion in the hall, he kisses her
again, and she kisses him back, in the most

ludicrous display of igorance I've ever
witnessed. "Well, I'm going," I tell
Alexa. "At least, if I can find a way
out. Think I could fit through that window?
Okay, probably not. Thanks for the company."
I stand, but before I can take a step, she puts

her hand on my forearm. *Take me home?*
I actually rode with Lainie. Looks like
she's got more on her mind than me,
and it's a very long walk in the rain.
Or even not in the rain. But you know—
I'm babbling, aren't I? Her grimace

makes me smile. "I happen to admire
those who babble, and if you can help me
safely escape the morass, I'm more than
willing to drive you home, milady." Now
I'm babbling, but I think she likes it.

She Takes My Hand

You go first, and fast.
I'm going to be sick. Got it?

I do. If there's one thing more
imperative than watching a fight,
or even winning one, it's getting
the hell out of the way of a likely
vomit blast. I'd duck myself.

"Too much beer! Move, man!
You like the smell of Pabst puke?
Out of our way!" Like magic, the mob
parts, and we hustle by the human heap
on the floor—Vince pounding on . . . ?

No clue who. And I really don't
care. Best of luck, Marsh. Sweet
little actress Alexa keeps her
fist to her mouth, approximating
the sounds of imminent upchuck.

We escape into the mist-mellowed
night, laughing and surfing mud
all the way to my truck. I open
the passenger door, sort of boost
her up inside. "Quite the performance."

I thought so myself. She looks at me
with eyes the approximate color of ripe
blueberries, and in those eyes I find
recollection of a time when Alexa
and I might have merged into coupledom

had I not fallen instead for her best friend.
Well, her then-best friend. The tiniest tip
of her tongue comes to rest against her
upper lip and I know what she wants and
for some insane reason, I sway toward her,

wanting to kiss her, and I am a millimeter
away from doing exactly that. "I can't."
It comes out a hoarse croak. "Sorry."
She pulls her feet inside, and I close
the door, walk around to the driver's side,

climb up beneath the steering wheel.
Wordlessly start the engine. We withdraw
to separate cubes of space, only feet apart,
but a universe away from each other,
both of us wondering what that meant.

We Are Quiet

For a mile or so.
Very quiet. Finally,

>   she tosses a pebble into the silence.
>   *You're really in love with her.*

Splash. Glug, glug, glug.
"Hayden is easy to love."

>   *Really?*

"Really."

>   *I don't see it.*

"Why not?"

>   *Because you two are not
>   the same kind of people.*

"That's true. I'm a guy
and she's definitely not."

>   *You know what I mean.*
>   She's starting to get pissed.

"Actually, I'm not sure I do."

*Come on. She's a raging Jesus
lover. You're anything but.*

"Well, there is that. . . ."
The small injection of humor

goes unnoticed, or ignored.
Doesn't that bother you?

"Once in a while." More like
often, but I keep that to myself.

She reflects for a second or two.
Don't you want to, you know . . . ?

Okay, this word duel grows old,
not to mention hard to keep up
with. "Don't I want to what?"

She tsks irritation. *Stop being dense.
Don't you want to have sex with her?
Because I'm pretty sure she's not*

*going to do that. Not without a ring
around her finger and a Bible verse
before—God-inspired foreplay.*

Enough!

"Why in the hell is everyone suddenly
so interested in my sex life? Mom's
positive I'm getting some, you're sure
I'm not. And Marshall thinks I need
pharmaceuticals to masturbate."

> The last, of course, is total bullshit,
> meant to elicit a reaction, and it does.
> Alexa snorts laughter. *Wh-what?*

"Nothing. I made up the part about
Marshall. Just wanted to see if you
were paying attention. But I did have
to defend my actions—or lack of them—
to my mom. Just because she got knocked
up her senior year, guess she figures—"

> *Wait. Your mom got pregnant . . .*
> *with you?* Now she's way too serious.

"That's what they tell me. I was born
approximately five months after
a fancy shotgun wedding. Pretty sure
my grandfather wishes he'd pulled
the trigger. Then again, pretty sure
sometimes my dad wishes so, too."

There's a Lot More

To this tale of regret, details gleaned from Dad's
inebriated ramblings. Confessions not confided,
but rather overheard. Like how he was a junior

at UOregon, a star forward on the Ducks
varsity basketball team, and head-over-heels
in love with another girl the night he met Mom,

who was much too young to be hanging out
at a frat party. How, despite a team prohibition
against alcohol, and a personal vow to remain

faithful, he went ahead and indulged in a drink
or four, which loosened his inhibitions enough
to make him forget about the love of his life

and engage in a fifteen-minute ride-of-his-life
with a wicked eighteen-year-old wild child
from out in the sticks. How, despite the guilt,

and swearing to himself he'd never again
cheat on his girlfriend, when Mom showed
up at his door he invited her in for an encore.

Three times they had sex, that was all, but
apparently that was more than enough to get
Mom in a family way, and even though

his heart belonged to someone else,
he agreed to do the right thing and marry
Mom, losing both the love of his life

and his shot at a career in the NBA. Not
to mention, gaining a wife who rocked it
in bed but was pretty damn boring otherwise,

followed by a couple of problematic sons,
an upside-down mortgage, and a tidy job
only made interesting by the coaching gig.

Now all they do is play the blame game,
especially after what happened with Luke:
If only; you should have; why did you?

But that's a lot to say before I drop
Alexa off, so I hold it all inside
and make do with this: "The last thing

I want for myself is a shotgun wedding."
I expect her to reply with a comment
about the availability of birth control.

Instead, she says, *So, you're afraid
of your life becoming complicated,
and Hayden makes that easy for you.*

I Want to Deny It

But I can't, not completely. So I stutter,
"B-b-but, that's not why I love her.
She's beautiful and smart and sweet . . ."
And uncomplicated, yes, and I really
don't need complications in my life.

> *You're right. She's all those things, but*
> *there's something else there, a nasty*
> *little undercurrent. I mean, I thought*
> *I knew her, but . . . Just, be careful.*

Second time tonight someone's told me
to be careful while referencing Hayden.
I should probably jump to my girl's defense,
but Alexa's right. Hayden can be snippy.
"No worries. I can fight her off if I have to."

Alexa's laugh is warm, rich gingerbread,
and I'm glad I didn't have more to drink.
I most definitely share my father's genes.
Don't want to have his history in common,
too. But I don't have to worry about that

with Hayden, do I? Suddenly, it strikes me:
Alexa hit *that* nail square on the head.

If There's Anything Worse

Than the professional psychotherapy I endure,
it's amateur pysche dissection, intentional or not.

Spot on or not. So I'm happy when I turn off
the main road into Alexa's unassuming, well-kept

neighborhood. I attempt a return to small talk.
"So, what are you up to the rest of the weekend?"

> Her shrug releases the scent of her leather
> jacket, a hint of some citrusy lotion. *Not much.*

> *Filling out college applications and FAFSA*
> *forms. Tedious and silly. I'm not going far.*

"Me either. UOregon, and I'm thinking about
taking a year off before that. But when I told that

to Mr. Wells, he acted like it was a dead-
end alley to residence behind a Dumpster."

> *Well, I think it's a great idea, especially*
> *if you explore a little of the world beyond*

> *the Willamette. Everyone should travel*
> *before they decide where to settle down.*

I pull over on the dirt shoulder in front
of Alexa's small tract house, which

is shuttered by the night, no hint of light.
at the windows. "You here all by yourself?"

> As a matter of fact, I am. My parents went
> to the movies in Eugene. They won't be back
>
> for a while. She feathers my hand with her
> fingertips. Want to come in and play?

I lift her hand from mine, bring it up
to my lips, kiss it gently. "You tempt me,

milady. However, I shall have to decline
your generous offer. Perhaps another time."

> Fine, she sniffs, but at least she smiles.
> In that case I'll just have to go play alone.

I watch her walk to her door, appreciate
the arc of her hips, their metered swing.

I could change my mind, follow her in.
Instead, I'll go home and play. Alone.

Well, Not Quite Alone

It's a little after midnight, and Dad still
isn't home. Postgame on Friday nights,
he regularly goes out with his buddies
and gets wasted. On more than a few
occasions, he's arrived home courtesy
of a designated driver, usually a wife,
called out into the cold to save her husband's
butt, not to mention his friends' butts.

They never call Mom, who is home
and passed out on the sofa, snoring
like a chain saw above the soft play
of HBO on the TV. She is on her back,
long reddish hair a tumble of waves over
the pillow, her face worry-freed by sleep,
and in this one glimpse, this momentary
standstill of time, she is the mother

I always imagined she could be—warm
and caring. Not pierced, heart and soul,
by fragmented dreams and splintered
memories. But now she rolls to one side,
her sleeve lifting to expose a freckled arm
and nicotene-tattooed fingers. Her forehead
creases, the skin beneath her chin slackens.
She looks old. I think she was born that way.

I Trudge to My Room

In no mood anymore to play, alone or
otherwise. My cell is on my bed where,
apparently, I left it. Wow. I never even

missed it, which seems to have pissed off
the love of my life: *WHERE THE HECK R U,
AND WHY WON'T U ANSWER UR PHONE?*

Sheesh. (Heck!) If I didn't know better,
I'd think she was jealous or something.
I flash back to less than a half hour ago,

smell the perfume of orange over leather,
feel the dance of Alexa's fingers against
my hand. I did nothing. Except, maybe, lust

a little. But lust without follow-through
doesn't count as infidelity, right? Too late
to call her now, I text back: SORRY. FORGOT

MY PHONE. BUT SEE? HOME EARLY. MISSING
YOU. There. That should do it, and if not,
tomorrow could be either very interesting

or a boatload of boredom. At least I won't
be hungover, though the way my shirt
smells, I could probably get that way just

sucking the spilt beer off it. I strip, slip
into flannel pants and a well-worn T-shirt,
tiptoe down the hall to the laundry

room, and throw my stuff in the washer.
On the way back, I grab a blanket from
the stash above the dryer, cover Mom

to warm her dreams. Turn off the TV.
Hopefully Dad will let her snooze
right there until morning. Depending

on his mood—good drunk, or evil—
he might. If she's really lucky, he'll
be blasted enough to not even notice

she's missing from their bed. I flop
on my own mattress, roll up in the down
comforter, try to shake the moist chill.

The face of my cell tells me I've received
a new message. *1 A.M. ISN'T EARLY.* Guess
that answers that question. Next door

in Luke's room, I hear a train whistle.
"It's only one now," I whisper to no
one. It's not like Hayden is listening.

It Would Be Nice

To sleep in just one freaking Saturday
morning. But, no. It's barely eight o'clock
when I startle awake, words crashing
over me, and into me, like a landslide.

Where were you?

Why would you care?

You could have called.

You're not my fucking mother.

Don't talk to me like that!

You barely qualify as my wife!

Remind me not to get married in my
lifetime! What is it about marriage
that makes people start to hate each other?
Then again, sometimes I wonder if what

initially attracted those two to each other
wasn't, in fact, hate. Is it love that makes
sex good, or would any emotion, equally
weighted, create the same kind of passion?

That's Assuming

Their sex was passionate,
and why would that thought
even cross my mind? Beyond
the thin drywall membranes

enclosing my room, doors
slam. One. Two. They've gone
to their separate corners
for now, but it's only Saturday,

Day One of the Martin Luther
King Weekend standoff. I lie
very still, listening to myself
draw breath, trying to remember

a holiday when this miserable
excuse for a family actually
had fun. Way back when Luke
was little—maybe not quite

three—we drove to the coast
for Fourth of July and camped
on the beach, just the quartet
of us. Mom and Dad set up tents

and a big canopy, and beneath
it, a fold-out picnic table.
The place wasn't real crowded.
Most everyone wanted to watch

the big fireworks displays,
so they stayed close to city
"hullabaloo," as my kindergarten
teacher used to call such chaos.

I would have been just past
old Mrs. Mueller's class then,
and now twelve years dissolve,
just like that. Funny how your mind

works, but I can see that day
as if peering through a reverse
time telescope. I taste the tang
of the salt mist, feel the breeze

lift a forest of goose bumps
off the wet skin of my stick-
thin arms and legs, right up
through the sand crusting them.

But What I Remember Most

Is the music of Luke's little kid giggles
and Mom's lilting gossip while Dad
chopped wood for the campfire.
I've rarely felt as complete as I did
that day, eating half-cooked hot dogs
and digging for sand crabs and dodging
surf, showing off to my brother what it meant

to be a boy at the beach on the Fourth of July.
Mom sneaked off a time or two to smoke;
Dad quietly sucked down beer, pretending
not to notice. Mom was drinking lemonade
from a big cooler, only when I accidentally
sipped from her cup, it tasted sharper than
mine. I knew what that meant by then.

As the afternoon wore on, Luke and I grew
tired from sand-castle building, but not nearly
as drowsy as Mom and Dad. Once or twice,
I caught them kissing, and that was rare indeed.
At six, I didn't think much about them being
in love, so it surprised my naive eyes that they
sure looked to be that way. I will never forget
the flush of raw happiness that brought me.

Once It Got Dark

Dad went to the car, returned
with a surprise—a small footlocker
filled with fireworks. We had to wait
for the wind to die down, and I could
see Dad grow antsier as time passed.

> Finally, he decided, *I think it's safe
> now, boys. Let me get the lighter.*

Mom handed him the butane stick,
cautioned us to take the fire danger
closer to the wet sand at the water's edge.
Luke and I watched Dad set up a row
of spinners and cones and funnels

> in front of some big, gnarled driftwood,
> to block any breeze off the water.
> *Here we go. Ready? Stand back.*

Crackle! Whistle! Whoosh! Okay, compared
to giant sky explosions, it was a small
display, but Luke grabbed my hand, took
one step behind me, peeked out from
around my back, not even pretending

> bravery. Then Dad handed each of us
> a sparkler, showed us how to hold them

at the very bottom of the sticks.
Careful. These babies are hot, hot, hot!

Hot, hot, hot, repeated Luke, and then
Dad lit the end, igniting the sizzle spray.

"Wave it, like this!" I demonstrated,
but Luke held his sparkler straight up
and down, right up until one of those
tiny white embers lodged itself in a pore
on his arm. He threw the offending stick

into the sand. *Ow! Ow! Stupid hot.*
Then he held up his arm to show the blister.

Dad blew. *Jesus H. Christ on a crutch!
How can my son be such a pussy?*

His temples pulsed anger noticeably.
"Hey, Dad. He's just a little kid, okay?"
Defending my brother, that was my job,
even way back then. Dad, of course, was two
sheets to the wind. I see clearly in hindsight

what I was blind to then. In retrospect,
the next part isn't really such a shocker.

It Sure Freaked Us Out Then

There were more fireworks
inside that footlocker—

> bottle rockets
> Roman candles
> firecrackers
> a couple of M-80s.

All illegal in the state of
Oregon, which outlaws
personal possession of
fireworks that—

> fly
> explode
> travel more than six feet on the ground
> or twelve inches in the air.

And boy, they did every
bit of all that! Dad lit them
methodically, laughing
like a lunatic as they—

> flew
> exploded
> shot into the air, with a great
> whoosh of fuel before blowing wide.

Dad's lame attempt
at Fourth of July family fun.

No One Laughed

Except for Dad, and that was totally
swallowed up by the chaos of noise.

Down the beach, people
shouted, a chorus of *Hey!*
What the hell was that?
That's illegal, isn't it?
Someone call the ranger!
(And someone did.)

>Luke screamed
>and scrambled toward
>the tent, tripping over
>his feet and crying even
>louder because of that.

>Mom came running,
>yelling at Dad to *Grow a brain!*
>Though it was obviously much
>too late, and the one he made
>do with was stewing in alcohol.

I plugged my ears, but
couldn't block out the tornado
of sounds, which were scarier,
somehow, than the bottle rockets.

So Much

For sweet family memories.
The rest of that one devolves
into a cacophonous blur of arguments
and explanations and Dad talking
his way out of going to jail,

> *I thought those were only taboo*
> *in residential areas. So sorry . . .*

but only because the park ranger
happened to have witnessed Dad's
outstanding play for the Oregon
Ducks once upon a time,

> *Holy Pete! I'll never forget that*
> *game against Purdue, when you . . .*

while Mom kept shushing Luke,
whose sniffling began to wear on
my nerves. I had to agree with Dad.
Luke was a wuss, even if he was just
a baby, and Mom kept him that way.

> *Quiet now, little man. Everything's*
> *okay. No more booms. I promise.*

All I wanted was for everyone to
shut up so I could listen to the low chuff
of surf and the chatter of wind against
the nylon tent. I remember muttering

into my sleeping bag, "Camping's
supposed to be good times. Not like
it is at home. Why can't we ever
just have fun?" But no one heard,

and no one answered. Pretty much
the story of my life, at least where
my parents are concerned. Too caught
up in their personal tangles of pain,

disappointments, and tomorrows
made murky by yesterdays. I'm damn
sure never going to exist that way. No
sir, it's all about living fearlessly today.

And to do that, I have to get out of bed.
All's quiet on the western front, so I do
the bathroom thing, then head to the kitchen
where, I hope, the coffee is already made.

No Such Luck

Guess my parents decided to sleep
off their late nights, rather than fight
them with caffeine. At least the silence
indicates slumber somewhere. Two doors
slammed, though. Mom must have chosen
Luke's bed. Dad never goes in that room.

Good thing I'm familiar with the Mr.
Coffee. I measure the grounds, add extra,
wanting the brew stiff. I fill the reservoir
with cold water, hit the on switch, and as
the machine starts a slow drip, happen
to glance over the kitchen counter into

the dining area, where my essay still
decorates the table. Most of it is stacked,
facedown. But one section remains right
side up, spread slightly, as if someone has
recently been reading (rereading?) it:

> And what of this "Imago Dei," this supposed human
> creation "in the image of God"? Theologians and
> philosophers differ in their interpretations, but basically,
> were one to believe in the scribblings of Genesis,
> everything started with God. An entity of some kind.

(Who knows his precise nature, or exactly what his origin was? The Bible isn't real specific about infinity, pre-Genesis.) But God was powerful. No, invincible. The flawless source of all love and reason. Intellect defined.

I suppose it makes a certain sense, if you were all that, you'd want to play around with creation, if it was your preferred pastime, and to believe the scriptures, it was his. Not to mention, a talent. If I were to buy into the whole theory, I'd like to know if the Earth was his first try or if he'd had some practice. I mean, seven days from oblivion to Eden, fully functioning. Now that's some serious handiwork!

And his crowning achievement—Adam and Eve. Created in his image, so flawless, like him. Except for that little thing called free will, something he owned in spades; therefore, they got it, too. And all that free will led to disobedience, the fall away from enlightenment. Still, God, the wellspring of love, offered them salvation through forgiveness. Not through an offering plate, or because they fell on their knees, repeating Hail Marys. Mary—that Mary, anyway—didn't come along for quite a few years!

I Almost Quit Reading There

I have read it before, more than
once. But the next few sentences
are underlined. By whose hand,
I haven't the slightest clue.

> Even if you can swallow the idea of God, the concept
> of Imago Dei defies comprehension. Humans aren't
> inherently good—a ludicrous proposition. Instinctively,
> people are barbarians. Cannibals, even. They eat each
> other alive, get off on torture, inflicting pain. This is not
> the image of the Gospel God. If God is love, and God is
> infinite, love would by definition be infinite. But love,
> for most, is a means to an end, and even in its purest
> form, it is fleeting. Not infinite. Therefore, there is no
> God. Simple logic.

The Mr. Coffee beeps, and I'm
drawn away from the table to
the steaming pot of lush-smelling
hot liquid. As I pour a cup, add

a heaped teaspoon of sugar,
no cream, I think of the words
that come next, the segue to
part three of my essay, the best

part. And, I'm sure, the scariest
to those trying to discern some
subtext I didn't really intend,
at least, I'm pretty sure I didn't.

The bridge from Imago Dei to
my little brother, who did not
have to die, is, and I conjure it
strictly from memory, where
it replays several times every day:

> The Imago Dei mythology moves straight into the realm of cruel fantasy when you consider my little brother. If any human ever to walk the face of this earth represented love, it was Luke. So if he, in fact, was God's image, why would the benevolent creator's faithful have played such a heavy hand in his demise?

Strong and just sweet enough,
the coffee I gulp can barely
shore me up against the crashing
tide of depression. Maybe two cups.

Two Cups

Plus thinking about spending time
with Hayden today. Hope she's not
still pissed. Girls sure do get irritated
easily. Trying to keep them happy
is a game. My problem is, I'm not
always sure of the overarching rules.

It seems to be okay that:

She went to a game without me.
She chose her friend's company over mine.
She drank too much soda, ate junk food.
(Just guessing, but it's a decent guess.)
She watched other guys be athletic.

But it's probably not okay that:

I went to a party without her.
I put up with a friend's company instead of hers.
I drank some beer, smoked a little weed.
(She'd just be guessing, an accurate guess.)
I talked to another girl, drove her home.

Okay, it's weighted a little unevenly.
Still, overall, I did absolutely nothing
wrong except try to enjoy myself
without my girlfriend coming along.

They Say a Solid Offense

Is the best defense, and I'm going
with that. I wait until a decent hour—
eleven o'clock on a Saturday is decent,
right?—and I go ahead and call my lovely.
One ring. Two, and that's enough. "You up?"

Of course. I was in early last night.

Snippy and inaccurate. "You texted
me at twelve fifty-six. That's late.
Oh, and just by the way, I was home,
and had been." Not exactly true either.
But let's play the game. "Why are you mad?"

Long sigh. I don't want to fight.

"Good. I don't either. In fact, I want
to do whatever the exact opposite of
fighting is. I love you, Hayden. Now
what should we do today?" Outside
it's still cold and drizzly. Go figure.

I don't care. Mall walk? Movie?

We Settle on Both

I pick her up just after lunch for the drive
into Eugene. I watch her exit her house,
spin to wave at someone inside before
turning back toward me with a sincere
smile. This day is looking up. She floats
along the walk, ethereal in some gauzy
skirt the color of greening spring, plus

a darker, emerald sweater, which hugs
every perfect curve of her body. Was it just
yesterday I last saw her? Why don't I
remember her looking this way? Nymph
is the word that comes to mind. Not
the dirty kind, but the kind who consorts
with the gods, lowercase *g*. Stunning,
that's what she is, and more. Breathtaking.

We will not argue. We will not argue.
It's a good mantra. Almost as good as:
We will kiss. We will touch. We will
kiss. We will . . . Okay, probably not that.
But the thought makes me grin, and
my smile is the first thing she sees when
she opens the door and ducks her head.

>   *What is it?* she asks, voice all maple
>   syrup sweet and butter smooth.

"Nothing. I was just watching you
and thinking how you remind me
of spring. Come over here, okay?"
She blushes an incredible shade
of rose, but scoots as close as
the arm between the seats allows,
and that's plenty close enough

for me to cup her face in my hands,
tilt her chin up just so, and realize
my mantra. Actually, both of them.
Because kissing like this, there is no
way we can argue. She closes her eyes,
but I keep mine open, watching the subtle
movements of her body. Yes, she looks
like spring, and tastes of winter mint.

But her scent is summer—toasted
skin. Hint of apricot. A potpourri
of flowers haloing the silk of her hair.
I'm holding Eden in my hands, and
it makes me glad there is no God
to take this garden away from me.

Except . . .

Except

Her cell phone buzzes inside her bag.
She jerks away, breathless, and reaches
down to check for the text. "What is it?"

> *Let's go.* She waits for me to start
> the truck, motor away. *It's from my dad,
> who was spying on us out the window.*

I try to avoid her father, who does
not approve of his daughter dating
anyone. Especially me. "And . . . ?"

> *He said he hoped we wouldn't repeat
> that performance in public, and to
> consider what Christ would want.*

"In my admittedly limited understanding
of the New Testament definition of
Christ, he is the foundation of all love.

Considering how I feel about you, that
would put Christ sitting solidly on the arm-
rest between us. I think you're safe."

> She reaches over, circles my knee
> with gentle fingertips. *If I didn't believe
> I was totally safe, I wouldn't be here.*

"Does your dad ask about the . . . uh,
personal stuff we do? I mean, it's not
like we're shacking up in motel rooms."

> Her fingers stop their circular orbit.
> *Well, that isn't exactly how I put it.*
> *I said you're a complete gentleman.*

I purposely drop my jaw. "But . . . How
could you say such a preposterous thing?
I mean, everyone knows *that's* a lie!"

We both crack up, and Hayden's
left hand relaxes on my leg while her
right turns up the volume on the radio,

> which happens to be tuned to Liquid
> Metal. A deadly guitar riff screeches
> into the space around us. *Ugh! How*
>
> *can you listen to that?* Like magic,
> we've got boy band pop. *Good thing*
> *Dad doesn't know you like that stuff.*

"Or what? He'd refuse to let you see me
because I'm obviously in league with Satan?"
I wait for her smile. Instead, she shrugs.

I Should Drop It

Don't really know why
I feel the need to defend
myself, or my taste
in music. Anyway,
she knows what I listen to.

This is the first time
she's overtly associated
it—and so, me—with
something as unsavory
as the King of Lies.

"That would just be
your father's opinion, right?
You don't believe metal
is the voice of the Devil?"
Does anyone in their right
mind actually buy into that?

> *My dad is a hard-core*
> *evangelical, but he does*
> *allow me a mind of my own.*
> *I prefer not to listen to death*
> *metal, but not because I think*
> *it's satanic. More like a lot*
> *of irritating, random noise.*

We've Been Going Out

For close to a year, more than long
enough to confess music tastes.
"Why didn't you say so before?"

> I don't know. Guess I didn't
> want to sound like a nag.

Fair enough. But, "So, why
tell me now?" And also, just
by the way, why change the channel
without asking if it was okay?
I mean, if only to be polite.

> Another shrug. *Why not?*
> *We should tell each other*
> *what's bugging us, right?*

Uh-oh. Tension grips
my shoulders like giant
hands, squeezes. Quick.
Mantra one. We will not
argue. We will not argue.

"Of course." I grit my teeth.
"Is there anything else
bugging you besides my music?"

I Half Expect a Tirade

Or at least a short
list of complaints.

I party too much.
I'm kind of a smart-
ass. I drive too fast.
I eat like a hog. I don't
much like her friends.

But no. She smiles, then
brings those coral gloss
lips against my cheek,
tickling it when she says,

> That's the worst thing
> about you, and the rest
> doesn't matter. You're not
> perfect, that's a fact. But
> your imperfections are
> part of what makes you
> you. And that's who I fell
> in love with. Surprises.

> She's full of them. Like
> now, she dials back to Liquid
> Metal. *For you, I can even
> handle this. Once in a while.*

Loving This Girl

Is a roller-coaster ride.
Protracted climb.
Serious drop.
Loop until your stomach
threatens to lose it,
jerk to the right, spin
left. Coast to a stop.
Disembark.
Get back in line.
Do it again.
And again.
All in the name
of chasing a thrill.

Is the rush worth the effort?
Most of the time, hell yeah.
But then come those moments
when I'm really not sure.

Guess it's a good thing
those moments
are few
and far
between.

In Addition

To different tastes in music, we have
a similar wide divide in our ideas

about what constitutes a good movie.
I'm all about action. She likes romance.

Usually one or the other of us has to
compromise. Today, we find one that has

both violent revolt and tender love scenes.
That is providential. What's less fortunate

is some of those love scenes involve
nakedness and sensual discovery, resulting

in downright hot sex. I can't speak for Hayden.
Don't even know if girls react in the same

way to such visual stimulation, but I am
completely turned on and sitting next to a girl

who's every bit as beautiful as the one
on-screen, and I've rarely been quite

this uncomfortable, and all I can think
of at this exact moment is Alexa

asking, *Don't you want to, you know?*
My arm is around Hayden's shoulder,

and I am adrift in the current of her hair,
spilling across my chest. The sudden grip

of desire is so wicked, I can almost believe
there is, in fact, a Satan playing some vile

game. I move my hand to the left, whisper
trace the outward curve of her breast.

She doesn't protest, but rather sighs
into the heavy fabric of my shirt, and now

I wonder what it would be like to "you
know" with her right here, right now, zero

hesitation, just please, please, let me
love you like that. But now the screen

lights with battle, and in the barrage I hear
my mom, hear my dad, hear Hayden's father,

all shouting, *Be careful! Don't ruin your life
like I did!* And, *What would Christ think?*

From Satan to Christ

In about twenty seconds, all because
of a flush of passion. And that is made
all the weirder considering neither S
nor C means one damn thing to me.
Consider the poor kid who stumbles
through life in the shadow of both.

The credits roll and as we exit,
I ask, "Did you like the movie?"

> *It was pretty good, I guess.* She slips
> her hand into mine, steeples our fingers.
> *Some parts were better than others.*

I wish I could read her, know for sure
she means what I think she does. But
I'm not about to ask her to clarify.
I unlock our hands, tuck her slender
shoulder beneath my arm, kiss the beat
in her temple. "I love you. Know that?"

> Her arm circles my waist and she tucks
> a thumb in my back pocket. *Yes, Matthew,
> I know that. And I kind of love you, too.*

Kind Of?

Hope she's not trying to tell me
something. We cruise the mall
like Siamese twins until something
in a window catches her eye, severs
our connection. As she exclaims over

the latest Coach purse, my eyes scan
ahead, and I'm dismayed to see Lainie
heading our way, elbow to elbow
with Vince. So much for breakups.

I hope Marshall is still in one piece.
Vince gives me a curt nod and Lainie
coos, *Oh, hey, Matt,* pulling Hayden's
attention away from turquoise leather.

This could go poorly, and does instantly,
when Vince rather obviously checks
out my nymph. Lainie's voice frosts.
Hayden. Huh. She considers what to say,

and I think she might spare me. But
the green-eyed monster wins out.
Her mission is now to hurt Hayden.
I'm surprised to see you *here.* Her words
stab and the "you" twists the knife.

No Escape

I'm in trouble now.
I should have known.

> Hayden: *Really? Why would
> you be surprised to see me?*

> Lainie: *Because of last night.
> I kind of thought maybe Matt
> and Alexa were a thing now.*

> Hayden (a serious shade of red):
> *Last night? What do you mean?*

> Lainie (ignoring my evil glare):
> *Sorry. Sometimes I read too much
> into things. Guess I was wrong.*

I can either stand here
like a wuss and wait
to be leveled, or act
like a man, invite
the solar plexus punch.

"Alexa was at the party
last night. I drove her home."

Acting Like a Man Is Overrated

Especially when it means hurting
someone you love, and Hayden
is stung, even though she hangs on
to a good percentage of her dignity,
at least in front of Lainie (the bitch).

> *Oh, that,* is all she says, refusing
> to publicly cede ground.

Something simmers beneath
the surface, though, sizzling
like hot oil. Vince senses it, too,

> decides to dodge the pending spatter.
> *Let's go.* He gives Lainie
> a decent push, ignores her complaint.

Hayden watches their retreat,
mostly as a way not to look at me.
I reach for her, but she sidesteps.

> *Will you please take me home?*
> Sssssssplatter! It blisters.

Hope it doesn't leave a scar.

She Walks Two Steps

Ahead of me all the way to the truck.
It's a struggle to stay behind her,
considering the relative lengths
of our strides, but if I'm lucky,
maybe her quickened pace
will burn off a little anger.

> Luck is not my best thing.
> We are barely out of the parking
> lot when she spits, *Alexa? Really?*
> *I thought Marshall was your date.*

Reverse déjà vu?
"I did take Marshall to the party.
What Lainie forgot to mention
was how she climbed all over him,
trying to piss off Vince. . . ."

> *Lainie and Marshall? Whatever.*
> *Anyway, what's that got to do*
> *with Alexa?* Cavernous breath.
> *That's why you got home so late.*

"Listen. Lainie drove Alexa
to the party. When she hooked up
with Marshall, Alexa needed
a ride home. That's it. Nothing

happened between Alexa and
me." Except for my wanting to kiss
her, and her slightly disparaging
remarks about Hayden. But that's
nothing much. Nothing, really.

It's maddening when the truth
(mostly the truth) isn't enough.
You know how I feel about Alexa.
I can't believe you'd do this to me.

"Hayden, I didn't do anything
to you, and I didn't do a damn
thing with Alexa except make
sure she got home safely. Please
don't be mad. I would never
jeopardize what I have with you."

Seethe. That's the word.
She's seething. *You're wrong.*
You already jeopardized it.
End of debate. I drop her

off and if her dad is watching
out the window, he's gloating
about what he sees. No kiss. No
goodbye. No see you tomorrow.

Infuriating!

Why won't she listen?
Why won't she believe me?
Will she just stay mad for
a little while, then automatically
forgive me? Why do I doubt
that? Girls hold grudges
longer than guys do.

Except, that's not exactly
accurate, is it? I mean,
there's Dad. And there's me.
Dad, who'll always blame
Mom for his fizzled dreams.
Not his dick. Not his warped
sense of morality.

Me, who will never
forgive those who played
supporting roles
in the Luke melodrama.
No, I can't forgive them,
and the only narrow windows
of forgetfulness I enjoy
are when I'm with Hayden.
Therein lies a big problem—
I need her more than
she'll ever need me.

The Person

I'd really like to choke
is Lainie. She's the impetus
for all levels of this mess,
and it's probably good
she's nowhere within reach
right now. Stinking troublemaker.
What is wrong with people like her—
those whose greatest pleasure lies
in destroying others? Bitches,
bullies, and broadcasters-of-shit.

And for what? To feel mildly
better about themselves,
try to scrub away a chunk
of the cancer eating them up
from the inside out?

They're like well-fed Rottweilers,
tearing into an entire flock
of chickens, just to watch feathers
fly and get off on the piteous
squawking. All fangs
and slobber. Zero sympathy.

I Give Hayden's Temperature

A few hours to drop a degree or two.
It's Saturday night, and both my parents
have gone out, but not with each other.
Retreated to their separate alcohol-soaked
corners. One, to talk sports and regret.
The other, to discuss God and loss.

What's it like to spend an entire
weekend together as an intact family?

Hayden and I were supposed to have
dinner together, post-mall. I'd planned
on Thai. Instead, I microwave half-assed
beef broccoli, chase it with a couple
of Dad's beers. He won't miss them,
and the carbonated buzz sounds inviting.

Guess I'm burrowing into my own
alcohol-infused sanctuary. Alone.

I turn on the TV for company as I eat,
random noise to fight the suffocating
quiet. It weights this house, threatens
to drop it down into a sinkhole of memory.
How do I escape it? Where can I go?
What can I do? Maybe Luke had the right idea.

Buzzed but Anxious

I won't sleep right away, so I tune into
old action movies on cable. Before it gets

too late, I call Hayden, apologize again
for doing nothing wrong, although I don't

reiterate that last part. "Will I see you
tomorrow? I'm still jonesing for Thai."

Even bounced off a satellite, thousands
of miles above us, her voice sounds cool.

> *I don't know. I've got church, and after,*
> *Mom wants us to visit Nana.* The tough

old crow lives in a retirement complex,
but not because she needs care. More like

because she needs company. Most of her
circle has moved away or journeyed on

to the Old Folks' Mansion in the Sky.
"Please think about dinner. And what you

want to do on Monday. I love you with all
my heart." Please don't desert me, too.

I Crash Late

Still alone, anxiety shimmering
around me like an aura. Though
it's cool in the house, I lie on top
of my blankets, somehow too warm
to go under. Every room is empty,
and silence-bloated, so the blood

whoosh in my ears sounds like
the bellow of swollen surf. I try
to relax my muscles, but I feel like
a winter kill, left to freeze overnight.
My therapist gave me relaxation
techniques to try at times like this.

I imagine floating on my back in
a warm, salty sea. No effort. Eyes
closed to the gentle sun against
my face. Now I create a mantra,
a rhythmic chant: "Ohm. Ohm."
Before long, it changes: "Omega."

The last. The ultra. The end. I sink
beneath the surface, no light, no air,
but oddly no fear, and it doesn't hurt
not to breathe. Is this what death is?
I have nowhere immediate to go,
so I let the current tug me at will.

It carries me to some sort of undersea
grotto, at least it seems I'm underwater
still, until I bump up against a graveled
shore. A thin finger of light pokes down
from an opening in the rock above.
I crawl onto the beach, find myself

completely dry. Breathe in. Exhale.
I am alive. I hear footfalls in the gloom
ahead, the slam of a door. "Hello?"
I call, to no reply, so I investigate.
Along a narrow corridor flanked
by slick black granite. A sudden whisper

of fear lifts goose bumps all over my body,
and I know I have to hurry, or it will be
too late. I break into a trot, chanting,
"No, no, no." And now I'm running
down the hall in this very house. "No!"
Luke's door is locked, but the knob

is no match for the adrenaline screeching
through me. The first thing I see is his
feet. He's still wearing his left shoe;
the right has fallen beside the chair
lying sideways on the floor. Then I look
up at his face. It's plum blue. And he's smiling.

No! Please, No!

My own scream yanks me awake, and I fight
the black glove of night pressing me against
my bed. I turn on my side, curl into a capital

G, knees against my chest, sucking in air around
an immense exhalation of sobs. The clipped rhythm
of bare feet informs me Mom is home, and aware.

> She bursts through the door, flips the switch
> beside it, flooding my room with ochre light.
> *What's wrong?* She looks at me. Understands.

"I'm f-f-fine," I stutter, though it's obvious
I'm anything but. "I haven't . . . I just . . .
It's been a while since I've dreamed about it."

Mom approaches slowly, almost warily.
Something melts, her sharp edges blur
and she puddles on the edge of my bed.

> In a rare gesture, she strokes sweat-damp
> strands of hair off my face, combs them
> with tobacco-perfumed fingers. *I still dream*
>
> *about him, too. But not like that, and I'm*
> *sorry this is the way he comes to you.*
> *He mostly visits me as a little boy, before . . .*

She Leaves the Sentence Unfinished

Her unspoken words trail
like breeze-disturbed smoke,
pale and thin, toward the ceiling.
But I know what they are.

> *Before he knew.*
> *Before we knew.*
> *Before anyone knew.*

I wish she wouldn't talk.
Wish she'd remember that
even when things weren't insane,
you couldn't have called them good.

> *Before he grew up.*
> *Before he grew aware.*
> *Before he grew into himself.*

All I want her to do is keep
weaving her fingers into my hair,
comforting me like good moms
do when their children hurt.

Clatter and Cursing

Shake me awake. I'm still lying on top
of my bedspread, covered by billows of
afghan. I remember last night. Mom's hands.
Grief, tremoring in the thick mantle

of silence between us. I inhale regret,
listen to Dad crashing around in the kitchen,
punctuating every dropped pan or lid
with invective. Sunday morning and

the lift of silver light informs me noon
isn't far away. Mom will be at church
while Dad fights his hangover with
beer, or maybe vodka. Hair of the dog,

or pelt of the wolf. No school tomorrow,
coupled with the cupboard chaos,
I'm guessing he's chosen the latter.
How is it possible for a multiple-

championship-winning basketball
coach to be such a loser when it comes
to domestic responsibilities? How can
anyone so egotistical about his career

completely lack self-respect in regards
to his home and family? I could just
lie here, ignore his tirade. Instead, against
all that is sensible, I fold up the afghan,

straighten the covers, slip into flannel
pants and a clean T-shirt, go see
what, exactly, his current problem
might be. When I get to the kitchen,

he is bending over a raw egg spill,
semi-mopping it up with paper towels.
A tumbler of something tomatoey sits
on the counter. Bloody Mary pelt of

the wolf, I'm guessing. His attention
is so raptly focused on the goo that
he hasn't noticed me yet. I could sneak
away. Instead, I offer, "Need some help?"

Which startles him and when he tries to
jump, the hand clutching the slippery
paper towels slides, lurching his whole
body forward toward the fridge.

Bam!

His forehead slams into the stainless
door. Then he windmills into reverse,

> splatting backward on his ass. *Fuck!*
> *You trying to kill me, you little prick?*

"Nice parental vocab, Dad." Not that he's
ever been the warm, fuzzy type. I extend

my hand to help him up, but the gesture
goes unappreciated, and he finds his feet

all on his own. When he turns to face
me, I can't help but wince at the knot

popping up, purple-black, just above
the bridge of his nose. "Ouch. Sorry."

It would make sense for him to yell.
Instead, he chooses obnoxious laughter.

The Bloody Mary on the counter must
not be his first. Might as well play smart-

ass. It's expected of me. "You're supposed
to scramble eggs in a bowl, you know."

I go to the cupboard for my favorite
Pyrex container. Dad downs his drink

and watches me expertly crack two eggs,
depositing them in the bowl without

so much as a sliver of shell. I beat them,
add a dash of half-and-half, seasoning salt,

and pepper. Then I melt a little butter
in a frying pan, pour the yellow mixture.

> *Look at that, would ya?* His voice
> is sandpaper-textured. *When did you*

> *learn how to cook?* Luckily my back
> is turned so he can't see my eyes roll.

"Really, Dad? I've been cooking
since I was a kid. God, wait for you

or Mom to do it, Luke and I would
have starved to death." It was harsher

> than I meant it, and he responds
> in kind. *You just fattened him up for . . .*

His Last Sentiment

Drops into the sizzle-pop of eggs.
I think about letting them burn,
but then the kitchen would smell
like butt, so I yank the pan off
the flame, push it onto the countertop,
which, fortunately, is granite.

"Enjoy." That's what comes out
of my mouth, but what I really mean
is, "Hope you choke on them."
And as I start to leave, I mutter
an under-breath amen: "Dickhead."
Apparently, it wasn't qute far enough

>under my breath because he's quick
>to cross the floor and grab my arm.
>*What did you say?* V8 and vodka
>can't quite conceal the smell of stale
>sleep on his breath. His eyes move, side
>to side, as if trying to focus, and I really

think he might be considering violence.
"Want to hit me, Dad? Go ahead, if
it makes you feel like more of a man."
The remark is unwarranted. He hasn't
touched me since I was around nine, and
even then his spankings didn't hurt.

His Grip Loosens

But he doesn't let go completely.
I know what he wants is an apology.
Whatever. No skin off my nose.

"I'm sorry I called you a dickhead,
Dad, but your insensitivity pisses
me off. You were shitty to Luke

when he was alive, and now you're
worse, if that's even possible. He's dead.
Respect him for that, if nothing else."

> He flings his hand off my arm as if
> it burns. *Respect? Goddamn pussy,*
> *that's what he was. Goddamn cow—*

"Stop it! He was gay, okay?
That didn't make him a pussy.
Stop calling him that, would you?"

> *He was a coward, and a waste*
> *of talent. I can't stand crap like that.*
> *Not from any kid, but especially*

> *not from one of mine.* He slugs
> down his drink. *No goddamn*
> *wonder those boys gave him hell.*

"No! Don't you dare defend them.
What is wrong with you? Luke
was your son, and pretty much all

he ever wanted was for you to be
proud of him. Yes, he had talent.
But he worked his butt off trying

to be the absolute best basketball
player to ever walk on this planet.
Not for attention. Not for fame.

Not even so he could have a friend
or two. He did it for you, Dad. And
you denied him." All his tension

releases suddenly. He shoulders go slack
and, impossibly, his eyes water. I have
never seen my father cry. Never. Not even

at Luke's funeral. He disintegrates now,
and I'm not sure which one of us is more
embarrassed about my witnessing the event.

I Have No Idea

How to react.
Hug him?
Slap him?
Break down
and cry with him?

How do you find sympathy
for someone who has never
once offered it to you,
especially when that someone
happens to be your parent,
a person whose arms
should always be open wide?

This is a moment
of weakness, nothing more,
and likely never to be repeated
in my presence. So why
does any part of me wish
it might be the door
to a whole new father-
son relationship?

It's Over

Almost as soon as it began.
He turns his back, sucks down
his drink. Starts to make another.
Then he notices the frying pan.

Goddamn eggs are cold.

Time to retreat. "Mix 'em up
with mayonnaise and pickle relish
and slap 'em on bread. Egg salad
sandwich." I leave him to consider

my suggestion, and as I start up
the hall, Mom comes in the front
door, all smiles, at least until
she notices the look on my face.

What's wrong?

I shake my head. Nod once toward
the kitchen. "Dad and his eggs got
into it. Not pretty." I lower my voice.
"He and Bloody Mary are melting down."

So Much for Her Smile

She glances toward the kitchen,
wheels and heads for their room

instead. Personally, I'm escaping
this place before everything turns

to excrement stew—a simmering
pot of shit. It's well after noon,

and Hayden should be finished
with church. But just in case,

I text her rather than call. HEY
LADY. YOU READY FOR ME

TO PICK YOU UP? She doesn't
respond immediately, so I go

ahead and dress in my favorite
jeans and a dove-gray flannel shirt.

> I'm in the middle of brushing
> my teeth when her text finally

> comes. *GOING BOWLING WITH*
> *WITH MY YOUTH GROUP. PIZZA*

> *AFTER. FINISHED AROUND FOUR.*
> *I'LL CALL YOU WHEN WE'RE DONE.*

This Time

It's an emotional one-two punch
striking my solar plexus.
One: anger.
Two: jealousy.
One.
Two.
One.
Two.
Straight to the gut.

Powerful blows
in repetitive action.
How
could
she
do
this
to
me?

My resident little voice
of reason—the one who
always talks me down
from the reactive cliff—
seems to have
vacated my cranium.

Can't Sit Around Here

Waiting for the figurative knockout
blow. The interior turbulence
is building, and if I don't want
it to shake me apart, I'd better
find a way to release it.
Only one thing I know
can accomplish that.
It resides in a lockbox
beneath the seat of my truck.

Technically, I need
a concealed carry permit
to keep my Glock 34 there,
and I can't get that until
I'm twenty-one, despite
having taken the course.

Pistol and instruction were gifts
from Dad, which led to a memorable
eighteenth birthday, both because
of the most unexpected presents
and the fight that instigated
between him and Mom.

It Started

The moment I opened the box.
Unloaded, unpolished, unpacked
from its wrappings, still the Glock
looked remarkably deadly.

> Mom: *A gun? Are you insane?*
> *He's not mature enough for a gun.*

> > Dad: *Plenty of kids his age have guns,*
> > *and he needs to excel at something.*

> Mom: *What are you talking about?*
> *He's at the very top of his class.*

> > Dad: *Academically, yes, but he sucks*
> > *at sports. Team sports, anyway.*

> Mom: *What do sports have to do*
> *with this? Shooting isn't a sport.*

> > Dad: *Don't be an idiot. Haven't*
> > *you ever heard of hunting?*

The volume of their argument
increased as the tension escalated.

Mom: *You hunt with a rifle. This is*
a handgun. Only serial killers
go hunting with handguns.

Dad: *Target shooting is a sport,*
too. You can do that with a handgun.
Don't you know anything?

Mom: *Why are you attacking me?*
Do you really think this is a good
idea, all things considered?

Dad: *You mean because he's seeing*
a ther-a-pist? (Disdain evident.)
Maybe this is all the therapy he needs.

Mom: *He has no idea how to shoot*
that thing. What if he accidentally
puts a bullet through someone's head?

Dad: *You don't have to worry*
about that. I signed him up for
a course at Jessie's range.

That wasn't quite the end
of the "discussion." But I tuned
the rest out about there.

Dad's Motive

For buying the gun remains
murky. But I was fascinated
immediately, and he proved
right about a couple of things.

Shooting is therapy.
And I'm really, really good at it.

I practice a lot at Uncle Jessie's
range. He says I should enter
competitions, and maybe I will.
But not till I'm unbeatable.

Not that I worry a lot about
what Dad thinks of my talents—

or lack thereof. But for once
it would be nice to prove to him
that his disappointment of a son
is not only good at something

besides academics, but he is,
in fact, the absolute best.

Sunday on a Holiday Weekend

Uncle Jessie isn't here at the range,
playing NRA-butt-kissing owner,
and I'm pleased about that. I love
my gun, but I despise gun politics.
I don't want to massacre little kids,
I just want to hit bull's-eyes on targets.

If they happen to resemble some Al
Qaeda goon, well, that's a fortunate
bonus. The Glock 34 is a competition
gun. Quick to load and reload. Smooth
slide action. Not too much recoil, at
least if you grip it correctly.

Dad showed me the basics—how
to load and check for chambered
bullets. Where not to put my thumb
to avoid the backward kick of the slide.
The Weaver stance, which is his choice,
one leg slightly behind the other.

But Uncle Jessie taught me finesse
and nuance. How to bring the gun up
from the holster, right hand positioned
correctly to shoot without the aid
of the left if need be. Where to place
the left and how to utilize it for maximum

control and cushion. How to focus
most on the far sight, rather than
the near, which actually blurs just
a bit because of concentrating so hard
on the other. The Isosceles stance—
feet parallel, upper body forward

and triangular to the plant, allowing
free side-to-side swing at the waist.
The last is more important for taking
out moving targets. Uncle Jessie knows.
He was infantry in Iraq. Lost an eye
to shrapnel on his second tour. After

his discharge, he had a choice: go
to Portland, live with his parents,
and design video games; or move
to his grandparents' property and farm.
Didn't want to do either, he told me.
Fake shooting on-screen is for pussies.

*Farming is for fools, but I've always
loved this piece of land.* The shooting
range was his compromise. And damned
if he can't hit bull's-eyes square despite
his handicap. *It only takes one eye to
sight, son. But you go ahead and use two.*

I Use Two

For a couple of hours. I'm off
my game a little today,
and I'm pretty sure my lack
of concentration has to do
with still being pissed.
The initial earthquake
of anger has receded.
But the aftershocks keep
coming in rhythmic succession.

Finally, I give up, pack it in,
and go home, where it's very
quiet. Dad's sleeping off
his tough morning. Mom's
gone. I wash off the gunshot
residue, put on a clean shirt.
It's probably not enough.

Hayden does not share
my passion for shooting,
and she can always smell
gun on me after I spend time
at the range. One time I told
her it was better than smelling
something else on me.

She didn't appreciate the joke.

Four O'Clock

Arrives. Goes. Four ten.
Four fifteen. Four twenty.
By the time her call finally
comes at four twenty-five,
I'm pacing. A big ol'
simmering pot of pissed.
I consciously lower
my boiling point
before I detonate.

Deep breaths. Liquid Metal,
turned way up loud,
the blazing beat absorbing
what's left of my anger.
By the time I reach Pizza
Hut, I'm mostly in control.

Until I turn the corner, see
them standing beneath the eaves,
backs to the building, bundled
against the cold. Hayden. Jocelyn.
And some guy who's in his early
twenties. Though he's a head
taller than me, he's slender.
I could kick his ass if I wanted
to, and maybe I do. As I pull

to the curb across the street,
two things are apparent.
Jocelyn is flirting unmercifully
with him—hardly "Christian,"
and I hate how familiar that sounds.

But what I despise
is how his eyes completely
overlook Jocelyn, despite her best
efforts, because they are locked
on Hayden. She says something,
and he smiles, and there is way
too much obvious affection there.
I tap the horn to ruin the moment.

Hayden turns, waves, and
her smile is all for me. I think.
She gives Jocelyn a quick hug
and as she starts away the guy
touches her arm, redirecting
her attention toward his goodbye.

I definitely want
to kick his spindly ass.

She Crosses the Street

And I get out of the truck, wait
for her. I want him to see me greet
her with a kiss, and more, I want
him to see her kiss me back.
I hope she can't hear the anger
hissing in my ears, or see the way
it's crawling, crimson, up my neck.

I pull her into me for said kiss, gaze
fixed over her head on the guy,
who is most assuredly assessing
every move she makes. The hiss swells
into a growl so I close my eyes, reach
for her mouth with my own, silently
pleading with her to prove how very

much she loves me. She rewards
me with a swift, dry osculation,
then slips out of my arms and walks
around to the passenger side. I follow
closely, open the door to let her in.
"Do I smell like onions or something?"
I don't give her a chance to answer

before shutting the door. Sometimes
jerkish behavior is sort of called for.

We Are a Half Block Away

Headed toward where, I have no clue,
when I snap, "Who was that guy?"

> She acts all innocent. *What guy?*
> *Oh, do you mean Judah?*

"Judah? What kind of a name
is that?" Lame, that's what kind.

> *Judah. As in Judah Ben-Hur?*
> *He's our youth minister.*

"Oh, really? Are you you sure?
He's kind of young for a minister,

don't you think? Has anyone
checked his credentials?" Snarky,

> and she does not appreciate the snark.
> *He's still in the seminary, Matt.*
>
> *He has a one-year internship at our*
> *church, working with Pastor Bohart.*
>
> *Judah believes he's been called*
> *to youth ministry. He's so inspirational!*

If She Gushed Any More

She'd drown in her own gushiness.
I want to yell. Instead, I grumble.
"Inspirational? Looked more
like robbing the cradle to me."

> *Robbing . . . You're kidding, right?*
> She plasters on a ridiculous grin, but it
> vanishes when she analyzes my expression.
> *Wait. Don't tell me you're jealous?*

"Let's see. We were supposed to spend
the afternoon together, then go out
for Thai. Instead you go bowling and eat
pizza with your perverted youth minister.

First of all, when have you *ever* gone
bowling? And second, his eyes were
crawling all over you. No wonder
you're so hot on youth group lately."

> *As for bowling, there's a first time*
> *for everything. I sucked, but so what?*
> *And as for the rest, don't be ridiculous.*
> *Christ called me to youth group.*

"That's amazing. Did he use a phone,
or just shout your name down from on
high? Nah, that can't be it, or I would
have heard it, too." I'm on thin ice

but I can't seem to stop skating.
"I mean, an all-powerful God would
have a pretty loud voice and all, right?"
Damn. I might have just fallen through

the veneer. She's steaming. *Why
are you being so nasty, Matthew?
If you really think I'd cheat on you,
and with a minister, no less, maybe*

*we need to rethink our relationship.
I can't believe you have such a low
opinion of me. I didn't eat pizza,
but I'm not hungry. Take me home.*

I'm almost there already, but now
I want to apologize. Except, I don't.
She's infuriating! How can she make
me feel so bad about being right?

And, Worse

How can she make me feel
so rotten about tomorrow
being a holiday? Apologize?
Don't apologize? Pretty sure
this isn't salvageable, but
I'm damn sure going to try.

"I'm sorry, Hayden. I know
you wouldn't cheat on me. . . ."

Hardly Christian, after all.

"Yes, I was jealous, and it's
an obnoxious thing to be. . . ."

Pretty much like you were
approximately two days ago.

She's softening, and I really
should stop right here. Even
realizing that, my mouth keeps
motoring. "But that guy has got
a definite thing for you. By the way,
you do realize that Judah Ben-Hur
is a *fictional* character, right?"

Emphasis on the word that means "fake."

Too Much

I went too far; of course I did.
The barrier that had just started
to crumble reconstructs, solid.

> *How can you be so condescending?*
> *You don't even know Judah.*

I suck. She sucks. This sucks. So,
suck it up. "You're right." Deep breath.
"I don't know him, and I don't want to.
But I don't want you to be mad at me.
I completely trust you, Hayden."

I wish that were true, but the fact is,
I don't completely trust anyone.
And when I reach for her hand and
she jerks it away, I have to wonder
if it's just out of anger, or if some
ugly ulterior motive is at play.

As I pull into her driveway, stop
the truck to let her out, I withdraw
into pouty juvenile mode, "Why
wouldn't you kiss me back there?"

> *I don't know, Matt. Who were you*
> *trying to impress? Me? Or him?*

Valid Question

One she doesn't allow
me time to answer.
She storms toward
her door without so
much as a wave, or
even a backward glance.

Damn, she is something—
anger evident in the way
she tosses her hair and
thrusts her hips side to side.
She is haunting. Daunting.
High maintenance, but
totally worth the effort.

Any guy with a libido and
half a brain would want
to possess her, and if that
includes Fake Minister Judah,
why should that surprise me?

If I'm not careful, I'll lose
her, and that could spell
the end of Matthew Turner.
So why do I seem hell-bent
on chasing her away?

I Spend the Next Thirty-Six Hours

Wondering if I've done exactly that.
It's a struggle not to go crawling up

to her door on my hands and knees.
Except, wouldn't her father love that?

Two major quarrels over the span
of one holiday weekend, and that

doesn't even include the ones I had with
my parents. By Tuesday, not a single

word from her, I'm wrecked. I fake
my way through English and calculus,

concentration impossible. I don't see
her in the hallways, wonder if she's even

here, until the lunch bell rings. I find
her in the cafeteria, surrounded by

her posse of believers, who are no doubt
discussing the relative merits of their youth

minister. When I gesture for her to join
me, I'm terrified she'll shake her head.

Instead, she says something to her friends,
grabs her book—*The Perks of Being*

a Wallflower, I can tell by the cover—
and comes over without hesitation. She tilts

her chin, reaching for a kiss. Relief upwells.
I whisper in her ear, "Thank you," encircle

her with one arm, and acknowledge
her gift of forgiveness. This is the kiss

I wanted two days ago. The one that makes
everyone in this chili-stinking room understand

that Hayden and I are in love. Unfortunately,
it draws the attention of Ms. Hannity,

> who happens to be passing by. *Break it
> up, Mistah Turnah. This isn't HBO.*

"Sorry. Couldn't help myself. As you
know, self-control isn't my forte."

> *Yes, well, work on that. Some things
> are best done in private. That is all.*

Arm Still Firmly Wrapped

Around Hayden's waist, I steer her
to a more private place—a table way
in the back of the room. As we pass
the deli cart, I grab a ham sandwich.
"Want something?" Who says chivalry
is dead? But Hayden shakes her head.

> *I'm eliminating carbs for a while.*

Don't be ridiculous. That's what
I really want to say. Instead, I go
with a much more generic "Why?"

> *Prom's coming up. I want to fit
> in the dress I bought. We are going?*

What kind of an idiot boyfriend
would say no, even if he quite
reasonably thought prom was nothing
but a money-sucking nightmare?
"Of course. Can't wait." We sit

and Hayden watches me unwrap
my approximation of a delicious meal.
Rather than have her stare as I scarf
it down, I direct her attention back

toward the Bible-thumpers' table,
where Jocelyn and friends seem
to be in deep discussion. "What's up
with them? Have they discovered
a lost gnostic gospel or something?"

She smiles.
That's good.
I think.

> *In the last five minutes? Don't think*
> *so. No, they're planning our spring*
> *break retreat. We're staying at a hostel. . . .*

Spring break.
Retreat.
Hostel.
And . . .

"Don't tell me. Judah is going."
Suddenly my lunch is flavorless.

> *Well, of course. It was his idea.*
> *A week of meditation, communion,*
> *and spiritual awakening. Don't*
> *look at me like that, Matt.*

Don't Look at Her

Don't say a damn thing. Spring break
is still weeks away. Who knows what
might happen by then? I bite into
my cardboard sandwich, concentrate
on the tabletop. "I can't give you a ride
home today. I have to see my therapist."

Mom made the appointment, insisted
I show up, *No matter what, no excuses.*
I could blow it off anyway, except
it might do me good to talk about this
crap with Hayden. I sure as hell
can't talk to *her* about it. She's dug in.

> *That's okay. I can ride with Joce.*
> *What about the game tonight?*

I've only gone to a couple, and there
are only a few weeks left until
the play-offs. I shrug. "If you're going
I guess I will, too." Better to kiss a little
butt than reevaluate our relationship.
"Will you wear that green sweater?"

My Therapist's Lair

Is in a modern building with a big,
sunny atrium smack in the middle,
circled by brightly painted offices,
all designed to fool patients into
believing things are better than they
seem. But let's face it. Body-sick
or brain-sick, we're all here because
it pretty much sucks being us.

I arrive five minutes late, still have
to wait another ten because I'm unlucky
enough to have the only therapist
on earth who's willing to go fifteen
minutes over, to be absolutely certain
her clients will make it through
the week without overdosing or parking
on the tracks, waiting for a train

to oblivion. I read about a California
town where suicide-by-train was almost
like a party game for a while. Four kids,
separate occasions, jumped right in front
of moving commuters. Ask me, that's
a seriously messed-up way to go out.
Then again, so is a rope around the neck.

At 4:16

The door opens and out comes a girl,
maybe thirteen, and the kind of thin
that can rarely be accomplished without
an eating disorder. Martha tells her
she'll see her next week, then invites
me into her den with a jerk of her head.

> *How are you doing?* She steps back
> to let me by. *It's been a while.*

Several weeks, in fact. I canceled
a few. "Forgot" a few more. Poor
excuses, as Mom would say. "I think
I'm solid, but apparently my parents
are worried about my currrent stability
because of an essay I wrote for school."

> She gestures for me to sit, goes
> around to the far side of her desk
> and extracts some papers from a pile.
> *You mean this. Your mom faxed it.*

"Why don't they just put it up on
a billboard and let the whole damn
town see it? Anyway, it's not so awful.
I don't get why it's making people nervous."

Martha Reminds Me

Of Mrs. Claus, or would, if I were
to believe the North Pole lore.

> She clears her throat. *I can understand
> their concern, Matt, although it seems
> to me there must have been a fair amount
> of catharsis in what you wrote about Luke. . . .*

I loved my brother more than anyone in the world. He was this amazing little person, dropped into my life by accident. Neither Mom nor Dad wanted another child, and I have no idea what random series of events created Luke, but I was the happiest kid ever when he came along. I've always had to work hard at keeping friends. I'm a smart-ass by nature and always manage to say the wrong thing. But no matter what words came out of my mouth, Luke was always there for me. Until he wasn't.

Like most guys my age, I never really thought about what it meant to be gay, other than it was something shameful, something I sure as hell wouldn't ever want to be. So when Luke first started talking about his sexuality, I thought he was putting me on. Luke was one hell of an athlete, and a primo basketball player. No way could he be gay; that's what I believed. His wrists were anything but limp; they could throw three-pointers and layups all day.

All I knew was the usual stereotypical misinformation. And I was the only person Luke felt safe confessing to. So how did I react? "Don't joke about shit like that," I told him enough times so he went silent. But eventually, it became clear he wasn't joking. Once I knew it was true, it vexed me at first. Then I got scared. For him, and for me. But the thing was, nothing had changed. Luke was the same brother he'd always been. It took a little time to understand that, a little longer to accept it.

It was a lot harder for my parents. One of the things I've always hated about jocks is the way they pick on kids who are weaker, and that is the general perception of homosexuals. My dad is a jock through and through. The idea of his son being gay totally messed with his head. What a waste, is what Dad thought, and, How could you do this to me? You could see it in his eyes when he looked at Luke. That pissed me off.

But what made me even angrier was how some supposed love-thy-neighbor Christians mocked my brother. A couple of them organized a regular hate campaign, and they were ruthless, relentless pricks. Eighth grade was a nightmare for Luke, who was afraid to go to his locker, where he would be pushed, poked, pantsed, and otherwise provoked. They'd follow him down the hall, calling him "fag" or "dick licker." They'd offer their own dicks for him to lick. Hetero-freaks.

Almost worse was the online harrassment, which was not only cruel, but also deviously creative. You'd think churchy people would be embarrassed to download porn, then Photoshop someone's face into the pics—that someone being Luke. You'd think they'd have better things to do than to post said pics not only to Luke's personal social networking pages, but also to the high school basketball team's Facebook page, which is how Dad first found out. No wonder he took it so personally, huh? Luke was outed to his father and to the entire community at the same time, and in a most humiliating way.

And those troglodytes who orchestrated that claim to serve the architect of love? Where would a true God stand on their actions? Would he actually forgive them on nothing but the strength of a Sunday prayer? No, those dudes are tumbling straight toward a brimstone bubble bath, and if it meant they'd fall in a little sooner, I'd happily give them a push.

God is an invention of mankind, an excuse to exist, and to thrive, in a subhuman state. Government must become and remain a servant of humanity. It cannot, and will not, with a religious figurehead at its helm.

Cathartic?

Up to a point. "Yes, it felt good
to put it down on paper, I guess."

It would feel better wrapping
the paper around those guys' heads

and duct taping it really tightly
around their necks so they'd have

reading material on that trip to hell.
But I probably shouldn't say so.

> You don't see anything in what
> you wrote that could make some
>
> people a little nervous about
> what you might have planned?

"Planned? Martha, the only thing
I have planned is graduation.

I can't see a thing beyond June.
Wait. That didn't come out right.

What I mean is, I'm not sure
about college or a career. But that

has nothing to do with planning
an act of mayhem. I have no desire

to go to prison, or to join Luke,
whever he is or isn't." That is sincere,

and I guess that's how I sound
because she visibly relaxes.

> *Well, that's very good to hear.*
> *To be frank, I'm not too concerned*
>
> *about you planning some vicious*
> *act of revenge. But let me ask you*
>
> *this. How honest were you? And not*
> *just with your readers. How honest*
>
> *were you with yourself? In my opinion,*
> *your essay lacks critical truths.*

See, This Is Why I Hate Therapy

Everyone else is all worried about
assessing possible outcomes—
seeking the meaning of selected
words as if they're hieroglyphics.

Martha wants to deconstruct
the storytelling, take it apart until
she exposes the infrastructure
of my psyche. "Like what?"

It's a challenge, and she's equal
to it, of course she is. That's why
my parents pay her the big bucks,
relatively speaking. My parents

      are actually pretty damn cheap.
      She tilts her silver-tipped head.
      First, despite your tendency
      toward sarcasm and acerbic

      wit, you've never exactly been
      a loner, have you? From what
      I've been able to discern,
      you're kind of an A-list kid.

What List?

That was so not the question I expected.
"A-list? On my best year, I doubt
I even approached the B-minus roster."

She smiles, but I know she'll keep on
me unless I dig down and unearth
a reasonably honest answer. "Well, sure,

yeah. I have friends. But, you know,
since I got together with Hayden,
I prefer spending time with her."

> *But in your essay you said you had to
> work to keep friends. Did you perhaps
> lose a few when Luke came out?*

Oh shit. I see what's she's doing.
She's good. She's very good. "Come
on, Martha. Why ask questions you

already know the answer to? Besides
our resident Bohemian woods dwellers,
Cottage Grove is a relatively conservative

community. All those factory workers
may love their weed and claim to be all
about equal rights, but let's face it.

We're eighty percent white-bread here,
and don't much talk about which way we
lean, and if you figure high school jocks

into that mix, this wasn't a great place
for Luke to come into the world gay,
you know? Man, I begged him to play

straight, and he acted the part pretty
well. Whatever his attraction, it's not like
he was out cruising for boy dates anyway.

He was too young to have the first idea how
to go about such a thing. But then the wrong
person overheard the wrong conversation,

and that person, well, as I'm sure you've
already intuited, he was supposed to be
my friend, but that's how the whole thing

got started and . . ." Vince and I were
pretty great friends growing up, in fact.
We ran in a pack—Marshall, Vince, Doug,

and me. Luke always wanted to tag along,
which would have been okay had I been
in charge. But the other guys didn't think

he could keep up and were mortified
to have a little kid attached like a tail
whenever there were girls around,

especially since most females found
Luke just "so darn adorable." Then, as
we got older, my buddies and I were doing

things no younger brother should witness.
"Yeah, I was defriended because of Luke.
Obviously they weren't very good friends."

Only Marshall didn't blink an eye,
mostly because, big confession, his favorite
uncle is gay: *Big effing deal. Why should*

*I care if Uncle Ken is in love with a dude?
It's not like he gives me all the filthy
details. And man, can that Taylor cook!*

*Tell Luke to be sure and find someone
who knows how to make homemade
pizza.* See, that is why I love Marshall.

But I leave that off the table. "Anyway,"
I tell Martha, "I still have decent friends,
not to mention a girlfriend to die for."

Tongue Slips

Are making this conversation
so tiresome. Martha stares at me
quizzically. "Not literally expire
for. Man, can't I use a colloquialism
without inspiring paranoia?"

No comment. Instead, she asks,
What about your nightmares?

I could lie, but what's the point
of therapy if I don't admit, "I still
have them from time to time. But
not nearly as often as I used to."

She looks unconvinced. *When
was the last time you had one?*

Confession, I've heard, is good
for the soul. And that's why I'm here,
isn't it? "A couple of days ago."

Her gray head nods expectation.
Did something specific trigger it?

Just hours ago I was dying—er,
I mean, anxious—to discuss Hayden
with an impartial third party. Yet, now

reluctance forms like a big glob
of phlegm in my throat. "I—uh—I'm
not sure. Maybe it's because . . ."
Oh, what the hell? "I think it had

something to do with Hayden. We got
into a couple of arguments and I started
thinking about losing her. I don't know
if I could handle losing someone else."

> *I hate to point this out, but loss
> is inevitable. You're young and . . .*

Even as my mouth spills the words
"I know," my head swivels side to
side in the negative. "Okay, I know
we're young. But why does that have

to mean we can't last? Some people
who fall in love in high school stay
together for the rest of their lives.
Why couldn't that be Hayden and me?

I hate how people make promises,
then turn around and break them.
I hate how everything good turns
to shit eventually. I hate when . . ."

I'm Panting Anxiety

Wheezing air like I just completed
a dozen wind sprints, Dad yelling

at me to *hurry. Move it. Why can't you
run like your brother?* Yeah, Dad.

Luke outran me all the way to hell,
which is about the time I started getting

mild anxiety attacks. Guess I'll have to
catch up to him there. Martha sighs.

> *Deep breaths, Matt. In.* Pause. *Out.*
> Pause. *Remember what I showed*
>
> *you last time.* She lifts her hands,
> rotates her palms upward for in. Pause.

Turns them toward the floor for down.
Directing my breathing like a symphony.

It's fascinating to watch, and without
really thinking about it, I collect myself—

oxygen intake and blood pressure start
to normalize, and I can breathe comfortably

again. "Man. You are really good.
Do you come in a portable model?"

> She grins. *The whole point of therapy
> is giving you the necessary tools to use*
>
> *on your own, so a portable me is
> unnecessary. You should be practicing*
>
> *this exercise at home. Proper oxygen
> intake always makes a person process better.*
>
> *I almost hesitate to return to our earlier
> discussion, but why are you worried*
>
> *about losing Hayden? You obviously
> care very much about her. Do you not*
>
> *think she feels the same way about you?*
> She sits patiently while I consider

the straightforward question. "I do,
at least most of the time. But lately

we seem to argue a lot, and since I know
you'll ask, over ludicrous stuff like jealousy."

The Soft Chime

Of an alarm means our session
is technically over. Technically,
because Martha refuses to honor
alarms. She shuffles in her seat.

> *Our time's up, I know, but*
> *I can't let you go without*
> *saying that jealousy is far*
> *from being ludicrous.*
> *It's the impetus for many*
> *bad things, including breakups.*

And now we slip into a short,
terse-because-we're-already-
running-a-few-minutes-late Q & A.

Q: *Who's jealous? You or her?*

A: "Both of us, actually."

Q: *Are the reasons real or imagined?*

I almost say hers are invented,
mine one hundred percent spot-on,
but that even sounds warped to me. So,

A: "I really wish I knew."

Beyond the Inner Sanctum Door

There is noise in the waiting room.
Martha's next victim is also running
a little late, which gives Martha

> the leeway to add, *Well, since I can't*
> *talk to Hayden, you'll have to do it. Open*
> *up. Tell her what's bothering you,*

> *without accusation. Discourse is a two-way*
> *street, though. Be sure to ask what's on*
> *her mind, and listen without comment*

> *until she's finished. Communication*
> *is the key to success in any relationship,*
> *but you have to be forthright. Love is a fragile*

> *thing, easily destroyed by dishonesty.*
> *Just remember to be honest with yourself*
> *first. Otherwise, there's really no point.*

She smiles at my obvious eye roll, stands
to let me know I have been dismissed.
All right, then. Go forth. Cause no mayhem.

Decent Session

I leave, feeling marginally better
about myself, Hayden, even my lack
of friends. They were nothing
but deserters, and who needs
traitorous pals blurring the focus

of your life? Perspective. That's exactly
what I needed today, and Martha is great
at allowing me a broader view without
accusing me of being a freak for not
having it in the first place. She's okay.

I wish Mom would talk to her instead
of bending her pastor's ear, expecting
the dude to be a human conduit to
the Great Therapist in the Sky. But
my parents seem to believe therapy

is only useful when you're young
and not quite over your brother's
suicide. What about the self-inflicted
death of your favorite son? At least,
your favorite until it turns out he's gay.

I Almost Call Martha Myself

When I get home and find Mom well
on her way to an alcohol-fueled meltdown,
instead of busting her butt not selling real
estate due to the economy. She's in the den,
knees tucked beneath her on the window
seat, and the gentle light through the glass
does nothing to soften the blotchiness
of her face. She's been crying for a while.

"What's wrong?" I ask, certain
I don't want to hear her answer
or jump into this conversation.

> Too late. *He. Wants. To leave. Me,*
> *Matthew.* Tobacco spices her breath,
> and gin punctuates the sentence.

"Dad?" Ridiculous question, like,
duh, she means Dad. "Did he say so?"

> She coughs up a laugh. *He never*
> *says anything, does he? Not even*
> *when Luke . . .* Fresh tears splash
> from her eyes. *No, he hasn't said*
> *so yet. But he will. And I don't know*
> *what I'll do when he finally finds*
> *the guts to tell me that's what he wants.*

What Would Martha Say?

I draw from today's session, put on
my best therapist face. "I have no idea
exactly what brought this on, but just

today I was informed by an expert that
communication is the key to every
relationship. Why don't you just ask

him if that's what he's got on his mind?
I mean, there's no use stressing over
something that may not happen at all.

And even if that is his plan, isn't it
better to know for certain now, rather
than wait for him to spring it on you?"

> She regards me with swollen eyes.
> *It isn't real until he makes it real. Until
> then, it's better to worry in private.*

I should just let it drop, but what
the hell, I've got a little time to kill,
and I shouldn't be the only one forced

to regurgitate his secrets. "I'm going
to be real direct here, Mom. Seems to
me you and Dad haven't had much

of a relationship for a long time.
Would it be the end of the world
if the two of you got a divorce?"

>Her body visibly tenses. *I need*
>*a cigarette.* She straightens her legs,
>preparing to stand, but takes the time

>to answer. *No, Matthew, the world*
>*wouldn't end. But I can't let that*
>*happen, because then, he'd win.*

Not sure which Mom I hate seeing
more—the broken-down blubbering
one, or the steel-hearted bitch.

I watch the latter go off in search
of a nicotene fix, and as I get to my
feet, notice a newspaper Mom left

folded back to the announcements
page. My eyes skim for offending
news, settle quickly on a divorce notice:

Plaintiff Lorelei Crabtree versus
Defendant Dale Crabtree . . . Lorelei.
Dad's old girlfriend just became free again.

Which, to a Point

Explains Mom's weeping jag.
But I still don't know
if she was crying from fear
that Dad might leave her

or crying from anger because
now it might be a little easier
for him to make that choice.
But does he even know

about Lorelei? If she lived
in Cottage Grove, of course
he would. It's a very small town.
Everyone is privy to the other's

business. But Lorelei stayed
in Eugene. The city isn't huge,
but it's big enough that neighbors
don't know their neighbors unless

they make it a point to say hi.
Big enough so you can live
there without the people next
door knowing your history,

which might include the fact
that the love of your life left you
for some other girl he got pregnant.
Big enough so the news you're

divorcing the replacement love
of your life just might get buried
on the announcements page
where no one bothers to look.

Except Mom. Personally, I think
she's crazy, and if Dad would even
consider divorce, with all
its repercussions, on the strength

of such a big MAYBE, he'd be
crazy too. And if Lorelei actually
encouraged such a thing, she'd
be the most insane person

of the bunch, because as Creswell
Grandma would happily counsel,
*Once a womanizer, always
a womanizer.* Or, why make

the same mistake twice?

Sage Advice

Why don't more people adhere
to the practice? Personally, I'm
going to make it my motto: *Mistakes
are easy to come by. Why make
the same one twice?* Maybe I should
print it on T-shirts and sell them.
My customer base would be huge.

By the time I eat, change, and leave
for the game, Mom and her Marlboros
have vacated the front porch, though
the ghost scents of both linger. I'd like
to say, "Poor Mom," and mean it, but
I hate when she acts all pathetic even
more than when she plays badass.

It's hard to feel sorry for someone who
will put her own happiness on hold,
especially when, by her own confession,
the only reason she chooses to do that
is to interfere with the possibility of Dad
"winning," as if, other than on the basketball

court, he could ever be a real winner.
He's already lost way too much.
We've all already lost way too much.

I Purposely Miss

The freshman basketball game,
not only because Luke should be
starring in it, but because watching
Cal Stanton play starting forward
instead would push me right up against
the edge. Watching Dad coach him
would shove me all the way over.

Cal was always jealous of Luke's
innate ability. Like Dad, the work
ethic part of the equation escaped
him completely. In elementary school,
Luke always got picked first, a trend
that continued in middle school, where
the basketball coach immediately

recognized his talent. In seventh
grade, Luke was the team's most
valuable player. Funny how something
like that buys instant popularity, with
teachers as well as classmates. That
included girls, and I think it was about
then that he started to realize his same-

sex attraction. Here these pretty
little girls were wanting to make
out, and what he told me was, *It
doesn't feel right. I mean, shouldn't
it make me horny?* Which made me
uncomfortable, but not because I
immediately went to "My brother's gay."

I just wasn't prepared to hear him
vocalize the word "horny."
Regardless, had he remained in
the closet, today he would probably
be a freshman superstar. Instead,
Cal found out, and revenge was his.
It's hard to believe a fourteen-year-old

kid could have such a vicious agenda,
but he was determined that Luke would
never make his first high school team.
To top it all off, Dad had a heavy hand
in that, too. Because when those pics
went live, he told Luke not to bother
trying out, he wouldn't let him play.

He Claimed

It was for Luke's safety.
That something bad might
happen to him in the locker
room, or on the game bus.

He claimed whatever bullying
Luke was suffering then would
only get worse in high school.
He even suggested Luke might

want to consider private school.
A boarding school, maybe boys
only, if that's what he wanted.
He was smart; he'd do well at

a college prep academy. Some
of them even had basketball
teams. To Luke, the implications
were clear: *Play ball anywhere*

but here. And: *No matter how*
good you are at academics or
sports, I will never accept you,
let alone be proud of you.

Dad Refused

To defend Luke and I have refused
to support Dad by going to any
of his games this year. Not that he cares

any more about my being there
than he did about Luke playing for him,
champion material or not. I'm only

going tonight to placate Hayden.
I've never seen Dad shoulder any
blame for what Luke did, other than

that one weak moment the other
morning, and I'm not really certain
he admitted anything except passing

on pussy genes. I'm relatively sure
he'd believe *that* DNA leapfrogs
generations. But even without accepting

responsibility, what about love,
Dad? Didn't you ever love Luke?
Or me? We were never really sure.

I Get to the Game

Halfway through the JV rout,
Cottage Grove ahead by eighteen
points. Go Lions! The gym is packed,
and I scan the crowd, looking for Hayden.
There she is, near the top of the bleachers,
flanked by her do-gooder girlfriends.
Whoopee. This is going to be great fun.

Paused by the door, I happen to overhear
a couple of people talking about the earlier
game. Sounds like the freshmen lost.
Too bad, so sad. You can't win 'em all,
Dad. Considering both the JV and varsity
teams are perched on the topmost rung
of the leaderboards, he's probably not too upset.
Championships there are all but assured.

Wonder if steamrolling games ever
gets tiresome, or if in some small recess
of his brain he might actually prefer
a close score once in a while—something
that would require exceptional coaching
skills to achieve the desired result.
Is it all about winning, or does he still
love the game for the game's sake?
Okay, probably a stupid question.

The Varsity Game

Is also a blowout. The most
exciting thing about it is Hayden,
a hint of summer in that wants-
to-be-touched green sweater.
It's all I can do to keep my hands
to myself, although I do rest one

on her knee, relatively politely.
Unfortunately, Jocelyn and
the Biblette crew are sticking
to Hayd's opposite side like hot
taffy, so she gabs through most
of the game, and not to me.

Later, I will most definitely
communicate my displeasure,
and without accusation, if such
a thing is possible. Martha,
my dear, why didn't you explain
exactly how to accomplish that?

For the Moment

I smile and give a jock cheer every time
one of our guys dunks a basket. Dad
glances my way once in a while.
Is he happy I'm here? Or pissed that
I'm drawing attention to myself? Causing
a scene and all. Which takes me back . . .

To my aunt Sophie's wedding. Mom's sister
defines Oregon hippie, so the whole affair
took place in the woods, trilling birds and
acoustic guitars providing the music as
the bride and groom skipped down the aisle
to pronounce their simple *Let's do forever
together*s in front of a mail-order minister.

After that came one helluva party. Sophie's
husband, Uncle Shawn, grew bud for profit;
green haze wreathed the trees. My grandparents
didn't last much past the carrot cake, but
the rest of the wedding goers stayed well
beyond that. Dad didn't indulge in the weed,
but hit the champagne bottles hard, followed

that up with harder stuff. Mom watched,
uncomfortable, while the younger crowd
wandered into the trees to do what buzzed
kids do—get more buzzed, and hopefully,

get lucky. What is it about weddings that
exacerbates the horny in people? Anyway,
Luke was in the eighth grade, and though
he'd come out to me by then, the rest of
the family was still in the dark. But everyone
knew about Shawn's nephew, Jeremy, who
at fifteen was open about which way he leaned.

That evening, he was leaning hard toward
Luke. It was the first time, as far as I knew
then or now, that any guy had ever come on
to Luke, who was obviously attracted.
I watched, half fascinated, half freaked
out, as Jeremy and Luke connected.

Not overtly. I mean, no tongue play or
inappropriate touching. But you could tell
they liked each other from the start. It was
in the way everyone else seemed to disappear,
poof! Nobody there but the two of them.
In retrospect, I think I was a little jealous
of the idea that Luke might come to care

about someone else more than he looked up
to me. Back then I would have said no, I was all
for anything that made him happy. Denial
is a powerful thing. It makes you believe lies.

Booze

Is also a powerful thing,
especially when you're not
used to imbibing, and Luke
definitely was not. But the post-
nuptial spirits flowed freely, no
one caring about which direction

and, encouraged by his new
"friend" to match him drink
for drink, my brother managed
to consume a lot. Of course, so
did I, so I didn't really notice
until Dad came storming across

the clearing where we were sitting—
Luke next to Jeremy, and me beside
our pretty little cousin Persephone
(yes, I know!). I'd been paying more
attention to her than to Luke, who,
as I was about to find out, had been

> "making a scene," though it
> was obvious to no one but Dad
> until the second he thundered,
> *What the fuck are you doing?*
> *Do you want everyone to think*
> *you're a fag or something?*

The Slur Factor

Was to the nth degree, but the loud
factor was even worse. Everyone
homed on the unfolding melodrama.

Especially when Jeremy responded
before Luke could even react. *What's
wrong with fags? Personally, I love 'em.*

Which might have been okay, except
Jeremy was easily as drunk as Dad,
and actually leaned toward Luke as if

to give him a sloppy kiss. Dad reacted
poorly to that, grabbing hold of Jeremy's
collar and jerking him to his feet. I thought

he might haul off and punch him straight
in the face, and tried to divert such action
with a moment of levity, launching into

the last verse of "God Save the Queen."
Most people wouldn't believe I actually
knew the lyrics to the song, but it so happened

I'd learned them for extra credit on a history
project I'd done the year before. Talk
about fortuitous coincidences! To the tune

of "My Country 'Tis of Thee," "From every
latent foe, from the assassin's blow, God
save the Queen." That cracked up Persephone,

Luke, and Jeremy, who spit laughter
in Dad's face, initiating an apoplectic
bloom of scarlet in his booze-puffed cheeks.

Any chance at situational lightening
immediately dissolved. *What's so funny,
you little shit?* By then, people were

moving in our direction, so I felt
emboldened. "Aw, come on, Dad.
In my humble estimation, that was

hilarious. Hope there aren't any Brits
here, but if there are, I'm very sorry.
Didn't mean to be offensive." I'd like

to say Dad cooled off right away, but
it took Uncle Shawn's intervention
to make him disengage from Jeremy's ruff.

Now who's making a scene, Dad, that's
what I wanted to say, especially as Luke
withdrew to safety behind his superjock facade.

That Was His Fortress

Fragile as it was. He despised
hiding behind the pretense,
but he hated more:

Pissing off Dad.
Worrying Mom.
Embarrassing me.
Losing his friends
and me losing mine.

All because of who he was.
How he was born. Who
he was programmed genetically
to love. Although, tell
that to Dad, he'd claim
you were insane, that no
gene of his could possibly
be responsible for gayness.

The funny thing is, until
his meltdown at Aunt Sophie's
wedding, I'd never before
witnessed Dad's raging
homophobia. Did he only
hate "gay" when it so obviously
manifested itself in his son?

I Watch Him Now

One minute to go in the game,
Cottage Grove leading by sixteen

points, but he's not celebrating yet.
In fact, he paces the sideline, yelling,

Move it! Watch the block!

Pressure, pressure, even more pressure.
That's how he coaches and, hey, who

am I to argue with a winning strategy?
Hayden et al scream right along with him.

I slip my arm around her shoulder, pull
her ear against my lips. "We already won."

Then, in a bold bid for attention, I run
the tip of my tongue along the contours

of her auricle. Great word, and interesting
that the term for outer ear is also a part

of the heart. Are they physically connected?
Could the way into a girl's inner chamber

in fact be licking her ear?

Apparently Not

Hayden gives me an inelegant
elbow to the ribs and hisses,

> *Stop it. Do you want everyone to see?*

Before I can respond, tell her
I really hope the entire world
sees, the buzzer rings. Game over.

The crowd is on its collective feet,
our side cheering, theirs sighing.
One or two look like they might define

poor sportsmanship. I can see more
than one raised middle finger. Lame.
It's just a freaking game. Hayden and I

trail the Biblettes down from the bleachers.
As they start toward the exit doors, I figure
I'd better ask, "I'm driving you, right?"

> She hesitates. *It's late, and a school
> night, and I've got a chem quiz tomorrow. . . .*

"I swear I'll take you straight home and only
bum a kiss or two for my effort. Don't worry.
It's too dark for your dad to play spy."

I can tell she's thinking about saying
no, so I tempt, "Please? I want to tell
you about what my therapist said."

Success! She taps Jocelyn's shoulder.
Matt's taking me home. See you tomorrow.

That nets me a wicked glare from
Big J, but then she shrugs and hurries
ahead. Score one for me, and why not?

It's only fair that I win once in a while.
The teams are finished shaking hands.
Dad's at the end of the line, looking . . .

My first thought was "proud," but I realize
a more accurate word would be "smug."
Maybe he's the one who those guys

were flipping off. Whatever. I wave
and he reciprocates. "What got into
my dad? He actually acknowledged me."

Don't be so melodramatic, Matt.
Why wouldn't he acknowledge you?

"Me? Melodramatic?" Only if truth is melodrama.

Outside

The usual mist has turned to out-and-out
downpour. I halt Hayden beneath
the wide overhang. "Stay here and I'll bring
the truck around." It doesn't take long,

but by the time I return, she's standing
alone, haloed yellow by sodium light,
an angel. If there were any argument
for a heaven, or even paradise on earth,

there it is, embodied by my beautiful
Hayden. I park on the sidewalk, close
as I can, so she doesn't have to take
more than three steps in the rain. Still,

when she climbs up into the truck,
her long hair drips, and her makeup
smears beneath her eyes. I think about
making a joke, but she looks fragile,

so wordlessly, I reach into the center
console, extract a tissue, and gently wipe
the black streaks away. "Have I ever told
you you're amazing?" I expect a love-

       sponged response. Instead, she pushes
       my hand away. *I think we'd better go.*

Seriously Stung

I put the truck into gear, pull
into the stream of cars leaving
the parking lot before I say,

"What's wrong?"

I don't know.

"Of course you do.
Talk to me."

I can't tell you.

"Martha says—"

Who's Martha?

"My therapist, but you
should know that. I've
told you her name before."

*Guess I should pay
better attention. What
does she say?*

"That relationships struggle
without open communication."

I don't mention the fact that I
was supposed to be the one
communicating my displeasure.

Martha's right, but . . .

"But what?"

*But sometimes I worry
if I tell you what's on
my mind, you'll freak.*

"Come on, Hayd. You know
I'm the benevolent King
of Cool. What's the problem?"

She thinks it over. Finally
decides to take Martha's advice.

*It's just you always say
things like I'm amazing.
And you kiss me like you
really love me . . .*

"I love you with all my heart."

So why don't you want me?

Want? Wait

Just hold on one freaking second.
Is she saying what I think she is?
"I'm not exactly sure what you mean."

> I mean, if I'm so amazing and
> beautiful and all, why don't you
> ever try to have sex with me?

Holy shit! She was saying what
I thought she was. "I—I—I'm kind
of speechless, Hayden. It's called

respect—for you, and your beliefs.
I just never thought . . ." Not for one
second did I consider she might be

> like my mother was at her age.
> You could have at least given
> me the chance to say no. I feel

> like you say all the right things,
> but you don't really mean them.
> Maybe I'm not so attractive, or

> maybe there's something else
> going on, something a whole
> lot worse, like . . .

Oh Man

I think I set myself up with all that
communication business. "Like what?"
We're closing in on her house,
so I pull over a couple of blocks
away, just in case her dear old dad
has night-vision binocs or something.

> *Well, I talked to Joce about it and*
> *she said maybe the problem is*
> *you're like your brother.*

"Wait. You talked to fucking
Jocelyn about why I've never tried
to have my way with you? And wait.
The prevailing theory is it's because
I'm gay? Why, because if Luke
was there's a good chance I am, too?"

> Anger courses like a storm-swollen
> creek. *Judah says it's possible,*
> *that there does seem to be—*

"Okay, screw that! You talked to *him*
about me, too? What the hell is wrong
with you? Oh, I get it. This is the way
good Christians gossip, right? Bathroom
discussions, post-communion, about

how to make their boyfriends come on
to them, so they can feel all holy about
turning them down—sanctimonious prick
tease." I grab her hand, yank it into my crotch.
"You want to feel my boner? It won't take
much. Just wiggle your fingers a little.

Jesus Christ, Hayden, I am so not gay!
Do you have any idea how many times
I've left you and had to go home and jerk
off?" As if to prove it, my dick jumps
to attention. "There. See? Let's have sex
right now! Unzip me. This will be fun."

Stop it! She jerks her hand away,
and now somehow it's her who's
pissed. Her eyes spill pain-spiked
tears. *Why are you being so mean?*

"I'm not the one talking shit about
you behind your back! Might as well
give you something to bitch about
tomorrow. Anyway, I thought this is what
you wanted. Make up your mind, okay?"

I'm out of breath, and she's out the door,
stomping up the sidewalk in the rain. Fuck.

I Drive Home

Way too fast on the storm-slicked streets, but recklessness
feels good, feels right. This late on a weeknight, traffic

is light, but should I come across someone minding
the speed limit, I punch the accelerator, pass without

much thought. The abandon initiates a major head rush,
no foreign substance required. I'm buzzed. Buzzing.

It feels so good, I drive right by the turnoff to our house,
head out a deserted back road, almost daring some lazing

cop to fire up his engine and come after me. But I see
no cruisers. No other cars. Nothing but a fucking deer,

smack on the center line! "Oh, shit!" I hit the horn,
stomp the brakes, steer into the inevitable fishtail,

and somehow manage to correct without losing
the asphalt or catching the doe with my bumper.

Now I feel better than buzzed. I feel invincible.
At least, until I remember what brought this on

in the first place. One close call tonight is more
than enough. I drive home ten above the limit.

I Walk Through the Door

A little past eleven. The house is already
fast asleep, or at least pretending to be.
No need to expose the ruse. I'm still wound
up, and in fact the recent exhilaration, coupled
with the earlier conversation with Hayden,
has made me want a shower. And not a cold one.

I go to my room for clean post-soaping clothes,
and when I extricate my cell from my jeans,
notice I've got a text. Unbelievably, Hayden
has already apologized. *VERY SORRY. I WAS
TOTALLY WRONG. FORGIVE ME?* Bitch. I toss
the phone on my bed, grab fresh underwear,

a folded T-shirt, some flannel pants, try
to remember not to slam my way down the hall,
into the bathroom. By the time the water
steams, I'm hard as hell—from frustration
and anger and that incredibly close call
on the highway. I am a warrior, and suddenly

I understand the base desire of the conquerer.
Having no one to rape and nothing to pillage
but myself, I step into the hot water stream,
lather up with Mom's fancy rosemary bath gel,
and when I close my eyes, it is Hayden I imagine
ramming into, take extreme pleasure in her pain.

Marginally Satisfied

Skin and hair scented with rosemary,
I return to my room, check my cell.
Sure enough, there's another text:
YOU'RE NOT STILL MAD AT ME, RIGHT?

Had it really been her in the shower,
I might have found a small measure
of forgiveness, but as it is, hell yeah,
I'm still pissed. Thankfully, Martha

has prescribed medication for nights
like this, when I just won't sleep any
other way. The dosage on the label
reads, *Take one or two for anxiety.*

Since I already brushed my teeth
and won't be chasing the pills with beer,
I pop three with water, turn off the lights,
burrow in beneath my thick, heavy quilt,

wait for the plunge into paradise. My brain
begins to thicken, a not altogether unpleasant
sensation except for the way it coalesces
around a single word: forgiveness.

Forgive

Forgive.
Forgive.
Forgive.

Over and over,
smaller and smaller,
a receding echo.

Forgive Hayden.
Forgive Mom and Dad.
Forgive yourself.

And where did that come from?
Forgive myself for what, exactly,
you bastard internal voice?

I wait for the answer,
but before it comes, I'm falling,
somersaulting down into Shangri-la,
courtesy of Miss Martha's little helpers,
followed by a random echo:

Luke.
Luke.
Luke.

By Friday

I still haven't forgiven a single person.
Least of all myself.

On the surface, Hayden and I are fine.
Except, not really.

Dig a millimeter beneath my epidermis.
Blood trickles, chilled.

I told her I'm okay. With her. With us.
But I'm not so sure.

I don't know how to act with her.
What to do. What to say.

Should I tell her she's totally stunning?
Or insist she's hot as hell?

Should I coax her hand into mine?
Or maul her boobs?

What freaking role should I play?
Respectful boyfriend? Stud?

And maybe the biggest question of all:
Would the true Hayden please step forward?

Zero Communication

That's what we've shared in the past
three days. Yes, we've talked, about
weekend plans, and the game tonight—
it's moot, but Dad has to finish out
the season—and even about her campus
youth ministry meeting today. Looks like

I'm giving up Friday lunches to Judah.
Oh, as they say, fucking well. But as far
as commentary, I didn't even say that much
to her about my real feelings. Martha
would be so disappointed. I totally flaked
in the open communication department.

But now, walking her to the library,
where she'll turn her attention away from
me and toward her way-too-good-looking,
way-too-interested-in-her young minister,
thoughts churn in my head, turning my brain
into sour butter. I still have hold of her hand

when I say, "Here's something to ask Judah.
Is the reason he thinks I'm probably gay
because I don't believe in God? All atheists
aren't queer, you know. And conversely,
a strong sense of morality isn't exclusive
to those who dress up in their religion."

Now, *That* Was Communication

Succinct. Well-spoken.
But apparently Hayden
isn't much impressed.
Our fingers come unwoven.

> *Believe it or not, we have*
> *more important topics*
> *of discussion than you.*

"Since when?" I turn and
stride away before way
too much communication
vomits from my mouth.

I'm halfway to the lunch-
room when it hits me. What
could they be discussing
that's so damn important?

Every shred of bravado
disintegrates. For maybe
the hundredth time I wonder
if Hayden and I are destined

to cut loose from each other,
go separate ways. But this
time I also wonder if I care.

Skipping Tonight's Game

Is a given. That Hayden
and her minions will attend

without me is also obvious.
The question becomes what

will I do with my Friday night?
I find the answer three paces

behind me, when I turn, sensing
eyes on my back. "Hey, Alexa."

I pause to let her catch up.
"I don't suppose you witnessed

that little scene with Hayden?"
A pretty smile paints tiny lines

at the corners of her eyes. Dark
blue eyes. Almost violet.

> *I might have. Don't suppose
> you want to give me details?*

She falls into step beside me,
close enough so every now

and again the curve of her hip
bumps my thigh. Nice. Wait.

I'm mad at Hayden, but not
enough to be thinking what

I think I'm thinking. "It's probably
not PC to divulge our secrets."

Just as the words escape my lips,
Jocelyn scurries past. Her rabid bitch

glare catches me and her smirk
declares she has seen too much,

assumes even more. Suddenly,
I want to confide everything,

and dare to ask Alexa, "So,
what are you doing tonight?"

I Spend Most of the Afternoon

Thinking up excuses.
But Hayden doesn't even ask
if I'm going to the game,
so there's no need
to explain why I'm not.

In fact, the only thing
she bothers to say
at the end of the day is,

Call me later.

She does give me
a whipped-cream kiss,
sweet and light and lickable,
but definitely not
the "I want to turn you on"
kind, let alone the "stick
your tongue down my throat
so I can bite it off
and spit it out" kind.

Then she floats away
like a wispy cloud,
to be swallowed up
by the chatter tornado.

I think about my plans
for tonight and guilt churns
as I watch the twister
spin toward the door,
nothing but hot wind
and the tiniest bits
of substance, but a force
to be reckoned with.

Hayden does not look
back, doesn't wave goodbye.

"Love you, too,"
I whisper into
the cyclone's wake.

The words fall,
autumn-crisped
leaves, scattering
across the floor.

The Guilt

Has pretty much dissipated
by the time I pick up Alexa.

We left our plans for the evening
fluid. After all, this isn't a real
date. More like hanging out.

That's my story and I'm sticking
to it, at least if I can convince
myself that this intense attraction

I find myself feeling can't possibly
lead to more than great conversation.

But damn, this girl is hot. If Hayden
is a nymph, Alexa is a siren,
a temptress in black leather.

When she gets into the truck, she scents
it with some rich, earthy perfume.
Not sweet, and for that I'm grateful.

> *Hey*, she says. *Where are we going?*

I shrug. "Depends on what you want
to do, but there's no one at my house.
We could go there. If you want, I mean."

She grins. *Might be dangerous.*

"Scared?"

Of you? Hardly.

"Okay, then."

Decision made, I steer the truck
toward home. Anxiety tremors
suddenly, cartwheels in my gut.

Alexa's right, this just might be
dangerous. But I'm pretty damn
weary of playing it safe. I do have

to wonder, though, what her motives
are. Then again, what are mine?

Too Late to Worry

About piddling things like motives
now. Alexa is sitting on the sofa,
legs curled up under her, waiting
for me to bring her a drink. I pour
two bourbons and Coke, hers as strong
as mine. Maybe even stronger.

By the time I return from the kitchen,
she has shed her jacket, and the shiny
pewter shirt she's wearing fits like
a seal's skin, clinging to muscular flesh
in quite a provocative way. I hand her
the slick, sweating glass, take a seat

at the far end of the couch, where
I can admire the view, but be less
tempted to touch her. She takes a healthy
swallow, and then another, deciding
what to say. Finally, *So, tell me. Why
did you ask me here? Revenge?*

Straightforward, and I imagine
she expects nothing less from me.
Good. The truth isn't always pretty,
but it's easier than deception. "Maybe
a little. But mostly I needed a neutral
someone to talk to. You can be that, right?"

I Expect Her to Say

Of course. But Alexa prefers
to surprise me. She lifts her eyes

> level with mine. *I don't know.*
> *But I'll give it my best shot.*

How do I begin this conversation?
What do I really want to talk about?

> My hesitation makes her ask,
> *Is this about Hayden? Or me?*

"Both, I guess. I can't quite figure
her out, and I thought you could offer

a little insight." Her steady gaze falls
away, and I attempt to draw it back.

"You two were friends for a long time.
What happened?" A swelling hum

at the hinges of my jaw tells me
the alcohol is kicking in. Not sure

> if that's good or bad. Especially when
> she says, *Come on. You have to know.*

Now I'm not exactly sure I want
to know. Distraction may be called

for. I drain my tumbler. "Need a refill?
I kind of think I might." She hands me

her glass, follows me into the kitchen,
and watches me pour two more,

>   slightly weaker than the last.
>   *What if your parents come home?*

"Mom's at her sister's for the weekend
and Dad drinks to closing on Friday nights,

so we've got the place all to ourselves.
Cheers! Here's to rotten parenting."

We clink-and-drink. Unexpectedly,
she pushes very close, and looks up

>   into my eyes, flushing me with heat.
>   *You are what came between Hayden*
>
>   *and me, Matt. She knew how I feel*
>   *about you. I'd never do that to a friend.*

And Just in Case

I'm not sure what she's saying,
she rises up on her tiptoes, puts
one arm around my neck to bring
my face right into hers, and I know
she won't take no for an answer,
and the truth is I don't want to say no.

This time, we kiss, and it is not sweet
nor kind nor gentle. Our mouths mesh,
fevered and flavored with bourbon, and
there will be no turning away from what
must come next. "Finish your drink."
The words fall away from my lips

and into the hollow of her throat. We
both take a final gulp, leave our empty
glasses on the counter. I boost her up,
and she wraps her legs around my waist,
and this time when we kiss I can feel
a rush of heat at the V of her jeans, right

above my belly button. I don't think
I've ever been quite this hard, and it
didn't take pills or porn to accomplish
it, let alone a guy's physique. Gay?
Don't think so, Mr. All-Knowing
Pseudo Minister. I'll show you gay.

Alexa and I Kiss Again

Then she moves her mouth
to my neck, and her anxious
sucking at the pulse beneath
my ear leaves zero doubt.

"Come on." It's a hoarse croak,
someone else's voice. I've been
body-snatched, and I can't help
but feel grateful for that pitiful

excuse as I carry Alexa down
the hall toward my bedroom,
no second-guessing, full speed
ahead. But now I stop, put her down,

back against the door, pin her
there, hands above her head, palms
to palms. "I want you more than
I've wanted anything in my life

right now. But I can't promise
this means anything more."
Her heart thumps against my chest
and the blood coursing beneath

her skin lifts the heady scent
of her musky perfume mixed
with white-hot feminine lust. I'd
take her right here, but I need

> to hear her confess. *I understand.*
> *This is already more than I expected,*
> *or even could have hoped for.*
> *But just so you know, I'm going*

> *to do everything in my power*
> *to make you fall in love with me.*
> *Because I love you, Matt Turner.*
> *I have since the eighth grade.*

I can think of no proper
rejoinder, other than to open
the door, pick her up and carry
her to my bed, lay her carefully

> on top of the quilt. She starts
> to get undressed and I move to
> turn off the light. *No. Leave it on.*
> *I want to see you, want you to see me.*

I've Only Been With

Two other girls, one older (and my instructor),
one younger. (I was the one who schooled
her.) Neither cared about pleasing me,
only about my bringing them to orgasm.
Both had body image problems and insisted
we play in the dark. This is something new.

I watch Alexa unsheath a near-perfect body.
Where Hayden is all soft curves, Lex
maintains the taut angles of the distance
runner she is. The whole time she keeps
those spectacular eyes on me. Finally

       she says, *Well? Don't just stand there.*

She doesn't have to invite twice.
I'm naked. We're skin against skin.
I'm in her mouth. My tongue's in her.
I'll finish too soon. She won't let me.
We tarry. Accelerate. Move into slow

motion, lights on, eyes open, and for
the first time, I experience a woman's
ascension and ultimate, ecstatic release,
punctuated by a heart-shattering,

       I love you! Oh God, Matt, I love you.

Heart Shattering

Because as she brings me all the way
there I can't echo her exclamation.
Afterward, we lie knotted together,

neither of us wanting to move, and
both a little afraid of what the other
might say. But eventually one of us

has to rile the silence, and this is
heavily on my mind. "I'm not sure
Hayden and I can make it. But I don't

know how to stop loving her, and even
if we do break up, I'm afraid a ghost
of that love will haunt me forever."

> *Is that such a bad thing?* Her fingers
> work through my hair, brush my scalp,
> and it just feels so good. *I mean, love*
>
> *is energy, right? So it doesn't die.*
> *It just changes forms. Evolves,*
> *I imagine, then burrows into memory.*
>
> *Real love, anyway. I think it's easy*
> *to confuse love with other things.*
> *Lust, for one. Need, for another.*

Am I Confused?

No. I love Hayden. But then,
why am I here? Can you love
one girl with all you are, from
the depths of your soul,
but still share this kind
of intimacy with another?

My feelings for Hayden
didn't start with lust. Desire,
yes, but not just for her body.
I fell for her spirit—her humor.
Her innocence. Her loyalty.

Need? Well, that is a much
more difficult call. And
this is not the time to make
it. I kiss Alexa softly. "Who
knew you were a philosopher?
Who knew I liked intelligent
women?" We kiss again, but
I stop long enough to ask,
"Do you think lust can evolve
into something deeper?"

God, I hope so.

An hour later, I almost do, too.

I Am Pulled from Sleep

Into darkness, disoriented from
dreams, and by the steady breathing

beside me in the bed I share with
no one. I inhale the scent of woman.

Alexa. Snoozing beneath my quilt.
I nudge her. "Hey. We fell asleep."

> She chuffs like wind through leafy
> boughs. *I know. I turned off the light.*

"I should take you home. Your mom . . ."
She backs up into the curl of my body.

> *It's okay. I told her I was staying
> at Lainie's. I'm prepared like that.*

Maybe so, but I was definitely
not prepared for anything like this.

What about my dad? What about
Hayden? Wasn't I supposed to call?

If she texted me and I didn't respond,
I'll catch hell when I talk to her. And

what if she somehow finds out
about this? Alexa wouldn't bust me,

would she? But now I remember
what we shared last night, and the slip

of her hot silk against my skin brings
me full-on erect in three seconds flat.

She is, indeed, a siren. "What are
you doing to me?" I'm helpless

here in the dark. At least, until
morning. At least until I can

consider just what the fuck
I've done. To Hayden. To Alexa.

Most of all, to me.

Uncharacteristically

I wake early, without an alarm.
Must have something to do
with the movements and sounds
of the girl sleeping next to me.
I lie very still watching her tread
her dreams, wonder if I'm sharing
those with her, too, as well as my bed.

Was this how Dad felt waking up
next to Mom that first time—
awash in guilt, yet fulfilled in
a whole new way, and wondering
if he could ever find such overwhelming
satisfaction with the girl he loved?

Something I never before thought
about—were he and his Lorelei
having problems, issues impossible
to wade through? Was their relationship
doomed before Mom managed to
obliterate it? Or would it somehow
have survived, if not for a baby. . . .

Wait. Baby? Shit! We never . . .
I never. Oh man. I was drunk.
We were drunk, and she never said
a word. She should have, right? What if . . . ?

Alexa's eyes quiver open, find
me, and she smiles. *Morning.*
But then they must really focus
because she adds, *What's wrong?*
You look kind of freaked out. Did
you forget I was here or something?

"Nothing. It's just, I started
thinking we . . . didn't . . . uh, use
protection." I bolt upright into
a sitting position, heart racing,
all panicky. Alexa reaches out,

strokes my chest. *Hey. No worries.*
I told you I come prepared. I've been
on the pill for two years, mostly to
regulate my periods. I wouldn't have
made love to you otherwise. I mean,
you're really attractive and everything,
but I don't want you to father my babies.

I smile. "Believe me, no one wants
me to father their babies. Insanity
runs in my family." I kiss her forehead.
"Dad's probably sleeping. Let's sneak
into the bathroom for a shower. I'll
wash your back if you wash mine."

It's the Best Shower

I've ever participated in,
and it's definitely all about
the participation. We wash
each other's everything,
which leads to the need
for even more washing.

We towel off, bodies steaming
into the cool morning air.
"Just so you know, this is by
far the most sex I've ever had
in any one twelve-hour period."

> She laughs. *Ditto.* A short pause
> for effect. *Well, there was that
> one time . . .* Another pause to
> assess my reaction. *Hey, I was joking.*

"I knew that. Come here."
I dry long drips on her back,
lift her damp hair to kiss her neck.
For a few seconds, I didn't know
she was joking. And what's really
disturbing about that is how much

I cared.

Dad's Still Asleep

When I take Alexa home, but by the time
I get back, he's up, drinking coffee, and
it's weird, but I think he's waiting for me.

Had company last night, did you?

Oh man. Did he, like, *hear* us? My face
flares. "Uh, yeah. How did you know?"

She left her jacket on the couch.
It wasn't Hayden, I take it. Can't see
that girl wearing black leather.

Not to mention spending the night
in my bed, doing unmentionable
things to me. I'm so busted. "No."

Have some coffee. He watches me pour
a cup. *I wouldn't recommend overnight*
guests with your mother present.

No kidding. "I didn't plan for her
to stay over. It just kind of happened.
We were only supposed to talk."

He out-and-out guffaws, and I realize
how lame that sounded. *How cliché.*

Absolutely, and yet his easy dismissal
pisses me off. "I don't guess that's what
you thought when Mom came knocking?"

He looks surprised that I'd mention it
but decides to cowboy up. *We both
knew exactly why she was there, son.*

"But you let her in anyway, despite
being in love with someone else."
I don't shade the statement with opinion.

Now he assesses me, as he might
a complete stranger. *That's right, I did,
and it's something I've long regretted.*

Regret. This house is a sponge,
absorbing regret until it can hold
no more and disillusionment drips

through the bloated pores. If Dad
could do it all over, he wouldn't cheat
on his girlfriend with Mom. Wouldn't

get her pregnant, no need for a quickie
wedding. And of course there would
be no me. I think maybe I resent that.

Dad and I Rarely Talk

Let alone openly communicate,
but what the hell? Is one time
in eighteen years too much?
"Were you and Lorelei
having problems? I mean,
if you don't mind telling me."

> He thinks it over. *I guess*
> *maybe we were—the pressure*
> *of maintaining grades while*
> *excelling at sports is never*
> *easy. Figure in nurturing*
> *a relationship when what*
> *you really want to do on your*
> *off hours is party, well . . . But*
> *it was nothing we couldn't have*
> *worked through, and she might*
> *have forgiven me, except for . . .*

"Except for me."

> Unbelievably, he agrees,
> *Except for you.*

236

We Both Sip Our Coffee

Slurping into the silent gauze
between us. Someone has to rip
through it. "But you stayed with
Mom all this time. Did you ever
love her? Just a little, even?"

>   *Love is a funny thing. Sometimes*
>   *it barrels into you like an angry*
>   *bull. Other times it infiltrates you*
>   *like an alien vine, and no matter*
>   *how hard you resist, it grabs hold*
>
>   *and squeezes. That's kind of what*
>   *happened with your mom and me.*
>   *Believe it or not, we've shared many*
>   *happy days, and that includes having*
>   *you and Luke. Eventually, it becomes*
>
>   *a matter of scale. When the good*
>   *outweighs the bad, you stay. When*
>   *the bad is the only thing you notice*
>   *anymore, you think about your future,*
>   *or what's left of it, consider options.*

Makes Sense

But it seems to me
it's better to consider
options before you shrivel
into a bitter, old slice of regret.

"You don't know it would
have been better if you'd stayed
with Lorelei, though."

True. I don't.

Honesty. How refreshing.
"Mom thinks you're going
to leave her. Are you?"

I'm not sure.

Honesty. How unnerving.
"You know Lorelei and
her husband are divorced."

It isn't a secret.

Kind of evasive. "Are you
thinking about getting
back together with her?"

He Doesn't Respond Immediately

Just sits, staring out the window,
and after so much unusual
forthrightness, I have to wonder.
"Are you already back together?"
I guess he figures he has nothing
to lose when he finally confesses,

> We've been seeing each other
> for a long time, Matt. See, the thing
> about the barreling-into-you kind
> of love is, it leaves deep, wide scars.
> I tried, but I never stopped loving her.

My turn to focus on the world
beyond the kitchen glass, where
the sun has decided to appear,
its thin rays of winter light magnified
by water droplets on every branch,
every blade, every needle. Stunning.

A lump balloons in my throat.
"Why did you stay? All you did was
make Mom miserable, make me feel
like a failure, give Luke another reason to—"

> No! Don't you dare blame me for that!

Blame

It's not a game, not at all, but
suddenly I know, "You're the reason
Lorelei divorced her husband.
He found out about you?"

> *Actually, he always suspected,*
> *but chose to look the other way.*
> *She was the one who finally*
> *grew tired of the deception.*

Do people really do that—
pretend not to see something
so hurtful? "And Mom? Has she
been looking the other way?"

> He nods. *I figured she'd stop excusing*
> *it and either boot me to the curb*
> *or hook up with someone else. But*
> *as far as I can tell, she's stayed faithful.*

So, basically, crap relationships
run in my family. Genetically,
I'm predisposed to lying, cheating,
and having sex for all the wrong reasons.

One Last Thing

I wouldn't bother to repeat
it, but since I'm stressing
over how much holding on
is too much, I go ahead.
"You still haven't told me
why you've stayed with
Mom, despite everything."

He draws a long, slow breath.
First, it was because of you.
A boy needs his father, that's
what I thought, someone to
teach him to play basketball.
Then your mother miscarried
and had a breakdown. Not sure
you knew that. I figured it had
to be mostly my fault because

I was glad she lost the baby.
Then she got pregnant with Luke,
a speck of redemption, and now
I had two sons to worry about.
After that, I found satisfaction
in my professional life. Personal
fulfillment became less important,
and maintaining my marriage
seemed easier than shredding it.

Easier

Having sex with a person
you don't care about.

Easier.

Staying in a toxic relationship
because people might talk.

Easier.

Not having sex with someone
you do care about.

Easier.

Because if you have sex,
that might change everything.

Easier.
Easier.
Easier.

But who ever said the easiest path
is the one you should choose?

I Can't Remember

The last time I've gone fifteen
hours without checking my cell.
I expect a half-dozen texts from
Hayden, wondering where I am.
What I'm up to. Why haven't
I called? Surprise! Not even a "hey."

There is one from Alexa, though.
THANKS FOR AN AMAZING NIGHT.
I LEFT MY JACKET THERE. ANY CHANCE
YOU COULD DROP IT OFF? My first
reaction is, no way. My second
is, what the hell is my problem?
It's not like she asked me to move

in, she just prefers not to freeze
to death. She didn't even sign off
with "I love you." But she does love
me. She said so, and there was more
emotion in her single declaration
than in all of Hayden's halfhearted

reciprocations combined, and that
makes me angry. Why hasn't she
texted me? What's happened to her?
To us? Thinking back over the past
few weeks, retracing every step,
I can find only one answer. Judah.

My Personal Corner of the World

Has never been rich
with happiness. Overall, joy
has been in short supply.
It's funny, because when
you're a little kid, it doesn't
take much to spark satisfaction—
you master fractions or land
a ridiculous jump on your bike.
You go looking for fun,
create it with your friends,
and in my case, sometimes
with my little brother.

Yeah, I got that my mom
and dad were a little off.
Compared to, say, Vince's
ever-present, ever-interested
parents, mine were distant, cool.
But what did it matter? Once
Vince and I were out the door,
our playing field was level.

But my memoir was all
a single chapter then, unmarred
by major transitions. And now,
the pages are shredding,
my life disintegrating.

Luke is gone forever.
Hayden is a wild card.
Mom and Dad are melting
down completely, every vestige
of imagined stability in flux.
Will I even have a home
next week? With or without
one or both of my parents?
Everything is upheaval.

I need order.
I'm used to order.
Artificially constructed,
yes, I understand that. And easy.
That stinking word again.
Familiar pressure builds
in my chest. My breath
flutters like sparrow wings.

Inhale.
Palms up.
Exhale.
Palms down.

What will happen to me now?

Hold On

What will happen *to* me?
A thought strikes suddenly.

(Palms up. Palms down.) I've spent
my time here passively. Waiting

for some external stimuli to initiate
action through reaction. (Breathing

begins its return route to normal.)
Why can't I be my own stimulus?

If I want order, I have to take charge,
and there has to be more control in

claiming the wheel, deciding where
to steer, how hard to punch the accelerator,

when to pass slower-moving vehicles,
obstacles in the path of forward motion.

And the first obstacle I need to clear
is a certain youth minister impeding

the progress of my relationship with
Hayden. Yes, that's a great place to start.

It's Strange

Because I've always
believed girls despised
male aggression.

Yet Hayden claims
to feel unappreciated
due to my lack of it.

And Alexa was totally
turned on when I tapped
into a small reservoir of it.

Is there something
to that caveman's club?
Would Hayden love me

more if I dragged her
around by the hair?
Should I set loose

my inner Neanderthal?

What Have I Got to Lose?

I grab Alexa's jacket with every
intention of dropping it off later.

But first I head straight for Hayden's,
no forewarning call to announce
my imminent arrival. All the way
there, I summon my inner primitive

man, keep poking him with a sharp
stick. *Ugga!* I knuckle-drag the sidewalk
all the way to her front step, ring
the doorbell. Unfortunately, it's her

> father who answers, and his expression
> is somewhat less than welcoming. *Yes?*
> *Oh. It's you. What can I do for you?*

I give him my best caveman grin.
"What's up, Mr. DeLucca? Is Hayden
here? I'd like to take her out to lunch,
if that's okay." No *ugga*. One point for me.

> Except he's the one keeping score.
> He glances at his watch. *Lunch was*
> *two hours ago. Anyway, she isn't here.*

That's a double *ugga* for the man.
"Can you tell me where she is?"
My impatient toe-tapping isn't winning

him over. *Have you tried calling*
her cell? I'm not her secretary.
I don't schedule her appointments.

Wow. What a hairy Sasquatch dick.
But rudeness won't serve my purpose.

"I'm sorry, Mr. D., but what is it about me
you so dislike? I shower every day,
sometimes twice." Ooh. Way too civilized.

"I'm at the top of my class, kicked tail
on my ACTs." Kicked tail. Better. "And
I'm totally in love with your daughter."
Oops. I think I just went too far.

His eyes narrow into slits. *Don't you dare*
toss around words like love. You are
a teenaged boy with adolescent cravings.

But beyond that, you are headed down the low
road to hell and I don't want you dragging
my daughter in Satan's direction with you.

As I See It

I've got two choices.

Play defense.
My usual position,
and in a situation like this,
doubtless the right way to go.

Attempt offense.
Survival of the fittest.
Triple *uggas*, and if I opt
for this tactic, he'll probably
forbid Hayden to see me.

Good luck with that, Mr. D.

Better straddle the line.
"Just because I don't go to church
or sing praise hymns doesn't mean
I've been condemned to spend eternity
with some mythical pork-footed,

dual-horned demon. I'm a good
person. I treat Hayden right. I've
never even tried to have se—" Oh shit.
Now he thinks I'm gay. "And I'm
not queer, either. I mean, the reason
I never tried is because I respect . . ."

The Door Slams

Okay, Plan A went about as well
as I could have expected. Bet
the first primitives to develop
language enough to express
their feelings ended up spit-roasted.

Plan B. Caveman up and call, not
text, Hayden. She answers immediately,
as if expecting the communication.

> She is. *What did you say to my dad?*
> *He told me I have to break up*
> *with you to save my eternal soul.*

"Already? It's only been, like, sixty
seconds since your front door attacked
my face. And mostly what I did was ask
why he doesn't like me, then I listed

all my best points. Including the fact
I'm not gay, by the way. That really
seemed to impress him." Too far?

> *You didn't. Tell me you didn't, Matt.*

Guess that means too far.

But How Far Is Too Far?

Have I crossed enough lines in the past
twenty-four hours to have thrown away

everything I struggled to build and maintain
with Hayden, despite the odds? "So, does

that mean you're breaking up with me?"
If she is, I'm certain it has little to do

> with any edict from her father. *Oh,*
> *Matt, I just don't know. I still love*

> *you so much, but it seems like you've*
> *changed, and it makes me wonder why.*

What? "You think *I've* changed? It isn't
me who's different, Hayden. It's . . ." Stop.

Don't do this now. "Please. Let's talk face
to face. Where are you? I'll come get you."

Please don't say no. Please don't say no.
If she does, we're totally through, and I'm

> not ready for that. Apparently, she isn't,
> either. *I'm at Joce's. Give me an hour.*

Fifty-Nine Minutes Later

I pull to the curb in front of Jocelyn's house,
wait the extra sixty seconds so Hayden can't say
I tried to rush her, then give two beeps. She's out
the door immediately. She was ready for me, and
the rare winter sun burnishes the crown of her hair,
and I fall in love all over again. I can't lose her.

I pop out of the cab, haul around to the far side
of the truck, and open the passenger door. The closer
she gets, the more I want to kiss her. But should
I do it here? Now? Will it embarrass her? Should
I wait, or will she freak out if I do? Jesus, when did
we, she and I, become such a complex puzzle?

When she reaches me, I have no clue if I'm
doing the right thing when I hold out my hand,
a simple request that she honors. I pull her
as close as we can get without actually touching,
plunge into the smoke of her eyes. "I love you.
Damn if I can figure out if that's enough for you,

but it's the absolute truth. I don't want to say
too much, or too little. I don't want you to feel
offended if I ask if I can kiss you, because I'm
not sure what you want anymore, and it's scaring
the hell out of me, Hayden." I can't read a single
signal in the smoke, so I just ask, "Can I kiss you?"

I Hope She Answers

The way I know
she would
have a year ago,
or six months
ago, or even just
a few weeks
ago—with a tender
brush of her lips
against mine,
flint to fire the kiss
that could bring light
to the blackest corner
of the darkest room.

I search her eyes,
wait for that response,
or something close
to it. Instead, she says,

                    Not here.

I step back, offer to
help her up into the truck,
and as I do, notice
the black leather jacket
on the console between
the passenger seat and the driver's.

No Way Around

The explanation that must come,
still I hurry to secure both doors,
start the engine, and take off down
the road, so I'll at least have the chance
to give it. I keep asking what's wrong
with everyone else, when maybe
the real question is what the hell's up

> with me? Was this some subconcious
> stab at confession? Hayden picks up
> the jacket, sniffs the signature perfume
> permeating the leather. *Alexa. Jocelyn*
> *said she saw the two of you together*
> *yesterday. Don't tell me. You gave her*
> *a ride home, and it got a little hot in here.*

I was going to offer the ride home
excuse, minus the rest. But now I'd
better come closer to the truth, minus
any mention of getting hot. "Not exactly.
I'm sorry, but I needed someone to talk
to. About you. We talked about you.
I'm just trying to figure you out, Hayd."

I Don't See Hayden's Temper Often

But it swells to bursting now.
Figure me out? With Alexa?
What does she know about me?
Why didn't you talk to me instead?

I couldn't have asked for a better
opening. "I've tried to talk to you,
Hayden, begged you to stop closing
yourself off from me. Alexa knows
what it's like to lose you. I'm doing
everything in my power to make sure
she and I won't have that in common."

That quiets her for a second or two.
I keep driving away from town.
Away from her father, her friends,
her minister, out into the countryside.
She watches the landscape shimmer
beyond the window. Finally, a whisper
escapes her mouth. *What did she say?*

I have to stop and think about it.
Not sure I should bring up the part
about the reason Alexa and Hayden
are no longer friends, and that's really
about all she said before . . . Better make
up something. "She said you hurt her."

Hayden Sniffles

Is she crying? Oh man.
Not that. I hate it when she cries,
hate it more when I'm the reason.

> *I hurt Alexa? What about me?*
> *She quit being my friend because*
> *she was jealous you liked me better.*

Slight distortion of the facts
there, girl. Not that I'd say so.
"That's not exactly how she put it."

> *Oh really?* she hisses. *Tell me*
> *how, exactly, she did put it, then?*
> I pull off the main road, onto

a gravel logging track, but don't
dare go far. The woods-shadowed
mud would swallow us whole.

I turn to Hayden, whose entire face
is puffy from tears. "Please don't cry."
I reach for her hand, afraid

she won't give it, but she does,
and I kiss each finger, one by one,
on the very tip. "Alexa doesn't matter."

Pretty sure that's not one hundred
percent true in the larger sense,
but in the context of this conversation,

it's valid. "Look. Until a few weeks
ago, you and I were solid, or at least
that's what I believed. Something

has changed, and it isn't me." I take
her other hand, kiss those fingers,
too. And it's only the tiniest interior

voice whispering that I'd never have
to go to such lengths to prove my love
for Alexa. If I did love Alexa, that is.

> *I guess I have changed,* she admits,
> *but not in a bad way. I'm growing
> deeper in my relationship with the Lord,*
>
> *is all. I love you, Matt, I do. But spiritual
> love is more important than love born
> of the flesh, and that's what we have.*

She's Trading Me In

For Jesus. Can't imagine whose
idea that was. "I thought all love
came from God. What happened
to that? Don't tell me. Judah,
who's given you a whole new
understanding of the scriptures."

> *That's right.* Her eyes fill with
> something very much resembling
> adoration. But for the Lord, or for
> his earthly messenger? *Remember
> the last argument you and I had,
> about why you never tried—*

"Of course I remember. To be
clear, however, my only problem
was about your 'discussing' my
probable homosexual predisposition
with your friends and pastor."

> *I know, Matt. And when I told Judah
> what happened he said to put myself
> in your shoes, as Jesus would have
> us do. And then he laid the blame
> totally on me. He said I was at fault
> for believing my worth was determined
> by the artificial standards of man.*

Insane

The man.
The message.
The way she believes every word.
The control that gives him.

But I don't dare argue.
Mustn't contradict.
I can't fight him long distance,
even though I know those
artificial standards
he expects her to eschew
are his own.

He is a two-faced prick,
and the only way to expose
the one he so skillfully hides
is on his home turf.

"You're not to blame
for anything, Hayden, except
wanting to feel valued. I try very
hard to do that for you, but obviously
sometimes I fail. Still, I'm glad
he's making you look at things
through a wider lens. In fact, I'm impressed.
Do you have a youth group meeting
on Friday? I'd really like to come."

Unconvinced

Doesn't quite cover
her expression. Skeptical
isn't strong enough, either.
She studies me, as if looking
for my own hidden face,
or the alien crawling beneath
my skin, seeking egress.

> *Why?*

"Why do I want to go? Why not?"

> *Matt, you've never shown one
> tiny bit of desire to go to church
> with me, let alone youth group.
> So, why? What do you want?*

"Wow. What a cynic.
Okay, Hayden, I want
to see your Judah
in action; to try and wrap
my brain around the way
you feel about him;
to comprehend the power
of his message. I want
to understand."

Not Exactly a Lie

Though I hope she misses
the nuanced meaning,
and she seems to.

I'll ask Judah, okay?

"Okay, but it's his job
to win me over, right?"
Go ahead, dude. Convert
me and I'll shave my head
and relocate to Tibet.

Finally, a smile. *I guess it is.*

"So, we're okay, then?"
Can't believe I pulled it off.
"Is it okay for me to kiss you
now?" Please, please, please
don't say no. "No one will
see but that bear over there."

She jumps. But there's no
bear. *Matt! That was mean.*

"Allow me to make it up to you."
Unpredictably, she softens, lukewarm,
into my arms. Let the kissing begin.

This Kiss

Is a shallow winter
pool—watery,
much too cool.
It makes me shiver,
and not in a good way.

I try to dive deeper,
find the hot spring
I suspect lies hidden
somewhere
inside this girl I love.

I give it my best shot,
but she keeps reeling
me back
to the surface,

where the scent
of citrus-perfumed
leather
is overwhelming.

Sunday Morning

I wake earlier than usual,
no doubt due to the sunshine
flooding the eastern window.
A second sunny day in a row
demands a celebration. But first,

I text Hayden. DON'T FORGET
TO ASK JUDAH IF I'M WELCOME
ON FRIDAY. I PROMISE TO BE
THE PERFECT GENTLEMAN.
What I don't promise is that

I won't change my mind.
When I open my bedroom door,
breakfast aromas smack me
square in the nose. Mom's still
gone, so it's Dad who's claimed

the kitchen. Weirdly, he's wide
awake and smiling around his eggs.
Enjoying the silver morning, too,
I guess, and some strange air
of nostalgia engulfs me. "I'm going

to the range today. Want to come
along?" Holy hell. Did I just invite
my dad to go shooting with me?

Holy Hell

Is what his body language
screams, too. And in the span
of about thirty seconds, his
expression segues from surprise

> to pleasure to disappointment.
> *Seriously, thanks for asking, son.*
> *But I'm afraid I've got plans.*
> The tone of his voice is odd.

Husky. And I understand
immediately that his plans
do not involve his buddies.
He's doing something with *her*.

> *But next time, give me a little*
> *warning. I've been meaning to*
> *hang out with Jessie. The two*
> *of us aren't getting any younger.*

And Luke will never grow older.
"So you know, I'd give my left nut
to spend one more day with my brother.
Next time you should come along."

I Retreat

Before he can respond, exit the house
without turning around. When I start

the truck, I notice the leather jacket
on the backseat. Damn. I forgot to drop

it off. Oh well. Lex's house is on the way,
so it will be a quick stop. I'm almost there

when I notice the little tremor of nerves.
What does she think of me? What does

she expect of me? And a bigger question—
what do I expect of her now? I glance down

at the speedometer, which holds steady
at thirty-eight in a fifty mph zone.

My subconscious, reminding me I really
don't want this meeting, hope it won't turn

into a confrontation, or even worse,
a tear-fest. I hate when women cry.

Only Fitting, Then

That Alexa answers the door,
puffed red eyes feeding the black
streams striping her cheeks.
Déjà vu to the nth degree.

"Uh. Hi? I came to retu—"

She pushes straight past the offered
jacket and rushes out the door,
not much differently than I just did
at my own home a short while ago.

> *I need to get out of here.*

The words are tossed over her shoulder
as she hustles to my truck and jumps
up inside, like I'd invited her to do
exactly that. I can only watch, half

choking on a silent protest.

My head swivels toward a flick
of movement behind the window.
Déjà vu to the nth degree, except
the scowling face belongs to a woman.

She is Alexa, only twice her age.

Okay, What Now?

I retreat toward the truck, backward,
just in case the shrewish woman
decides to come after me. But I reach

my vehicle safely. Alexa stares out
the far window, not acknowledging
my presence. "Hey, lady. What's up?"

> *Nothing.* She doesn't turn toward
> me. *Would you please just take
> me somewhere? Anywhere but here.*

Would it do any good to say no?
I submit to her request. "Parental
problems?" I steer in the general

direction of town, hoping she has
a destination other than "anywhere"
in mind. "They seem to be in the air."

> *Mom found out I didn't spend
> the night with Lainie. Now, she'll
> probably suspect I spent it with you.*
>
> *I'm over eighteen, and technically
> able to sleep with whomever I please.
> She hasn't played Mama in too many*

years to think she can step in and
start orchestrating my life now. She
actually believes she can ground me!

"Maybe she's feeling neglectful.
Anyway, her plan for total Alexa
domination didn't work out so well."

She half laughs. *As if. The worst*
part was the names she called me.
Okay, it was probably the tequila

doing the screaming, but if anyone
else defamed me in such a fashion,
they'd be hearing from my lawyer.

The faux snooty tone of her voice
makes me smile. At least the drama
has become intentional. But now

I remember my original purpose,
and since the tear tap has emptied,
"So, where should I drop you off?"

I can almost hear her eyes filling
up again. *Drop me off? Can't I*
just hang out with you for a while?

No! No! No!

That's what I want to say.
That's what I need to say.
But what I actually do say
is, "I don't know if that's
such a good idea, Lex."

> *Why not? No strings. I know*
> *you're still attached to Hayden,*
> *but right now she's busy chanting*
> *liturgy and sipping God's blood.*

She's got me there. Still,
"I was planning on going out
to my uncle's shooting range
for a little target practice."

> *Really? Cool! Will you teach me?*
> *I've always wanted to learn.*

I can't believe she wants to go
with me. Hayden thinks firing
at bull's-eyes is paper abuse.

"I don't know . . ."

> *Please?* At my silence,
> she amends, *Pretty please?*

Oh, Why Not?

Truth be told, I'm sick
of spending weekends
mostly alone.
Anyway, it will give me
the chance to make
my intentions—
or lack thereof—
perfectly clear.

"Okay. I guess
you can come. But if
Uncle Jessie is around,
don't be shocked
by his missing eye.
And if he hits the deck
at the sound of gunfire,
it's the PTSD talking.
Iraq is responsible for both."

> Why does he own
> a shooting range
> if the noise freaks him out?

"You don't know
much about soldiers,
do you? They're all
about choking down fear.

That doesn't stop
just because shrapnel
forces them home.
Uncle Jessie loves guns,
believe me, and even with one
eye gone, he's a better shot
than most. But his brain
has been traumatized,
and what's A-OK
one minute might
set him off the next."

She thinks that over
silently and finally asks,
Have you ever seen him go off?

I could tell her
about the time some
guy fired a .50 BMG,
BLAM! at the exact
same moment a helicopter
*whoop-whoop*ed overhead.
Jessie nose-dived
into the dirt and I thought
he just might dig himself
underground, shoveling
with his forehead.

Or I could mention
a certain incident
involving an asshole
who refused to quit picking
on his son. Every time
the kid missed his shot,
the jerk-off dad bear-hugged
the boy into submission,
kicked his feet into a stance,
clamped his big old hands
around the smaller pair
and fired for him.

When the kid collapsed
in tears, his loving father
slapped the boy's face
his nose and mouth ran red.
Until Jessie stormed across
the field and beat that guy
into a gooey pulp.
Later, after a night in jail,
he told how he'd seen
an Iraqi kid left faceless
by a hailstorm
of American bullets.

*Some things drill right through
your skull,* he said, *and into your brain.*

I Could Share Those Things

But I'd rather hold them inside
and skip explicit explanations
that might make her afraid of him.

"I've seen some things, but for
whatever reason, I happen to be
a calming influence, at least that's

what my therapist calls me.
We've had late night calls from Quin—
that's his girlfriend—telling us

he's wigging out. If he'll take
the phone, I can usually talk him
down." Why couldn't I do the same

for Luke? The sudden shadow darkens
my mood. Perhaps a change of subject
is in order. "I think we need to talk

about what happened the other night.
It was great and everything. . . ."
Was it ever. "But I feel like

I took advantage of you and—"
The volume of her sigh halts
my words midsentence. "What?"

Don't you think I have a mind
of my own? You did not *take*
advantage of me. I wanted to be

with you. Look. Like I said, I know
you're still with Hayden, and
I never asked for any sort of

commitment. It's enough to spend
time with you, at least it's enough
for now. The sex was amazing.

If you decided to pull over for
a quickie, I'd happily comply, but
it isn't necessary, or why I'm here.

I love you, Matt, I do. She pauses,
then laughs, staccato. *Pretty sure*
there's a Bible verse that says, "Love

is patient." Dude, I'm the patient
love poster child. I figure if I wait
long enough, eventually you'll get smart.

Her Forthrightness

Is bone-chilling,
yet also refreshing.
Communication?

This girl is not afraid
of the word, which makes
me wonder out loud,

"What *are* you afraid of?"

> *What?*

"Are you afraid of anything?"

> *Well, sure. Everyone's afraid*
> *of something, aren't they?*

"Okay, so, like, what? Spiders?
Snakes? Chain-saw killers?"

> She laughs again. *Dad killed*
> *a chain saw once. Not pretty.*

"Young woman, I do believe
you're evading my question."

She Sucks in a Serious Breath

Exhales slowly, as if expelling
the air compressed inside her secrets.

> *I'm not afraid of spiders or snakes.*
> *I'm afraid of things I can't see.*

"You mean, like, gasses? Or all
the way down to the molecular level?"

> *Smart-ass. I mean like . . .*
> *Have you ever felt something*

> *brush by, but when you look*
> *to see what, there's nothing there?*

"Uh, not really. Hey, are you going
all woo-woo on me or what?"

> *Never mind.* Her voice is heavy
> with "pout." *Sorry you asked.*

"Oh, don't be mad. I've never
experienced anything like that,

or if I did, my conscious self chose
to ignore it. I don't like creepy shit."

Me either, and that's exactly
what I mean. I have experienced

it, on more than one occasion, and
my conscious self couldn't ignore

the way it made me break out
in goose bumps and lifted the hair

on my arms. And the weirdest thing
was, I know exactly who it was.

Who? Damn, man, woo-woo squared.
"Really?" This is either obnoxiously

interesting or something I want
to know nothing about. *Really.*

So, do I bite, or leave it there,
hoping it will go away? "Who?"

My father. He was killed when
I was a baby. I never knew him.

Killed?

That's what I ask,
increduously, and, "Why
have I never heard this story?"
I've known Alexa
since fifth grade.

>*She shrugs. It's not*
>*something that comes up*
>*in conversation. Like I said,*
>*I never knew him at all.*
>*My mom remarried*
>*when I was two, so Paul*
>*has always been "Dad" to me.*

"Hope this doesn't sound
morbid, but what
happened to your father?"

>*Nothing too glamorous.*
>*Wrong place, wrong time*
>*to be buying liquor.*
>*The store got robbed,*
>*and he was caught*
>*in the crossfire when*
>*the guy behind the counter*
>*pulled his own gun.*

I turn off the highway,
onto the gravel road to Uncle
Jessie's. The tires crunch
beneath us, the noise obvious
above our silent reflection.

Finally I ask, "So why
do you think your father
would come back to terrify you?"

> I doubt that's his goal, but I
> can't help being weirded out.
> How often do dead people come
> around to visit? Why would
> he drop by? Great question.
> Maybe it's lonely wherever
> your spirit goes when you die.
> Maybe he wants company.
> Or maybe he just wants me
> to know he's looking out for me.

"Would it make you feel better
to believe a dead someone
is looking out for you?"

> Better than thinking he's inviting
> me to join him in the Great Beyond.

The Sun Showers

Have encouraged a number
of people to the outdoor range.
Small-caliber weapons crack
the air, while larger ones
thud and boom. I assess
Lex's expression—fascination
and outright delight. This
could be a whole lot of fun.

We find an open target and
I demonstrate all the basics.
Safety first, of course—what
not to do if you want to remain
unscathed. Then grip. Stance.
Aim. The kick surprises her at
first, the barrel's awkward lift
making her miss the paper
completely the first shot or ten.

I show her how to compensate,
and we start again. Before long,
she's hitting the target reliably,
if not square center. Finally,
I take control of the Glock.
"My turn." I spend a few minutes
showing off and am reloading
when someone taps my shoulder.

I turn. "Hey, Uncle Jessie."
His long salt-and-pepper hair
is tied back away from his face,
accentuating the sharp angles
that run in the Turner family.
He is younger than Dad, but could
easily pass for his older brother.
He gives me a giant bear hug,
steps back and grins, then notices
Alexa, who is likewise grinning.

>   *This your girlfriend?*

I glance at Lex. "Not exactly."

>   His single eye does the work
>   of two, gives her a total once-over.
>   *Hmm. Well, she should be.*

"Uncle Jessie!" Lex doesn't blush,
but I do. "Um, this is my *friend*,
Alexa. I'm showing her the ropes."

>   *I know. I've been observing.*
>   *You could do worse for a teacher,*
>   *miss. This boy is a world-class shot.*

A Sudden Outburst

Of world-class cussing draws
all attention toward the far end
of the long row of targets,

where an immense, scruffy
guy seems to be wrestling
with a very large long gun.

> *Ah, hell,* exhales Jessie. *Gus.*
> *Better go help him out.* He starts
> away, turns back long enough

> to invite, *Quin's whipping up*
> *enchiladas. Why don't you two*
> *come to the house for dinner?*

Alexa's all for it, I can tell,
and I'm having frozen whatever
otherwise. "Sure thing," I call after

Uncle Jessie, who, in a half-dozen
superstrides, has reached Gus.
I can't hear what he's saying,

but I can see him coax the rifle
away from the hulk. He checks for
a chambered round, examines

the barrel, points out something
to Gus, who remains agitated. People
start packing it in, but whether it's due

to the commotion or simply because
the day is tipping toward evening,
who knows? Alexa shifts uneasily

from foot to foot. "Don't worry.
Whatever the problem is, Jessie can
handle it. You up for another round?"

Lex pulls her attention back toward
the Glock and me, but when she takes
the pistol, I notice the tension traveling

from her shoulders all the way down
through her arms, into her hands.
"You'll have to relax or forget it."

> *I'm trying,* she says. *But that man
> looks just this side of going bad. Reminds
> me of Paul after an all-night bender.*

"If he's been drinking, my uncle
will escort him out of here. Guns
and liquor are a toxic combination."

As If to Prove My Point

Jessie and Gus come ambling
toward us, Jessie carrying the rifle
belonging to the bigger man,
who has one arm slung around
Jessie's shoulder. After they pass
by, headed in the direction

of the main building, Lex finally
expels enough stress to hit the target
again. Her last shot is a dead-on
bull's-eye. "Way to go!" I offer
a high high-five, one she has to
jump a little for. Anything worth

> having is worth working for,
> as my Grandpa Turner says.
> I take one last turn, annihilating
> the target's center with eight
> straight perfect shots. *Awesome!*
> exclaims Lex. *I want to shoot like that.*

"You can, with practice. You've
got a good eye." I drop the clip,
pull the trigger one last time,
making sure no chambered
surprises await me, then wipe
the Glock free of residue.

I pack the pistol in its case and
as Lex and I swing toward the truck,
Uncle Jessie and Gus emerge
from the office. This time,
Jessie does walk Gus to his car,
the offending rifle nowhere in sight.

I tuck the Glock in its usual
under-the-seat hiding place, wait
for Uncle Jessie's return trip. As
he nears, I call out, "Hey, soldier.
Want a ride? Good time, guaranteed."
Jessie laughs; Alexa does, too,

> especially when Jessie responds,
> *How could I* not *have a good time*
> *with you? But enchiladas first.*
> *Any and all good times after dinner.*
> The house isn't really so far, just
> a couple hundred yards up the hill.

Walking distance, but I kind of
enjoy the chauffeur role. I open
the backseat door. "Oh, brother
of my father, your four-wheel-drive,
supercharged V-8 limo awaits.
Allow me to help you in, suh."

He Slaps Away

My outstretched hand, but he does
accept the ride, climbs up inside,

> with a heartfelt, *Jerkwad. I'll give
> you "suh" right upside your head.*

We all watch Gus back his beater
out of the parking space, head off.

"What's up with him, anyway?
And what happened to his rifle?"

> Uncle Jessie clucks his tongue. *I
> talked him into letting me work on*
>
> *that old piece of crap. The barrel
> is corroded, and I'm worried it'll*
>
> *blow his ugly-ass face off.
> But he loves that goddamn thing.*

> *I thought he might fight you for it,*
> says Alexa. *He looked belligerent.*

> *B-b . . .* Jessie detonates laughter.
> *Yep, belligerent is the perfect word*

for Gus, and I figure he was born
that way. But he wouldn't fight me.

We're compadres. He's a tad tweaked,
but four back-to-back tours to

the Middle East will do that to a guy.
I let him come out here for free.

He needs to blow off steam every now
and again, and I'd rather it be shooting

targets than most other things I can
think of. Anyway, you're safe with me.

We pull up in front of the two-story
frame farmhouse. The front porch sags

a little, but seeing as how the place
was built almost a century ago, all in all,

it's in decent shape. A trio of pit bull
mix mutts come around the side of the house

to investigate, wagging their stumps
at the sight of Jessie and his company.

The Dogs Grin, Exposing Fangs

Alexa hesitates beside the truck.
"I thought nothing scared you
except things you can't see,"
I tease. "Don't worry. Larry,
Mo, and Curly are friendly."

Unless you piss them off, amends
Jessie. Then he quickly backs off.
*But I told you, you're safe with me.
Now, come on inside. Quin doesn't
get to play hostess very often.*

Lex decides to chance her way
past the dogs, who sniff her as she
walks by. *Hope I don't smell like
bacon,* she says. But she's smiling,
and the Stooges go off in search

of squirrels or skunks, hopefully
the former. One time they got hold
of a nest of the smelly critters and
I'm not sure who got the worst of it.
The place smelled like eau de stink for days.

Today, However

It smells like sautéed
onions and peppers, stewed
chicken, and hot corn tortillas.
"Man, I haven't eaten homemade
anything in months."

> *Thank God my lady can cook,*
> says Jessie. *It's one of her best*
> *attributes.* He winks at Lex.
> *I won't say just what it is*
> *she's better at, but let me tell*
> *you, she's an expert!*

Tugging Lex behind me,
I follow him into the kitchen,
where Quin is lifting an oversized
pan from the oven. Quite
an accomplishment, considering
she's barely five feet tall
and thin as a spring shoot.

"Need help?" I move swiftly
across the floor, in case
she says yes, but knowing
that's highly unlikely.
She thumps the enchiladas
down on the counter, turns

to face me. *The only help*
I need from you is a hug.
She pulls me to her, obliges
herself, then pushes me away
again. *It's been too long. Why*
don't you ever come see us after
you're finished shredding targets?

I shrug. "Don't want to bother
you. And anyway, how do
you even know I've been here
and gone without saying hello?"

Her laugh is warm and throaty.
I know pretty much everything
that happens around here.
Now, who's this? Your girlfriend?

Lex and I exchange amused
glances. But before either
of us can respond,

Uncle Jessie says, *Not exactly,*
according to Matt, despite
how things might look. Regardless,
this is Alexa, and Matt's teaching
her marksmanship. Now, how
about a couple of brewskis?

The Invitation

Extends to Alexa and me.
Our mild protests are brushed
away like pesky mosquitoes.

> *You're both eighteen, right?*
> asks Jessie. *If you're old enough*
> *to fight for your country, you're old*
> *enough to drink a beer or two,*
> *especially as a complement*
> *to enchiladas. Nothing beats*
> *the spice like cold carbonation.*

It's hard to argue with that.
Quin abstains, "just in case
someone needs to play designated
driver." I don't mention I've driven
after drinking more than a beer
or two, not that it was the best idea.

We settle around the table, dive
into probably the best Mexican
food I've ever tasted.
"You should open a restaurant,
Quin. Where did you learn
to cook like this, anyway?"

I'm one-quarter mexicana,
gringo, she says, bastardizing
both languages. Mi abuela *taught
me. She'd be happy you like
her recipes. Eat up. There's plenty.*

The revelation is a surprise.
There's a lot I don't know
about people in my life.
I suppose I should change that.
The small talk continues
for over an hour. We discuss
Dad, which leads to basketball
and championships almost in the bag.

We move on to Mom,
and I can't help but mention
that she's been staying at Aunt
Sophie's a little longer than I expected.

> *Problems at home?* Uncle Jessie's
> question elicits a "maybe that's
> none of our business" glare from
> Quin. He responds, *Just asking.*

I shrug. "I talked to her
yesterday. She says she's trying
to get some things straight
in her head." I don't mention
the precipitating factors.

Quin inquires about college
and when I mention my lack
of concrete goals, Uncle Jessie
says, *Hell, I didn't have any idea
what to do with my life until after
the war almost stole it from me.
You've got time. Just don't join the army.*

Now we talk about the range,
the shooting club Uncle Jessie
is forming. Upcoming competitions.

*I sure do need you on my team.
You're going to join, right? I'll even
loan you my special Glock. It's a killer.*

That brings us all up short.
"Figuratively speaking, I hope.
As for the team and matches,
I'll think about it, okay? At least
if you promise to leave Gus home."

The Joke Falls a Little Flat

So I'm glad the sound of silverware
clattering against emptied plates draws

attention to clearing the table. As we
remove the dishes, conversation turns

to the side effects of war. Jessie
takes a long swallow of beer.

> *I know Gus can be off-putting,*
> *but he's relatively harmless.*

"Something about him made
Lex nervous. Probably the way

he screamed at his rifle as if
it were a flesh-and-blood enemy."

> *He yells sometimes, a product*
> *of traumatic brain injury.*

> *I don't think he even realizes*
> *what's coming out of his mouth.*

I study Alexa for a minute. "Funny
thing, she just told me on the way over

here that the only things that scare her
are things she can't see. Isn't that right,

Lex?" She answers with a half smile
that says it wasn't the least bit funny.

> *Things she can't see? Like what?*
> *Evil spirits?* His unpatched eye glitters.

"Something like that. A spirit,
anyway, evil or benign, who knows?"

I think about it for a minute.
Who better to ask than my uncle?

"So, what's your opinion? You've
seen people die. What happens?

Do they have spirits that exit their
bodies, rise up from the cadavers?

Do they float toward some distant
bright light, happy to be released?

Do some of them hang around,
maybe haunt people they know?"

His Answer

Is a hoarse growl, delivered
from a place inside his head
I'm sure he'd rather not revisit.

> You're right, Matt. I've seen
> lots of people die. Men. Women.
> Children. Even babies.
>
> I've looked into their eyes
> as they lay there, waiting.
> Never saw happiness or hope,
>
> not even in those that accepted
> what was, and those were few.
> Most fought for life, here on earth.
>
> Death was unwelcome darkness,
> something thick and suffocating.
> I watched them slip into that,
>
> and the only thing I ever saw
> in their eyes was fear. Do I believe
> in an afterlife, or a far-off heaven
>
> to aspire to? No sir, I don't. I do
> believe in evil, but only the kind
> that walks and talks, corporal.

297

Pretty much what I expected.
"So, you've never seen ghosts,
then? Never had someone

come back and haunt you?"
I notice Quin give him a look—
one that says, "Tell the truth."

> *Not unless you count dreams*
> *as ghosts. I do have nightmares,*
> *and sometimes dead people come*
>
> *to call there. Buddies. Especially*
> *one—Lil Dog, we called him, because*
> *he kind of resembled a bulldog.*
>
> *All he ever talked about was his girl.*
> *How they were getting married*
> *just as soon as he got home. Only*
>
> *he never made it. We were on patrol*
> *and a sniper nailed him. I radioed*
> *for a medic, but it was way too late*
>
> *by the time they got there. I held*
> *him as he died, all the time calling,*
> *"Sarah." He visits pretty regularly.*

On That Semi-Creepy Note

It's probably time to go.
I reiterate my promise
to consider the shooting club.

> *Maybe your girl—uh, Alexa*
> *will think about joining*
> *us, too?* Uncle Jessie winks
> like a one-eyed old lecher.

Quin elbows him,
tells him not to tease.

> *It's okay,* soothes Lex.
> *I'll think about it, but I'll need*
> *a whole lot more practice*
> *to be good enough.*

> *You come on out here anytime,*
> *with or without that nephew*
> *of mine. It was a pleasure*
> *breaking bread with you.*

> Then, to me, *You could do*
> *a whole lot worse than this*
> *young woman. Think about it.*

Before We Hit the Road

Alexa and I both check our cells,
and in unison exclaim,

"Shit."   *Shit.*

Then, in almost unison,

"What?"
          What?

Which makes us laugh, despite
the seriousness of the text messages
we've just read. "You first."

> *Mom says if I don't get my butt*
> *home "right this very minute,"*
> *I'll find all my stuff out front*
> *and she hopes I have somewhere*
> *to go. That was, uh . . . six hours ago.*

"Whoa. She was pissed. But
she'll have cooled off by now,
right? Not sure Hayden will have.
She texted me five times, wanted
me to pick her up after church."

In unison, "Shit." *Shit.*

Alexa's Stuff

Is not out front when we get there.
Either her mom forgave her, or
she convinced the Salvation Army
to come pick it up on Sunday.
"See you tomorrow. And thanks
for putting up with my family."

*I like your family. And thank
you for the great day. It was fun.*

We don't kiss goodbye, and she does
take her jacket. I watch her go inside,
hoping the reception she receives isn't
as frigid as the one I'm about to experience.
I return to a house emptied of people.

I can guess where Dad went, and even
though on one level I understand why
he's made this decision, it pisses
me off. His wife is still my mom.

It's a sobering thought as I call
Hayden, explain how I spent the day
with my uncle Jessie, talking
about the ways war changes you,
omitting his observations on death.
And, of course, zero mention of Alexa.

I Shower Off

The strange potpourri clinging to my skin—
gunpowder and oil, Mexican food
and beer. It was a good day, and

I'm totally beat. Dad still isn't home
by the time I crawl into Luke's bed,
drawn there for some strange reason.

I lie listening to the clock's soft tick,
inhale through my nose, exhale out
my mouth, big deep breaths designed

to help me relax into sleep. Slipping,
sliding, skating toward slumber,
I find myself wishing there was some

leftover essence of my brother in
this room. But it just feels deserted.
"Why didn't you give it more time?

You selfish little bastard. Why didn't
you wait for me? We could have
talked it through. Just a couple more . . ."

This is the only place I ever allow
myself to cry, and I give myself
permission now. My eyes burn, on

fire, and it's no more than I deserve.
Who was the selfish bastard, really?
"I'm sorry, Luke. Oh God, I'm just

so fucking sorry. I love you, little
brother." A torrent of tears rushes
over my cheeks, down onto my neck.

I turn on my side so the pillow can
sponge them. Please let me sleep!
Just let me fall into deep, dreamless

oblivion. Breathe in. Breathe out.
Almost there. Almost there. Breathe
in. Breathe out. Almost there. Al . . .

Someone taps my shoulder and I jump
awake. "Dad?" I bolt upright, scan
the darkness. "Dad?" I repeat, but there's

no one here. It's cool in the room—
Luke's room, that's right—but I'm
sweating. Must have been one crazy

dream. Uncle Jessie's words settle
around me: *He visits pretty regularly.*
Go away, Luke. I'm sick of surfing. . . .

Nightmares

The moment the word materializes
so does a memory. Not of last night's
dream, but a wide-awake experience
I have to fight with myself not to recall.
Sometimes the wrong part of me wins.

It was right near the end of Luke's
eighth-grade year and the harassment
was a full-on freight train. I came home
from school all excited about a summer
basketball program I thought Luke

would love and blew through his bedroom
door without knocking, just as he popped
a couple of Mom's antidepressants.
I knew she'd been on them for years,
but I had no idea Luke realized that.

He did, and exactly where to find them
in her medicine cabinet. "Hey, man, what
are you doing?" He looked so scared that
I tried to lighten things up. "Those Mom's?
Better be careful. Who knows what hormones

those things might be spiked with?
You don't want to end up a girl."
Some jokes buoy a heavy moment.
Others land with a thud, and that one
did the latter. Still, Luke tried to smile.

> *Maybe I already am a girl. That's*
> *what everyone keeps telling me.*
> Then he let loose his anger. *I'm sick*
> *of it, Matt! I just can't take it any more.*
> *And these things make me feel better.*

I'd be lying if I said I'd never tried
one, but I hated the way it made me
feel, and the prescription drug unit
we studied in health class helped me
understand why. "Do you have any clue

what they are or what they can do
to you?" I tried to explain that Prozac
is used to treat depression, and that in
teens it could sometimes lead to suicidal
thoughts. "You don't want to kill yourself, right?"

Despite the Prozac

Kicking in, he went off.

> *I* am *depressed. Don't you get*
> *it? I feel like shit all day, every*
> *day. Almost everyone despises me,*
> *and the ones who don't hate me*
>
> *are* so-o-o *disappointed. Dad wants*
> *to send me away, did you know that?*
> *To hide me at some boarding school.*
> *He can't even stand to look at me!*
>
> *I've visited websites, searching for help.*
> *You know what the prevailing advice is?*
> *It gets better.* It. Fucking. Gets. Better.
> *But no one can tell me how to make*
>
> *it through right now. Do I want to kill*
> *myself? Not all the time. But the thought*
> *has crossed my mind. Don't worry*
> *about the Prozac, I know what it is.*
>
> *I've investigated that, too, and I have*
> *to say the primary research—as in*
> *giving it a try—is working out better*
> *than I expected. Just don't tell Mom.*

He Made Me Promise

To keep my mouth shut.
I thought it would be better
to maintain his trust, but
I only agreed if he vowed
in return to come to me
before he made any crazy
decisions. He gave me his word.

And he kept it.

Unfortunately, I kept mine,
too, and how many times
have I regretted that?
Countless! Multiply
countless by the days
I've got left,

stumbling through life.

I'm desperate to escape
the chest-crushing guilt
of not speaking up
when I had the chance.
I didn't understand
the depth of his depression.

Never believed he'd do it.

School Was Almost Out

It was early June, the best
of summer closing in.
Surely time and lack
of proximity between
attackers and victim
would slow their drive
and cushion his pain.

Winter drizzle and spring
rain had left the hills green
beneath a warming crown
of sun. Creeks and lakes
teemed with hungry trout.
I'd take Luke fishing, just
like when we were little.

I'd make an effort to do that, even
though I was concentrating
most of my energy on Hayden.
But I didn't mind splitting
my attention and giving a little
to my brother. Who knew
we'd never go fishing again?

I Shake Off

The memory, bring myself firmly
back into the present, and as I

straighten Luke's bed, think about
how I've lately been splitting

my attention between Hayden and
Alexa. Why does Lex have to be

so much fun? Why can't Hayden
be more fun, more like she used

to be? When did she get so serious?
I think it was even before this Judah

person became such a big presence
in her life. I'm really starting to hate

that guy. Can't wait to meet him.
That is, if he wants to meet me.

Judah the Great and Powerful

"Absolutely" wants me to come
to a youth ministry meeting, so I can
"understand the power of God,
when many gather in his presence."
Judah's so anxious to impress, in fact,
that it's three weeks before it can happen.

Apparently, he had some seminar
he had to attend back east, followed
by a visit to his parents. It's a strange,
liquidy time—literally and figuratively.
The sun has disappeared again behind
a droopy, gray blanket, and a colorless

shroud has cloaked everyone's mood.
Mom returned from her sister's long
enough to pack more of her things.
Dad doesn't give a damn about that,
or anything but his latest basketball
trophy and new/old girlfriend, not

sure in which order. It was weird,
but for the minuscule time frame Mom
and Dad inhabited the same room,
rather than two people there, it felt
like there were none, as if each
negated the other's presence.

I suppose at some point they'll
have to talk, if only to discuss who
gets what and who lives where,
because it's obvious divorce is imminent.
I'm so used to hearing them argue
that the mutual silence was scary as hell.

Hayden is in a funk, and I'm almost
positive it's because of Judah's absence.
I've done everything I can think of
to cheer her up, from rubbing her feet
to suffering chick flicks to promising
something special for Valentine's Day,

with only short-lived success. But
when I ask what's wrong, she answers
with an inarticulate, "Nothing." I leave
it there. What else can I do? My instinct
is to run to Alexa, dump everything
on her. But I can't. Not fair to her.

Not fair to Hayden. For her part,
Lex has kept her word not to rupture
the fragile shell I'm tiptoeing across.
She smiles and says hi if we pass in
the halls, but nothing more, and her
smile is the saddest I've ever seen.

Arbitrarily

The day I finally get to witness
a youth ministry meeting happens
to be Friday the thirteenth. Something
portentous about that, I think.

Everyone takes their lunch, but I
seem to have no appetite, other
than for a good debate with the One
and Only Judah. His return has,

in fact, bolstered Hayden's mood,
and that makes my own temper
prickly. We walk hand in hand until
we reach the media center, where

she shakes me off like a spider.
Prickly becomes razor sharp.
"Does Leviticus forbid holding
hands? Or do I embarrass you?"

> Her sigh is heavy. *It's just not*
> *respectful to the Lord, you know?*

"Are you really worried about
what God thinks? Or is it Judah
who might be offended by us
showing a small sign of affection?"

She huffs, but offers no other denial
and I follow her into the library
meeting room, where maybe
twenty kids have gathered. Some

I don't know. Too many I do, and
if anything should offend God,
it's their presence. Hypocrites. Judah
notices Hayden, comes to greet us.

> He shakes my hand, firming his grip
> as if to prove a point. *You must*
> *be Matthew. Good name.* His eyes
> are aquamarine—blue, but barely—
>
> and they study me earnestly, seeking
> signs of weakness is my best guess.
> *Thanks for joining us. Let's get*
> *started. Our time together is short.*

He goes to the front and everyone
nods their heads for the opening
prayer. I sit in back, observing, and
it's soon obvious that motives

for attending this group vary.

The Female-to-Male Ratio

Is three to one,
and most of the girls
seem as enamored
with Judah the Charming
as Hayden is. Honestly,
his voice is rich and
his patterned speech
is almost hypnotic.

Brainwashing was his calling.

Barbara Rossi fidgets,
but that girl is pure ADHD.
Jocelyn scribbles
on a small piece of paper
balanced on her leg.
Taking notes, or
preparing to pass one?

About half the guys
are under the preacher's spell.
The others, including
my no-longer-good friend Doug,
have obvious ulterior motives—
the girls, whom they study
like scientific specimens,
the kind you drool over.

Prayer over, there's a quick
praise song, then Judah introduces
Matthew 5, otherwise known
as the Beatitudes.

> In his well-practiced lilt:
> *"Blessed are the poor in spirit,*
> *for theirs is the kingdom of heaven.*
> *Blessed are those who mourn,*
> *for they will be comforted.*
> *Blessed are the meek,*
> *for they will inherit the earth.*
> *Blessed are those who hunger*
> *and thirst for righteousness,*
> *for they will be filled.*
>
> *Blessed are the merciful,*
> *for they will be shown mercy.*
> *Blessed are the pure in heart,*
> *for they will see God . . ."*

There's more, but I quit
listening there, bemused
by the way those assembled
here claim to be disciples
and yet have no idea
what their Jesus was trying to say.

I Sit Listening

To Saint Judah explain it to them,
half in awe of his charisma,
half pissed off at his ridiculous
spin. My expression must
give me away, because he

> says, *You look confused,*
> *Matthew. Do you have a question?*

"First, it's Matt. And second,
yeah. Well, no. It's more of
an observation. You're talking
about mercy. Did you know
that a few of these people right
here in this room were among
those whose unmerciful bullying
drove my little brother to suicide?"

The room hushes as I level
my gaze toward Doug, who looks
away, then at Jocelyn, who doesn't.
Judah considers just how to answer.

> *I'm sorry about your brother,*
> *Matt, but you can't rightly*
> *blame anyone else for his decision.*
> *Luke was weak, and—*

Boom! "Excuse me, but what
would you know about Luke?
You weren't there to see the way
these hearts-overflowing-love
Christians brutalized him.
Luke took it as long as he could."

> *Suicide is the ultimate weakness*
> *of the mind, he argues. Homosexual*
> *behavior is weakness of the flesh,*
> *and a sin in the eyes of God.*

The room buzzes again, and heads
nod agreement. I steady my voice.
"There was no 'behavior,' dude.
Luke never got that chance. There
was only the way he was born.
When a baby's born, is that a sin?"

> *Of course not.*

"When a baby's born straight?"

> *Don't be ridiculous.*

"So how can it be a sin to be born gay?"

That Quiets Him

But not for long.

> *Most Christians believe*
> *homosexuality is a choice.*

"Most scientists say you're wrong,
and anyway, who are *you* to speak
for 'most' Christians? There are
plenty with open minds, and
even more who don't think
it's their place to judge."

> *We're—I'm—not judging*
> *anyone. Like God, I love*
> *all sinners but hate the sin . . .*

"Pulled straight from *The Big*
Book of Evangelical Truisms.
The seminary should teach
how to avoid clichés. Well, let
me tell you something about
my brother. Luke was the most
pure-in-heart person ever put
on this earth, so if there was
a God whose word was sincere,
he and Luke would be partying
down right now."

There's a Big Addendum

I'd love to insert
in this lopsided
conversation.

But if I did mention
how I'm pretty damn
sure Judah the Holy
has the hots for my girl,
said girl would for sure
disown me completely.

Already she's staring
at me, disbelief in her eyes,
and not a small amount
of anger. I back quickly
away from the black-hearted
youth minister theme.

> Judah backpedals, too.
> *Please don't think we're*
> *unforgiving here, Matthew,*
> *and if I seemed judgmental,*
> *I apologize. It's just, I try to live*
> *by the tenets of my faith, and*
> *adhere to the word of God.*

The Bell Rings

Partially obscuring my reply,
but I'm pretty sure Judah hears
it. "You should totally give
that a try. Blessed are the meek,
after all." You blowhard prick.

I don't wait for Hayden, who
I'm sure wants to stay after
and apologize for her bad taste
in boys. Tomorrow is Valentine's
Day. I'll probably spend it alone.

I'm almost to class when footsteps
pound up behind me. I turn, sure
it's Hayden, hungry to argue, or
maybe Marshall, with Presidents'
Day weekend party plans. But no.

> Unbelievably, it's Jocelyn. *Did
> you really have to embarrass her
> like that?* she snarls. *Oh, and by
> the way, Hayden agrees with
> Judah about the gay sex thing.*

"Y'all have interesting conversations,
but as I mentioned, there was no
sex involved, only self-awareness."

Whatever. Thinking about BJs
is as good as giving them. Oh,
here's another piece of information
you should know. The only reason
Hayden's still with you is because

of what Luke did. She was going
to break up with you, but afterward,
she couldn't. She felt sorry for you.
She. Still. Does. Each word is a slap,
and I'd really like to return every

one of them with a nonverbal,
totally physical, in-kind smack.
But what would that get me? Ten
seconds of pleasure, followed by
a little time in lockup, which would

only make her even happier. "I have
no clue why hurting me brings you
such pleasure. Probably because not
much else does, especially not your
Big Guy in the Sky, who I seriously

doubt you believe in yourself.
I know what you did, Jocelyn,
and if there's a hell, I'll see you there."

I Leave Her

Standing there, stuttering.

> *What are you talking about?*
> *I never did anything.*
> *Come back here!*

"Fuck off!" I call back
over my shoulder, amend,
"Fuck off and repent!"

Freaking bitch thinks
I don't know the role
she played in the smear
campaign against Luke?

It was Vince who first listened
in on a private conversation
between Luke and me, then
shared that information
with Doug, who passed it on.

But when Jocelyn heard,
she felt compelled to tell
her brother. Cal is also
a churchgoing sort—why
wasn't *he* at that meeting?

I would have loved to take
him on, too. To have accused
him right there in front
all those holier-than-thou
fakers of masterminding
the plan to drive Luke to suicide.
Okay, maybe that wasn't the goal,
but that was the end result.

I really did think things
had to get better once school
ended, but June was a goddamn
nightmare, especially after
someone posted those pics.
Couldn't prove who—not like
they bragged—but I knew
who was behind it.

Martha keeps telling me
that forgiveness is the path
to contentment, but some people
don't deserve forgiveness.
I think I've just added Judah
the Sin Hater to that list.

I Fake My Way

Through my afternoon classes.
Sit in the far back, pretending

to listen, when my mind whirls
Jocelyn's words like fruit in a blender.

Hayden agrees. Hayden feels sorry.
The only reason Hayden's still with

you. And my favorite: *Thinking about*
BJs is as good as giving them.

She can't be right about Hayden
wanting to break up with me,

can she? We'd had a few blowups,
but nothing major, and after Luke . . .

Things did get better. I'm not sure
how I would have survived the pain

without her. She propped me up
at the funeral. Talked me through

the depression, the immense guilt
I assigned myself. Now I hear Judah

You can't rightly blame anyone else.
Suicide . . . weakness . . . homosexual behavior . . .

How long has Hayden been confiding
secrets to Judah? Was he her confessor

before what happened? Did he have
anything to do with her wanting to

break up with me? Is she ready to do
that now? Because I won't let her.

I sneak my cell from my pocket, text
carefully, under the desk, so as not to be

detected using contraband technology
in class: SORRY IF I EMBARRASSED YOU

TODAY. FORGIVE MY BOORISH BEHAVIOR?
CAN I SEE YOU TONIGHT? WE NEED TO TALK.

> Her return text comes late in the day.
> *AREN'T YOU SICK OF ASKING FOR*
>
> *FORGIVENESS? WE DO NEED TO TALK.*
> *BUT NOT TONIGHT. GOING OUT WITH*
>
> *MY PARENTS FOR MOM'S BIRTHDAY.*
> *CALL ME TOMORROW.* Ominous.

Tonight, It's My Own Bed

Where sleep eludes me,
dipping in close to tease,
ducking just out of reach.
It's a hard-rhythmed dance,
syncopated with words.
H words:
Hungry
Heart
Heaven
Hayden Hayden Hayden
S words:
Sin
Sinner
Sorry
Suicide Suicide Suicide
M words:
Mercy
Merciful
Meek
Mourn Mourn Mourn
B words:
Blessed
BJ
Breakup
Blame Blame Blame
The repetitions are the beat
of a telltale heart.

The Harder I Reach

For sleep, the more frantic
the drumming becomes.
Snippets of past dialogues
reverberate inside my head.

Dad: *Goddamn pussy,*
that's what he was.
Goddamn coward, and
a waste of talent. I can't
stand crap like that.

Doug: *He's a dick licker,*
dude. He's gonna burn
in a fiery pit. Don't that
bother you just a little?

Hayden: *Maybe it's because*
you're like your brother.
Judah says it's possible.

Alexa: *I'd never do*
that to a friend.

Jocelyn: *She. Still. Does.*

I Turn on My Right Side

Flip to my left, jam my pillow
over my face. But nothing I do
can quell the stream of memories.

Finally, I give up trying to sleep
without pharmaceutical aid and
wander down the hall to the bathroom,

where Martha's sweet little helpers
await. I swallow two, head back
to bed. Passing my parents' bedroom,

I hear voices beyond the door. Dad's.
And one that's unfamiliar. Female.
Most definitely not Mom's. Damn!

Can't he wait until a day or three after
he and Mom are, in fact, divorced?
A woman in his room, in the gray

soup of early morning, can only mean
one thing. What if Mom came home
suddenly? That he isn't worried

about that can only mean one thing,
too. Why won't they just talk to me?
I've handled a lot worse things.

As the Meds Kick In

The conversations inside
my thickening head begin
to mute. Only one person
remains, more obstinate
in death than he ever was,
maneuvering this world.

> Luke, musing:
> *What if aliens came from*
> *more than one planet? And*
> *some of those guys sucked.*
> *Like, they were mean and*
> *stupid. And when they mated*
> *with monkeys, the people who*
> *came from them ended up*
> *being mean and stupid, too.*

I think you had something
there, Lukester.

> Luke, freaking:
> *Oh shit! Matt! Come here.*
> *Look what someone posted*
> *on my page. And check out*
> *the comments. Who? Who'd*
> *do this? Who knew? Who told?*

Not me, Luke. I never said
a word to anyone. Promise.

     Luke, coping:
     They'll get tired of picking
     on me sooner or later, right?
     They'll get bored, or something.
     Or find somebody new, someone
     weaker to prey on. Right?

I thought so, too, or I would have
gone after them. I didn't want
to make things worse for you.

     Luke, withdrawing:
     Why do they hate me?
     I never tried to touch them.
     Never even looked at them
     creepily in the locker room.
     He flashed his dick at me,
     asked if I'd suck it good.
     Who's the queer? Right?

Compelling question.
One I never asked that prick.
But I should have.

Plunging Toward Sleep

Unable to stop the fall
now, even if I wanted to,
still I remember one last,
the last, exchange, in fact,
I'd ever have with my
totally lost little brother.

> Luke, vacillating:
> *Hey, Matt? I love you.*
> *Not in a gay way, in case*
> *you think I'm also a perv.*
> *I wish we'd have more time.*
> *But I can't take it anymore.*
> *This is the only way out.*

Me, distracted:
"Hey. Don't mess around.
I'll be home in a while and
we can talk this through."

> Luke, deciding:
> *Tired of talking. At some*
> *point, you just have to find*
> *the balls to step off the chair.*
> *Hope saying "balls" didn't*
> *make you uncomfortable.*

Me, Dismissing

I thought
he was being
melodramatic.
Not like he'd never
been that before.

I told him
to wait. Expected
he'd listen. He'd always
listened to me before.

I should
have gone.

Should
have hurried.

Should
have pleaded.

I
should
have
promised
to make
it all
right.

I Ascend

From the depths of dreamless
sleep, surface the lake of late-
morning light. Lie motionless
for a minute or two, trying to
make sense of the hangover

rocking. Part pharm. Part guilt.
I crawl from the covers, limp
to the bathroom, in giant need
of a piss. On the return trip,
I remember the noises emanating

from the master bedroom and
pause in the hallway to listen.
Not sure what for, exactly, because
were I to catch wind of my dad
boinking his girlfriend in my mom's

bed, I'd probably blow it. Speaking
of girlfriends, I need to call mine,
and the importance of that thuds
in my head. I go to my room, locate
my phone, check for messages.

I find one. It's simple, and from
Alexa, not Hayden. *HAPPY V. DAY.*

I Think It Over

Decide to respond with
a simple, RIGHT BACK AT YA.
No use hurting her feelings.

Then I call Hayden, who
is surprisingly cheerful.
And why did I feel the need

to attach "surprisingly" to
the "cheerful"? Regardless,
"Happy Valentine's Day,

my beautiful lady. I made
a six thirty reservation at
Stacy's. Hope that's okay."

It's my family's favorite
special occasion restaurant,
not haute cuisine, but good.

"I was hoping we could get
together earlier, though.
I want to give you your present,

and I really do want to talk.
It's cool, but the sun is out.
We could take a walk or ride bikes."

She Chooses the Latter

Almost too enthusiastically.
This day will either be very,

very good or total suckage.
We agree to meet at Bohemia Park,

where we can catch the paved
bike trail that skirts the river and

Dorena Lake. Hayden's already
there when I arrive, and I catch

my breath at the way the afternoon
sun glints off her hair, haloing

that amazing face. I tuck her gift
in the pocket of my flannel vest,

unload my bike from the bed of
the truck, all the while staring at

my girl. I open my arms, and when
she slides into them, everything feels

as it should. We kiss, and my upside-
down world turns itself right again.

Her lips are soft puffs, flavored
raspberry, and suddenly I'm hungry

for more of her. Starving for her
skin, bare against mine, the warm

of her, the wet of her. Without
pulling back, I talk into her mouth.

"I love you. I love you. And I want
you." My hands underscore that desire,

>   and that makes her tell me, *Stop.*
>   *You're turning that old guy on.*

Sure enough, maybe ten feet away,
some creepster man is ogling us.

"We'd better go before he pulls
it out and whacks off right here."

>   *Matt! Sometimes you're really*
>   *disgusting, you know that?*

"Me? *I'm* disgusting? Disgusting
would be if he did pull it out. Let's go."

The Trail

Is in decent shape, considering
it's February. It's a little slick
in places where overhanging trees

have dropped leaves to rot in the rain,
but Hayden and I are familiar

with these, so use care. I let her
ride ahead of me so I can observe
her slender form, rather stunning

in clingy jeans. The river is high
along the mostly level terrain,

its song loud as it rushes over
the rocks. Too loud to talk above,
so we keep pedaling all the way to

the Dorena Covered Bridge.
It's a favored place for weddings

in the summer and fall, but few
want to chance the weather in winter,
so even on Valentine's Day it's quiet.

And this romantic location is where
we stop. We sit on the railing, and

I find myself slightly winded. "Man.
I need to get more exercise. I think
I've got enough air for a kiss, though."

She smiles. *Only if you promise
to be a perfect gentleman.*

"What for? There aren't any dirty old
men hanging around. And anyway,
you're the only one who's perfect."

The kiss is also perfect, and it's like
I've got the old Hayden back, the one

who fell as intensely in love with me
as I did with her. Is she really here
with me? Is it because we're so all

alone, away from her friends and father
and nonjudgmental minister who does

nothing *but* judge? The intensity builds
and my body responds, but I keep
my hands away from everything

they're begging to touch. "Just so you
know, being a gentleman sucks."

Her Response

Is an easy laugh,
and its music is infectious.
When was the last time
we laughed together like this?
It makes me bold enough
to reach into my pocket
for the little foil-wrapped box.

"Happy Valentine's Day."

> The size of the box throws her.
> She looks at me, a mixture
> of curiosity and fear
> in her eyes. *What is it?*

"Only one way to find out."
Still she hesitates,
and a mad jolt of fury
flashes. "Don't worry.
Even your Judah
would approve."

> Her entire body stiffens.
> *He's not* my *Judah.*
> *Does everything have to*
> *come back to him?*

Quick! Damage Control

Don't mess this up
now, dimwad. The anger
bolt fades to black.
"No. It doesn't, and I'm sorry.
Really, I am . . ."

(*Aren't you sick of asking
for forgiveness?*)

"I'm an idiot, okay?
A jealous jerk, and I know
it, and I'm trying desperately
to work on it. Just, please
take your present. I looked
all over to find just the right
thing, and I knew this was
it the minute I saw it."

(*We do need to talk.*)

Her shoulders relax,
but her hand quivers
as she reaches for the box,
opens to find an emerald
pendant shaped like an angel.
"To go with that sweater I like."

Hayden Melts

Into a sticky mess,
warm, luscious caramel.

> *It's beautiful! Thank you.*
> *But I—I . . . All I got*
> *you is a card.*

"I don't care. I just want
you to be happy. I just
want you to love me."

Now it's me who goes
all soft. "I don't want to
lose you, Hayden, and
I feel you slipping away."

She looks down at
the necklace, as if deciding
whether or not to keep it.
Then she lifts her eyes
again to meet mine.
Both pairs glisten tears.

> She hands me the pendant,
> turns her back, lifts her hair.
> *Fasten it for me, please?*

The gesture is incredibly sexy,
the wavy wisps at the nape
of her neck so beautiful,
that I fumble the clasp
twice. Finally, I manage
to close it. Then I lower
my lips to her neck.

"An angel for my angel."
I kiss the circumference
of skin just below her jaw,
turn her to face me.
She closes her eyes,
but instead of moving
my lips to hers, I open
the top button of her soft
flannel shirt and kiss down
the V to where the necklace
hangs. She trembles and I pause.

"Sometimes it's really hard
to stop. Don't you
ever want to?"

> *Of course. I want to right*
> *now. But I can't. I won't.*
> *Not until I get married.*

I Step Away

Seems to me like being here,
teasing me and tempting
herself, is little more than

a form of self-flagellation.
But I shall remain wordless
on the subject. I take her hand.

Overcome by romance—not
to mention the need to cool
things off just a bit—I say,

"Lots of people get married
on this bridge. You'd want
a church wedding, though."

> *Absolutely. I'd never consider*
> *any other kind. The reception*
> *could be outdoors. Not the ceremony.*

"Not even if your fiancé asked
you to change your mind?"
I'm treading rocky territory.

> I can tell because she extricates
> her hand from mine. *My fiancé*
> *would know me better than that.*

Nothing But the Truth

I sidestep the possible subtext,
eager to avoid upsetting the tenor

of this day. "Maybe we should
start back. A predinner shower

is probably in order." I sniff
my armpits dramatically. "Phew!

Definitely in order. Don't want
someone confusing me with the brie."

She laughs that crystal-pure laugh
and I think I may have crossed over

       that rough patch of ground. *Ever hear*
       of an invention called deodorant?

"Sure, baby. But even the strongest
antiperspirant can't touch this manly

smell." We hit the return, and when
we reach town, agree I'll pick her up

at six fifteen. She cycles to her house.
I take my truck and when I get home,

there's no one there. Not Dad. Not
Lorelei. But when I peek into the master

bedroom, there's plenty of evidence
of her visit, my dad's obsessive neatness

totally denied by the ridiculous state
of the bed. Unmade does not come close

to describing the blankets, tossed
to the floor, and the sheets, completely

untucked by whatever action they had
going on. And the most damning proof

of all—a pair of lady's lacy panties,
tangled in a pair of Dad's boxers at the foot

of the bed. Half-disgusted, half-envious,
I head to the shower, already hard from what

I just witnessed, coupled with my earlier
encounter with Hayden. But the scent

of the soap and the smooth lick of lather
remind me of only one person. Alexa.

Traitor

That's what I am.
A slimy
(satiated),
no good
(definitely
could be better),
cheating
(can't argue with that),
masculine stereotype.

I am a soap opera.

I dress in my best
imitation *GQ* outfit—
crisp chinos, button-down
chamois, decent suit jacket.
Think about a tie,
but decide against it.

No use going overboard.

Just for fun, I leave
my dirties in a small heap
in front of the clothes hamper.
At least there aren't any girl's
pretties piled in with them.

We Hit Our Reservation

A few minutes early and have
to wait. I'm admiring the angel
hanging in the scoop of Hayden's
green sweater when I hear a familiar

laugh at the back of the room.
It's Dad, and he's not alone, which
might not be so bad except pretty
much everyone here knows their high

school's basketball coach. And
they also realize his Valentine's Day
date is not his wife. "Excuse me
for a minute." I leave Hayden behind

and make my way to the offending
couple. Dad tears his gaze away from
Lorelei, who is not so all that, if you ask
me. "What do you think you're doing, Dad?"

> His smile slips, and his warm, open
> (totally foreign to me) demeanor
> ices over. *Uh, we're having dinner?*
> *This is my son Matthew, Lori.*

She turns concerned eyes my way.
They are the dark gray of summer
thunderheads. *So good to meet you,
Matthew. Wow. You look like your dad.*

"It's Matt. And pretty much
everyone else says I resemble Mom,
who my father is still married to,
by the way." I redirect my attention

to Dad. "Do you really think this
is appropriate? It was bad enough
having to listen to the two of you last
night. But a public display of affection?"

My voice has risen in intensity
and volume. Dad tries to counteract
that. *Please sit down, Matt, so we can
discuss this using our inside voices.*

The implication is clear—stop
acting like a child. The people
around us react nervously, and
so does the restaurant manager.

I Might Back Off

Except for the smug smile spread
across Dad's face. He doesn't give
a good goddamn about what anyone
thinks. Well, Dad, neither do I.
Anger blasts like a furnace, sears

my face. "You're embarrassing
yourselves! How can you sit there
acting like this is okay?" The entire
restaurant is staring pointedly now.

> *I mean it, Matt. Sit down before*
> *Paul over there kicks you out of here.*
> *You're the one who's embarrassing*
> *yourself, and us.* He stands, comes
> around the table, and takes my elbow.
> *Sit down or leave and we'll talk at home.*

"Excuse me, but I've got a dinner
reservation myself, so I don't think
I'll be leaving." But my own smile

> disappears when Dad nods
> toward the front of the restaurant.
> *Pretty sure you're leaving.*
> *Your girlfriend just did.*

I Catch Her

Several paces down
the sidewalk. "Wait!
Where are you going?"

>She keeps moving
>forward, in a quick, straight
>line. *Home. I don't need this, Matt.*

"Need what?"

>*To witness you being*
>*a jerk. What is* wrong
>*with you? I don't know*
>*who you are anymore.*

I grab her hand, tug
her to a stop. "Look,
I'm sorry . . ." That fucking
word again. "It's just I'm
having a hard time dealing
with my parents breaking up."

>She looks at me earnestly.
>*Why didn't you tell me?*
>*We never talk about what's*
>*important. All we ever do*
>*is argue, and I'm tired of it.*

I take her other hand, hold
her in place. "I'm tired of it,
too. How can we go back
to the way we used to be?"

She opens her mouth to say
something. Closes it again.
Shakes her head. "What?"

> *It's just, I'm not sure we can
> go back. You've changed
> so much since . . . Her voice
> dissolves into silence.*

"Wait, wait, wait. You think
it's me who's changed?"

> She nods. *After Luke . . .
> I mean, you're so angry
> and short-tempered.
> You never used to go off
> so easily, but now I never
> know if you'll be sweet
> Matt or crazy Matt.
> Sometimes you scare me.*

Whoa

It's like we're living in parallel
but totally disconnected universes.

"Hold on. First of all, have I
ever threatened or hurt you?"

>   *Not physically. But you've hurt*
>   *me with the things you've said—*

"Like you haven't? Hayden,
you've accused me of things

I didn't do. . . ." At least, I hadn't
at the time she accused me of it.

"You've basically called me
gay-like-my-brother. You've

talked crap behind my back.
You told me I'm going to hell."

>   *Hey. That was my dad, not me.*
>   *And I've already apologized.*

"Yeah. Me too. So can't we just
put all that behind us and move on?"

She looks down at our interlocked
hands. *I don't know. We're such*

*different people, with different
friends, different goals, different*

*beliefs. I'm not sure we'll ever be
able to reconcile those things.*

She looks back up, into my eyes.
I don't know if love is enough.

I lean forward, kiss her forehead.
"You're saying you still love me?"

She hesitates, too long, steps back
just a little. *Yes, I still love you.*

*But I love Jesus more, and I don't
think you can ever accept that.*

So it's not Judah I should be
jealous of, it's some guy who's

been dead for two thousand years?
"What are you saying, Hayden?"

Our Hands Unlace

And I think our lives have, too,

and I just can't let that happen.

I maneuver her back against

the building, place one hand

on each side of her face and

repeat, "What are you saying?"

(*Sometimes you scare me.*)

She looks scared now, but tips

her chin up, accepting the pierce

of my stare, and determination

glitters in her eyes. Determination

bordering on defiance. I almost

have to look away. But I hold fast.

And So Does She

This resolve is new, and
I can't help but wonder
just where—or in whom—
she discovered it.

> I've been thinking about this.
> Today, when you kissed me,
> it really did make me want
> to do more, and that wasn't
> the first time. Next time I might
> break down and say yes. And
>
> I don't want to do that. It's
> against everything God wants
> from me. Being a virgin on my
> wedding night is the best gift
> I could ever give my husband.

"But—but—I'd never
force you to do anything
you didn't want to do. And—
and I could wait—"

> You don't understand. I love
> you, Matt. But I could never
> marry someone who didn't love
> the Lord like I do. It wouldn't work.

I Break Out

In bitter, anxious sweat.
"When did you decide all this?
You didn't used to feel that way."

> *Look. I'm getting stronger*
> *in my faith journey. I didn't used*
> *to understand just how important*
> *it was. Now I know for sure.*

And now I know for sure, too.
"Because of getting involved
with your youth ministry."
I purposely don't say Judah.

> *Mostly, I guess. I learned how*
> *to listen, and now I can hear*
> *God talking to me. His voice*
> *fills me with awe. It's amazing.*

It's schizophrenic. "So this
means we're breaking up?"
She nods and I back away.

> *I think it's for the best, don't*
> *you?* She starts to unclasp
> the angel pendant, and a slow
> burn of anger prickles inside

my head. "Keep it. I bought it
because it's perfect for you.
It belongs around your neck."

Besides, what would I do with
it? "Let me ask you a question.
Jocelyn said you were going to
break up with me before what

happened with Luke. Is that
an accurate appraisal, or was she
just being her usual bitchy self?
Wow. She'll be happy, won't she?"

Now she can't meet my eyes.
I guess I was thinking about
breaking up with you before.
We were starting to pull apart. . . .

"So instead, you played me
for months? Did you think
without my 'loving girlfriend'
by my side to support me,

genetics would insist I put a rope
around my neck and step off
the chair, like my little brother?"

Intentional Strikes

That's what the words
are. I want them to hit
her hard, and they do.

> *No—I—why*
> *would you say that?*

"I don't know. Gay like
my brother, suicidal
like him, too?"

> *No. That's not it at all.*

Tears drip from her eyes
all the way to her cleavage.
Hope that angel knows
how to swim. "What, then?"

> She tucks her chin, forcing
> the angel to breaststroke. *Guilt.*

"Guilt?"

> *You were with me when*
> *Luke did it. . . .*

"So? That was my choice."

Now She Is Sobbing

Every inhale is a tear-racked
wheeze. *There's more. I know*
you always blamed Vince for
starting the rumors about Luke.
But you're wrong. It was me.

"What the hell are you saying?"
I remember Vince's denial,
so close to convincing, but I was
positive it had to be him. "Why?
You met Luke. I thought you liked him."

I did like him! I didn't mean for
anything bad to happen to him.
It's a miserable little whine.
It was just a horrible accident.

"Accident? There was nothing
accidental about the abuse
Luke took. How could you?"

I'm sorry! Look, one day a few
of us were sitting around talking,
and the subject of gay marriage
came up. I said homosexuals were
abominations in the eyes of God.

*Vince pulled me aside and warned
me never to say stuff like that if you
were around, and he told me why.
I made the mistake of confiding it
to Joce, and everything went wrong*

*from there. But as far as I know,
I'm the only one Vince told, and
only because he was worried about
my hurting you. I'm so, so sorry.
I've struggled with this ever since—*

"You know Jocelyn has a big
mouth! Why would you tell
her? What did you say?"

*Her eyes move past me to stare
at something across the street.
You and I had been together
for a while and you'd never tried
to have sex with me. I couldn't figure*

*it out, so I asked Joce if you could
be gay. She wanted to know why I
thought it was possible and I told
her because Luke was. I swear,
it just slipped out. Please don't hate me.*

I Disconnect

From her.
From her confession.
From yet another way
I find myself responsible
for the choice my brother made.

"So, you're saying you talked
to Jocelyn about my failures
as a boyfriend *before* Luke died,
and that conversation sparked
the bullshit that drove him toward
suicide? Look at me, would you?"

> Her reluctant eyes find mine.
> *You don't know how hard it's been*
> *to reconcile this, Matt. It's the main*
> *reason I've immersed myself so deeply*
> *in my faith. I needed God to forgive me*
> *so I can forgive myself. Judah says—*

"Shut. Up." Stay calm. Breathe in.
"Don't you dare bring up his name
to me again. You don't need God
to forgive you. Just crawl to your youth
minister for absolution. He'd love
to see you on your hands and knees."

Everyone Has a Breaking Point

And she has just accessed mine.
"Earlier, you said you don't know
who I am. All I can say is, I can't

believe I had no clue what a vile,
despicable person you are. How
could you hide all that from me?"

Maintaining calmness. "How could
you let me lose a friend, allow me
to believe him capable of that kind

of treachery, when in reality all
he was trying to do was be supportive
of my little brother and me?"

And now, I wonder, "Did you ever
participate? Do you by any chance
know how to Photoshop porn?"

No!

Starting to lose it. "How did it feel
when you found out about Luke?
Did you run to Judah for a hug?"

Matt . . .

Anger escalates. "Oh yes, I can
see it now. He told you not to worry,
it wasn't your fault. Luke was weak.

Maybe so, Hayden, maybe so.
But how did it feel, sitting beside me
at his funeral, holding my hand

while I broke down, acting as if you
gave a shit?" My hands clench, unclench.
"How could you pretend to love me?

How could you keep leading me on,
all this time, knowing this breakup
was inevitable? How—"

                    A hand falls on my shoulder.
                    *That's enough, son. I think
                    we'd better go on home now.*

          Thank you, Hayden says to Dad,
          then she turns and flees, as fast
          as she can go in ridiculous heels.

Dad Coaxes Me

Backward, toward the street.
Lorelei maintains a decent distance

between us, just in case I decide
to come away swinging, I guess.

Ten seconds ago, I just might have.
I wanted so badly to hurt Hayden.

Not to maim or scar her for life,
just make her beg for mercy a little.

Instead, I turn my back on her,
and I probably need to credit Dad

        with saving me from lockup tonight.
        You all right, now? he asks.

"Well, sure. Let's see. The girl who
I'm in love with turns out to be

a bullshitting bitch. But that's okay
because she just broke up with me,

after confessing how she's manipulated
me for over a year, not to mention

the fairly substantial part she played
in my brother stretching his own neck.

Before that, my father outed himself
quite publicly as a two-timing adulterer,

and the best part about that was when
I found his and his paramour's respective

underwear having boxer-panty relations
on the bedroom floor. Don't worry,

though, I didn't sniff! Oh, yes, it's been
quite a day, and not just any day,

but Valentine's Day, one I'll surely
remember. How was your dinner,

by the way? Looks like it's frozen crap
for me, or maybe I'll splurge on McD's."

> *You finished? Because self-pity sure*
> *looks poor on you. Just so there are no*
>
> *unpleasant surprises, Lori is staying*
> *the weekend. I'll take her home Monday.*

Sounds Like a Great Reason

To get wasted
and stay that way
right through Monday
night. A red, white, and blue
way to celebrate dead presidents.

I climb into my truck,
try to ignore the empty
passenger seat, start down
the main drag, headed for home.
Maybe I can beat Dad, hit the booze

cupboard before
he can try to stop me.
But there on the sidewalk,
tottering in heels, is a nymph,
too splendid in emerald green, and

I'm ecstatic that she
has to walk a mile home
on her toes. And I'm leveled
to know I'll never again pick her
up at that house, with her prick father

peeking out from behind
the window blinds, promising
my best can never, ever be enough.

I Arrive Home First

Pilfer a tumbler of Jack.
Dad will probably miss it
sooner or later, but I don't give
a shit. What's he gonna do,
make me give it back?

I go take a piss, hope
I don't have to do it
again when Dad is grunting
over that woman. Lori.
Is that what he always
called her? Is that what
her husband called her?
Are three syllables
too difficult to deal with?
I swear, I'll never call
Alexa "Lex" again.

In my room, I exchange
my good clothes
for comfortable flannels,
down a couple of Martha's
little helpers, suck
in Jack Daniels as I turn on
some tunes. Judas Priest,
in honor of my little brother,

whose taste in music
skewed toward metal,
maybe to make himself
feel a little less gay. Did
Luke realize Priest's lead
singer was also gay?

I sit on my bed, waiting
for the hallowed buzz
to descend, eyes closed
in thought about this
evening's revelations.

I think about calling
Vince, but what would
I say? "Hey, buddy,
I know it's been almost
a year since I talked
to you, but I just found
out you were telling me
the truth all along. Sorry
I didn't believe you, but . . ."

But What?

But this: I needed someone
to blame, and he was the logical
choice, if you can even attach
the word "logic" to the emotional
battle I found myself embroiled
in. Still, why would I assume

someone I'd been friends with
forever would have betrayed
my trust in such a horrible way?
I certainly never assumed
my loving-but-considering-
breaking-up-with-me girlfriend

might have been involved,
even if she didn't mean to. Like
who wouldn't know telling
Jo-ce-lyn anything is tantamount
to announcing it to the world?

Dave Holland launches his epic
"Painkiller" drum solo and K. K.
Downing joins in on lead guitar.
And now Rob Halford's crazy
lyrics—*half man and half machine*—
make me want to kill my own pain.

One More Pill

Could only help,
right? Down it goes
with a hot gulp of
whiskey. Ga! Nasty,
but likely to do the trick.

I turn off the light,
embrace the cool hug
of darkness. In spite
of the frenetic music
in my ears, my body
relaxes and my brain
begins a slow whirl.

*We're such different
people.* That's sure
the fuck true. *Love
isn't enough.* Maybe
not for you. *I think
it's for the best.* Right.
Screw you. *So sorry.*
Kind of late for that.
*You were with me
when . . .* My choice.

Guilt.
Blame.

A Crash of Cymbals

Wakes me. Cymbals? Shit!
Judas Priest in endless loop, all
night long? I'm probably brain

dead. I yank off the headphones,
sit up in bed, or at least try to.
There's more than drums pounding

in my head. There's a goddamn
sledgehammer! The air reeks
of Jack Daniels and nightmare

sweat, though I can't remember
dreaming. Probably a good thing.
Now yesterday reincarnates,

good, awful, and hideous—bikes,
breakup, and ball-bashing
confession—in quick succession.

Two years ago, my life wasn't
perfect, but it was a cakewalk,
compared to what it's become.

All because of who Luke was—
a fluke meeting of sperm and egg—
and some people's animalistic need

to exploit perceived weakness
in others. Wonder which instinct
is stronger—survival of the fittest,

or the hunger for sex. Speaking
of that, I suppose my dad and Lorelei
are sleeping off their own appetites.

I slip down the hall to relieve
myself, make it all the way back
without hearing even a whisper

anywhere in the house. Then I fall
back into bed. Screw it. I have nothing
to do today, and unconsciousness

sounds better than breakfast with Dad
and his girlfriend. There's a little
Jack left in the glass on my nightstand.

I hold my nose, drink it down, hair
of the dog, to ease me into sleep and
turn off the jackhammering in my skull.

It's Dark

When I wake up, driven
from sleep into the velvet
black sleeve of predawn
morning by a dream so real

I'm still breathing hard
from running. I remember
it start to finish. Fade in:
Hayden and I are on a blanket

looking up at an evergreen
canopy. It's an incredible July
day, hot but not sweltering,
and she is wearing short cutoffs

and a pink tank top. I slide
my hand over the smooth skin
of her legs, push a little farther
than I ever have before and

she sighs into her laughter.
I lean up on one arm, bend over
to kiss her, and just as I do,
my cell plays three bars

of "Back in Black," Luke's
designated ring tone. I almost
don't answer, but he knows
I'm with Hayden and wouldn't

call if it wasn't important.
"Hold that thought," I say to
Hayden, who stares up at me.
Expectantly, I think. I can't wait

to see just how far she might
let me go, so when I respond
to Luke, it is semi-impatiently.
"Hey, bro. What's up? I'm busy."

> *Hey, Matt? I love you. Not*
> *in a gay way, in case you think*
> *I'm also a perv.* There's more,
> and I hear it, but my attention

is focused on my girl. Her skin.
The female scent of her I'm
suddenly aware of, one I want
to dive into and swim around in.

I Tell Him to Hang On

I'll be right there,
But Hayden is here,
inviting temptation,
and I don't pull myself
away until afternoon
fades toward dusk.

She is everything to
me in those two hours,
and even though we never
come close to shedding
our clothing, what we
do share is making me
hard right here, alone

in my bed. And I'm afraid
to reach the end of this
dream because I know
what's on the far side
of the door, so I refuse
to hurry. Refuse to run
toward its inevitable
conclusion. Fade out:

I could have saved him.

Three Hours Till Dawn

And the comfort
of daylight, I force
myself to lie motionless
beneath a threadbare sheet
of night. One word

pirouettes round and
round the black space
surrounding me. Blame.
Blame. Blame. Blame.
So easy to affix blame
to someone else.

I blamed Dad
for his steadfast refusal
to accept what could not
be changed. I blamed
his inexplicable homophobia.
Where did he learn to hate?

I blamed Mom
for her aloofness,
for wallowing in resentment
over circumstances she sparked.
If she'd only been more present,
if she'd only opened her arms
more often.

I blamed Vince
and Doug
and Jocelyn
and her miserable brother,
who still deserves a pummeling,
along with all his bastard friends.

I blamed middle school
for being a cesspool of nastiness.
Blamed Luke's teachers
and principal and counselors
for not doing their damndest
to protect him from harm.

I blamed the Bible,
when its words were not at fault,
only the way they're interpreted
by those too willing
to wield them like chain saws,
cutting others off at the knees.

I blamed Hayden,
once I knew what she'd done,
maybe not as much as the others
because, one: I didn't have
a lot of time to think about it.
And, two: I still love her.

Somehow I Avoided

Blaming myself,
at least consciously.
Funny how the brain
works. Can't deal
with it? Shut down.

But now, every time
I look in the mirror,
I will recognize fault
in the person I see.
And he won't be able
to deny culpability.

Now every dream
will return me to that
day, to that blanket,
to Hayden, who in
those hours was more
important to me than
discerning my little
brother's state of mind.

And forever, I'll know
I was all that stood in
the way of Luke kicking
over that chair. I failed
him, and he's dead.

The Sky Pales

Coaxing me out from under
the covers. Well, that, and my empty

stomach. I didn't eat at all yesterday.
All I did was sleep. I lost an entire

day to bad dreams and worse
certainties. But now I'm starving.

Too bad the kitchen is so disappointing.
Mom's the one who buys groceries,

as evidenced by the dwindling staples
in the pantry and toothless yawn

of the fridge. All that's in there is beer,
a little milk, and some wilty carrots.

There are waffles in the freezer,
at least. I scarf four, sans butter,

but heavy with the strawberry jam
I find hiding out in a cupboard.

By the time the third one hits my gut,
I'm treated to a carb-and-sugar rush.

It energizes my body, and my will.
I find the notepad and pen Mom uses

for her lists, write a note for Dad.

> Any chance you might buy
> a few groceries, or are you
> trying to starve me into
> submission? (Not working!)
>
> I'm going out to the range,
> where Uncle Jessie still
> awaits your promised visit.
> Why don't you stop by after
> you drop off your girlfriend?
> It's on the way home, you
> know. Oh, if you've forgotten
> how to get there, text me
> for directions.
>
> All my love,
> Your Only Son

I Consider Where

To put the note so he'll see it.
Refrigerator? Nah. Not unless
he's planning on beer for breakfast.

Counter? Too random. I settle
on taping it to the cupboard above
the coffeemaker, the one with mugs

for the French roast I'm sure he'll
brew. Or maybe Lorelei will make it
for him. How housewifey is she?

I'd like to skip the bathroom routine,
but man, I totally reek. Even gunpowder
couldn't mask *this* B.O. I manage

to scrub off the smell, dress, and slip
out the front door without a Dad
confrontation. It's a crap day, slick

and gray, kind of like my mood.
I've got a couple of hours until
Uncle Jessie will open the doors—

it's an inside shooting kind of day—
so I drive on over to the Koffee Kup
for a kup of koffee and some protein.

I'm sipping my joe, waiting
for my omelette, when who walks
through the door with her parents,

but Lex—A-lex-a. Three syllables.
When she sees me, she says something
to her mom, who nods a curt hello

in my direction as Alexa comes
over to my table. *Hey. How're you
doing?* Compassion dampens the bell

of her voice. "You know? How?"
Less than thirty-six hours
from breakup to broadcast news.

Her shoulders lift. Fall. *The power
of the Internet, you know? I never
unfriended her, so she still shows up*

*in my feed. Mostly, she was griping
about her feet. She said you made her
walk home from downtown in heels.*

"*I* made her? That's rich. She was
the one who chose Valentine's Day
to break up, in public, no less."

Even to Me

That sounded bitter.
I guess I am, but should I be?
"Sorry. The wound is pretty
raw yet. I'm sure it will scab
over sooner or later, though."

> *I hope so. Well, I should*
> *get back to my parents.*
> *Mom's giving me the "Hello,*
> *remember us?" look.*
> *You know how to get hold*
> *of me if you want to talk.*
> *Just so you know, I may be*
> *happy about it on a purely*
> *selfish level, but I'm sorry*
> *it happened like it did.*

Her fingers light softly,
like moths, on my hand.
It's a gesture of sympathy,
not invitation, and she leaves
everything there, ball solidly
in my court. She is all class.
I like it. I like her.
But I'm not ready to rebound.

My Omelette Arrives

I eat, thinking about girls
and class and love. I always
thought Hayden was classy,
but in retrospect, her proclivity
toward gossip and criticism
tarnishes her halo. Of course,

anger and hurt could very
well be influencing my current
opinion. Now another word
drifts across my line of sight,
like an eye floater against
a sun-startled sky: Secrets.

We are both guilty of keeping
them, but while infidelity—
a single lapse of judgment—
was a breach of faith, the things
Hayden kept from me were
soul shattering. I thought I knew

her, but I didn't. All I knew
was the person I wanted her to be.
The girl I believed suited me,
despite every fact to the contrary.
Her halo was never gold, or it
couldn't have rusted so completely.

I Arrive at the Range

A little past nine. There's only
one other car in the parking lot—
Gus's old gas-guzzler. I grab
the Glock, head on inside the office,
where Uncle Jessie is talking
earnestly to his veteran pal.

> . . . to Eugene to get that barrel
> looked at. I've got a friend who's
> a great smith. He knows his shit.
> I told him give it a thorough once-over.

> Kinda strapped for cash right
> now, answers Gus. My piece-
> of-crap car needs an engine
> rebuild and my rent just went up.

> No worries at all. I'll cover it
> and you can pay me back when
> things turn around. Meanwhile,
> you can borrow one of my guns.

> Well . . . okay. But did you
> tell him Fiona was my grandpa's
> gun? He'd better take real good
> care of her. She's one of a kind.

The Two Go Off

In search of a gun for Gus to use.
Pretty sure it won't have a name,
especially not one like "Fiona."

Did Gus name that rifle, or did
his grandfather? Was the older
gentleman a little off, too?

I grab some safety glasses and ear
protection, make my way out into
the big cement building that houses

the indoor range. People will show
up eventually, so I choose the farthest
of the eight lanes, preferring to have

only one person shooting beside
me. I spend a half hour wasting
ammunition, and just as I'm reloading,

Gus appears with a pistol similar
to mine. He settles in two stalls
away, but before he loads up,

                        he turns, signals for me to take
                        off the earmuffs. *Your uncle
                        says you're a crack shot. That so?*

I Guess I'm All Right

That's what I tell him, and
that leads to a shooting match
of sorts. "Of sorts," because
I'm no match for Gus, at least
not today. Though he claims
to be a much better shot with
a long gun, Uncle Jessie's Glock
is no match for him either.

Every bullet strikes the heart
of the target in a beautiful
round pattern, while most of
mine fly high or wide on either
side. I'm happy enough just
to hit the paper. Our magazines
empty and we come up for air.

"Wow, I kind of suck today.
Not sure what my problem is."

                    He studies me curiously.
                    What're you holding inside?

"Wha-what do you mean?"
I thought he was a psycho,
not a psychic. What does he see?

> *You're tense as a new grunt on*
> *perimeter patrol. What's up?*

Like it's any of his business?
Still, I offer, "Guess I'm kind
of pissed at the world right now."

> He smiles. *I know the feeling.*
> *You here blowing off steam?*

Not really his business, either.
Still, "Some of that, yeah. That,
and maybe plotting revenge."
It's supposed to be funny, but
the not-joke thuds between us.

> He thinks a moment, then says,
> *You know how they say revenge*
> *is best served up cold? I'd say*
> *it's best not served up at all.*
> *Revenge is a great motivator,*
> *but it doesn't help achieve*
> *the desired results. I've seen*
> *guys lose buddies, then go*
> *off half-cocked, piss fuel*
> *running through their veins.*
> *Things never turned out well.*

He's So Rational

I can hardly believe
it's the same guy who
was freaking out over
a misfire a few weeks ago.

I could argue that I was
kidding, I'm not out for
revenge, hot or cold.
But I'm finished arguing.

"Thanks, Gus. I'll keep
that in mind. Maybe next
week we can have a rematch?
I'll try not to come pissed."

> *Easier said than done,*
> *buddy. But sure, always*
> *up for a little competition.*
> *And by the way, when all*
>
> *else fails, go for a run.*
> *Hard to stay mad when*
> *you're breathing hard.*
> *Oxygen, that's the ticket.*

I *should* get more exercise.
"I'll remember that, too."

The Glock

Needs a good clean, so I go
in search of Uncle Jessie,
who's got both supplies and
expertise. He sets me up at
a table in the office, demonstrates
how to fieldstrip the gun,

> breaking it down into its major
> components—barrel, slide, guide
> rod, frame, and magazine. *Keep*
> *those safety glasses on, now.*
> *The last thing any living person*
> *needs is to get solvent in their*

> *eyes. You don't want to end up*
> *looking like me, do you?*
> He watches me brush the bore
> of the barrel, then run patches
> through till they come out residue-
> free. It's a long process, and people

start to trickle in. No Dad, though.
By the time the Glock is cleaned,
lubricated, and reassambled,
I'm starting to notice something.
"Hey, Uncle Jessie. Do you feel okay?"
He's sucking in short, shallow breaths.

Actually, no. My jaw aches, and
I'm having a hard time finding
air. Must be coming down with
a bug or something. But I can't
leave. Quin's in Eugene and there
are all these people. . . .

"I'll take over." He looks like death,
and I've got nothing better to do.
"The counter is pretty straightforward,
and if something unusual comes up,
I'll give you a call. Go rest. Kick
that bug before it really gets you."

He hesitates. The Turner men
do not easily relinquish control.
But then he winces, and whatever
caused that makes him decide, *Okay.*
Been thinking about an employee.
Why not you? I'll even pay you.

He gives basic instructions: Most
everyone is a member. Drop-in
costs for those who aren't. Services
menu. Anything else can wait a few
days. *Chase everyone out by five.*
Lock up and bring me the keys.

I Trade Him

The building keys
for my truck key.
"You drive up that hill.
I'll walk it. Gus says
I need more exercise."

He manages to wheeze
out a laugh. *Since when
are you listening to
what Gus has to say?*

"Since he started
saying stuff that makes
sense. So, go home and
chill. Have a big glass
of NyQuil or something.
I've got this covered."

And I do. It's a slow
but steady day, customer-
wise. No surprises. No
unanswerable questions.
Nothing I can't handle.

At Least, Until

Gus comes storming through the door.
Unceremoniously, he tosses Uncle

Jessie's pistol onto the counter.
"Hey, that's empty, right?" Last thing

I need is a renegade bullet going
through the wall and hitting a customer.

> *Shit, yeah,* he spits. *I may be ugly,*
> *but I ain't stupid. Where's Jessie?*

Now it's Gus who's on edge, as
evidenced by his concrete shoulders.

Defusion may be necessary. "Uh,
he's a little under the weather,

so he went home. Can I help you
with something? I'm ugly *and* stupid,

but I'll do my best." The sorry attempt
at humor seems to relax him a little.

> *Nah. Nothing you can do. I got*
> *a shitty call from my ex is all.*

Bitch wants to deny me visitation.
They're my kids, too, goddamn it!

His face is the color of cherries,
and his temples are visibly thumping.

Jessie said he knows a lawyer
who might cut a vet some slack.

I'm half thinking his ex might have
valid reasons. But what I say is,

"That sucks, man. How old are
your kids?" Why am I asking?

Sixteen, fourteen, and twelve.
I wasn't around much when they

were little. I don't want them to
forget who their dad is, you know?

Even when my dad's home, he's
not really around, so yeah, I get it.

"I'll see Uncle Jessie a little later.
I'll be sure and have him call you."

Everyone Has Vacated

The place by four thirty,
so I lock up at five on the nose,
hike up the hill to the old farmhouse,

fighting mud and incline.
I'm wheezing a fair amount
myself by the time I reach

the front door. "Uncle Jessie?"
I call as I go in, mostly to warn
Curly, Mo, and Larry, who might

not appreciate a surprise visitor,
if they happen to be inside. But no,
no sloppy pit-bull greetings.

Jessie's on the living room couch,
beneath a blanket, watching hockey.
"No basketball?" I set his keys

quite obviously on the coffee
table, so he'll know where
to look when he wants them.

> *Nah. Basketball was always*
> *your dad's sport. Not rough*
> *enough for me. I want to see blood.*

"I asked Dad to stop by after
he dropped off his girlfriend.
Guess he got tied up. Hell, maybe

he's got *her* tied up." Another joke
bites the dust. Uncle Jessie doesn't
laugh, but he does turn his attention

toward me, curiosity in his eyes.
"You didn't know about her?
It's been going on for a while."

> He shakes his head. *Wyatt and*
> *I haven't talked in a good*
> *many months. Doesn't surprise*
>
> *me much, though. In case you*
> *haven't noticed, men*
> *aren't monogamous by nature.*

Pretty sure there's a subtle
accusation to the statement,
but I'm not in the mood

to discuss my own relationships,
or lack thereof. "Oh really?
Does that include you?"

Hell no. Zero hesitation. *Matt,*
I'm a solitary soul. Quin's more
than enough company for me.

Anyway, she never gave up
on me when everyone else
figured I'd probably croak.

And she stood right by my side
when I came home a one-eyed
freak. Wouldn't be right, running

around on a woman like that.
Risk losing her for a shot
of poontang? Not on your life!

"Why didn't you marry her
then? Afraid you might change
your mind down the line?"

No. I was afraid she might, and
I wanted her to be free to leave
if she wanted. I wasn't a great catch.

Wrong, soldier. In my opinion,
you were an amazing catch.
It's Quin, back from Eugene.

In Simultaneous Measure

I flush with relief—
didn't want to leave
Uncle Jessie here alone—
and concern overtakes

> Quin, who scurries to
> the sofa. *Are you sick?*
> Her fingers probe
> his forehead for fever.

"He thinks he's coming
down with a bug. I told him
to get off his feet for a while.
Who knew he'd actually listen?"

> *Bug schmug. It's nothing*
> *a goddamn score couldn't fix.*
> *Come on, Kings.* The requisite
> implied exclamation point

> is totally missing. Quin
> decides not to mention it,
> instead asks me, *What's up*
> *with you? No girlfriends today?*

"Nope," I snort.
Not even one.

I Decline

Quin's obligatory
dinner invitation.

Mention Gus's request
for a number to call.

Remind them where
I left the office keys.

Give Quin a big hug,
beg off giving Jessie

> one, too. He's gracious.
> *Nobody needs a damn bug.*
>
> *Truck key's in the ignition.*
> *See you next week.* Pause.
>
> *Sorry about your father.*
> *Hope your mom's okay.*

"Thanks. I hope so, too."
She is on my mind all

the way home. Truthfully,
I have no idea how she is.

No Groceries

No Dad. No Lorelei, at least.
I'm one hundred percent
starving, but before I raid
my piggy bank and head off
into the rainy night in search

of cheap sustenance, I give
Mom a call. She seems surprised
to hear from me, adding more
guilt to the pile I'm already
suffocating beneath. "I miss

you. Just wondering when
you're coming home." I already
suspect her answer, but still
it's like diving into ice water
when she tells me she's not.

> *I thought your father would*
> *have told you by now. What*
> *would I do in Cottage Grove*
> *but wallow in resentment?*
>
> *Wyatt is determined to start*
> *over. I have no choice but to*
> *move on, too. I can stay here*
> *with Sophie and Shawn as long*

as I need to. Your grandparents
are getting older, and I'll be
closer to them. My church is here,
and it's brought me a lot of comfort.

On a brighter note, Sophie and I
have been talking. When we were
kids, we used to play dress-up and
fantasize about designer clothes.

We've decided to open a little
boutique in Eugene. I'm tired
of real estate, and I've got a nest
egg saved up. It's all in, baby.

A boutique? Like Eugene's a raving
fashionista scene. Whatever, I guess.
At least she's got a dream. "The last
time we talked about this, you said
you couldn't let Dad win."

I've rethought the definition
of winning. He's stuck in the past,
and there's a lot of sadness there.
I'm moving forward. It has to be better.

She Asks

About school, but is certain
I'm maintaining my grades.
As far as she knows,
I have nothing else
to worry about.

I tell her all's well.

She asks if I'm being
faithful to Martha—okay, if
I'm faithfully attending our
sessions.

I lie and say of course.

She does not query me
about "that girl," or if we're using
protection. Maybe she's aware
that we've broken up.

Maybe Hayden is in her friends network.

By the time we hang up,
I know a lot more about how
Mom is.

She still doesn't know jack about me.

It's a Bittersweet Ending

To a totally
unpleasant weekend.
Hurray for holidays!
Can I get a woot-woot?

I've lost my appetite,
but considering I've had four
frozen waffles and an omelette
in two days, I conjure the energy
for a trip to Subway. When I get back,

Dad's in the kitchen putting
away three bags of groceries.
Milk. Beer. Peanut butter.
Bread. Definite bachelor fare.
I help with the cans—fruit,
soup, beans, chili—and cereal.
At least he took a stab
at the four food groups.

We work in silence,
afraid we'll say too much
if we open our mouths.
When we're finished, I offer up
a single word. "Thanks."

You're welcome.

It's the Most We Say

To each other all week,
which proves to be a tough
one. I swear, I see Hayden
around school more now
than I ever did when I went
looking for her. One or more

Biblette is always with her,
and it's usually Jocelyn. If
she turns that haughty bitch
glare at me one more time,
I'm liable to go ballistic.
It's all I can do to keep walking.

Midterms are coming up, so
every class is choked with
monotonous reviews, totally
unnecessary unless you didn't
pay attention the first time. I did.
More than once, I'm called out

for zoning while a teacher is
talking. Every time I mutter
a lukewarm "sorry" when I want
to scream, "Teach us something
new for cripe's sake, or stop
pretending to be a fucking teacher!"

I Do Keep

My appointment with Martha.
Not to talk about Luke or Hayden

or any new revelations there,
but to discuss my parents' pending

divorce. "Mom moved out a few
weeks ago. She's not coming back."

> *How do you feel about that?*

"Like my life's being methodically
ripped into ever smaller pieces."

> *That's quite descriptive. Poetic, even.*
> *But this isn't really a surprise, is it?*

"Well . . . I mean, I knew they had
problems, but didn't expect them to

become so permanently unattached.
And I had no idea about Dad's girlfriend."

> *How do you feel about her?*

"She had no right to be screwing Dad
while they were married to other people."

*Do you think that was the root
cause of your parents' problems?*

"I don't know. But Lorelei made it
easier for Dad not to want to fix them."

How do you feel about that?

"Stop asking how I feel! Deserted.
Neglected. Unwanted. Unloved."

*Is that different from how you felt
before your mom moved out?*

Thud. Great fucking question.
"Probably not a lot." I hate Martha.

What about Hayden?

I did not. Come here. To talk. About
her. "I'm not sure what you mean."

*You told me you feel unloved,
but she loves you, right?*

She's either psychic or good at fishing.
"Not anymore. Not for a while."

And So We Arrive

At the heart of my overwhelming
feeling of loss. My parents
split emotionally years ago.
Intellectually, they were probably
never joined. Had they gone
their separate ways before Luke's

death, he and I would have been
like any kids faced with their parents'
divorce. Sad, yes. Angry, probably.
But we would have learned to cope
with it. Instead, both my parents
and my so-called girlfriend waited

until after Luke died to leave me.
Martha wormed all that out of me,
because she's excellent at her job.
What she can't tell me, however,
is where to find forgiveness. What
she can't tell me is how to move on.

Yes, I resent all three of them
for finding forward motion. But
more, I hate them for not carrying
me along. And while, thanks to Martha,
I understand the psychology, I'm not
looking for ways to forgive them.

So, Yeah

Short week or no, it's a crap
four days till the weekend rolls
around again. The few bright spots

I found all revolved around the girl
who loves me (she promises), but
who I can't quite accept as mine.

I'm not sure what it is. Not looks.
Alexa is striking. Not intellect.
She's smart, but not in a show-offy

kind of way. More like she understands
every off-the-wall reference you throw
at her. Definitely not the sex. That one

night was incredible, on many levels.
I crave that kind of intimacy
again, although maybe I'm afraid

of it, too. Because if love sans sex
could eclipse me so completely,
then annihilate me when it's taken

away, imagine the sheer power of love
coupled with passion, raw exchanges
of energy. A give-and-take of life force.

Scary, and Anyway

I've got some healing
to do—hard seeing Hayden
every day but not being
able to talk to her, or touch
her, or inhale her perfume.

Alexa understands that,
but she's also insistent
about walking next to me
if we share a hallway, or
sitting with me at lunch

        if I hang out on campus.
        They say puppies are good
        for mending broken hearts,
        she joked once. *Woof, woof.*
        You can pet me if you want.

The only other person
I've talked to is Marshall,
but he's so wrapped up in
his new girlfriend, Holly,
about all he was good for

        was a semi-impersonal,
        There's a better one out
        there, man. Go get her.

By Saturday

I still have no desire to go get
anyone or do much of anything.
But I can't lie around the house,
feeling sorry for myself and trying

to avoid my computer. I mostly
managed it last week, but every
now and again, curiosity tugged
me over to that screen, and Hayden's

posts. Believe it or not, she found
a way to blame God for the breakup.

> *Status update: single. God spoke*
> *to my heart and told me I've been*
> *distracted. My relationship with*
> *Matt weakened my dedication*
> *to the Lord, and made me forget*
> *what he expects of me. I've been selfish!*

Selfish? Duh. But I seriously doubt
she'd see things that way without
some outside counseling. Considering
the rest of her confession, I have no

doubt who's been playing therapist.
Hayden hears God when Judah speaks.

Can't Stay Here

Obsessing about it. Might as well
go out to the range, see if Uncle
Jessie could use some help.

I didn't ask for pay last week and
I won't ask this week, either. But
maybe it could work into a summer

job. I've been lucky up till now.
Mom didn't want me to work.
Concentrate on school, she insisted.

So she might have saved up a nest
egg. But all I've got in the bank
is birthday money and allowance.

On a whim, and a strange one, I pick
up the phone and call Alexa. "Hey.
Did I wake you? Good. Just wondering

if you want to work on your shooting.
I'm headed that way. Only caveat
is we might be tied up most of the day."

She jumps at the chance, and the half
of me who's scared warns the happy
half that I might have just made a mistake.

Turns Out

She's nothing but great
company.

We talk about school,
past, present, and,
perhaps, future.
She's set on the media
arts program at Lane
Community College.
I tell her I have no clue
where I'll be post-summer.

I mention my parents'
implosion, omitting
the ugly "whys."
She says her parents
would rather fight
to the death
than admit defeat.

We gossip about people
we know, including
Marshall and Holly,
an unlikely pair,
but seeming very happy
enmeshed in coupledom.

We avoid the subject
of Hayden and her posse.
But then Lainie comes up,
which reminds me of Vince,
and I think maybe Alexa
could offer me advice.

I give her the main talking
points. "I was positive
it was his fault, and now
I totally feel like an asshole,
you know? Do you think
I should try to apologize,
or just leave it alone?"

> She's so quiet I can almost
> hear her brain working.
> Finally, she says, *If you get
> the chance to try and make
> something right, you should
> take it. What's the worst
> that could happen?*

"He could dislocate my jaw?"

> *Or he might be relieved
> that you finally know the truth.*

File That Under

"Things I Never Even Considered."
Perspective is an amazing thing.
Sometimes it takes distance to find
it, and when you're not used to
looking very far beyond your invented
walls, it might take a fresh pair of eyes.

Speaking of eyes, when we go
through the office, Uncle Jessie turns
his away from his customer long
enough to notice who's with me.
He smiles and winks, and I shrug.
If it makes him happy, I'm happy.

The indoor range is hopping today,
almost every lane in use. We wait
a half hour until one clears, and I
spend that time reminding Alexa
of the basics, and hammering her
on safety, shooting this close to others.

When she's all set up, I watch her
for a few minutes. Her innate ability
is impressive. I tell her to stay as long
as she likes, I'm going to see if Uncle
Jessie needs any help, and I leave her
to her own devices. She'll be fine.

It's Been Almost a Week

Since I left Uncle Jessie
sweating under a sofa throw.
He should look better and
I suppose he does, but only
marginally. "Still got that bug?"

> He's sitting in an office chair,
> and I don't think he wants to
> get up unless he has to. *Don't*
> *know what's wrong with me.*
> *Just getting old, I guess.*

"This may be an off-the-wall
suggestion, but have you seen
a doctor? They get paid to tell
people what's wrong with them."

> *Screw that. I'd have to go all*
> *the way into Eugene. No time*
> *for that. Not for a couple little*
> *ass aches I can fix with aspirin.*

"Well, keep it in mind. And
if you need someone to watch
the place, I can take a day off
school. And while I've got you
on that subject, let's talk about

employment. Spring break's
coming up, and summer's not
far behind. You said something
about an employee, and I could
use a job. I know the ropes—"

> *Hey. I didn't pay you for last
> week, did I? Goddamn if I'm not
> getting senile, too.* He pushes
> down on the armrest to stand,
> wincing in pain with the effort.

"Sit. I don't need pay for helping
out for a couple of hours. But if
you hire me, you can toss a few
bucks my way. The Department
of Labor frowns on slavery."

> *Smart-ass. I think we can work
> something out. Especially if you
> bring that girlfriend to work
> with you every once in a while.*

I don't correct him. She may
not be my actual girlfriend, but
she's the closest thing I've got,
and that's good enough for now.

It's Close to Six

By the time I drop off Alexa
and make it home. It was a good day.

I got a job—will work weekends
and holidays, paid, for my uncle.

I made a decision to apologize
to Vince, damn the consequences.

That was encouraged by the girl
I'm starting to like a whole lot.

Why did I have to lose my heart
to Hayden, and when will I get it

back to give away again? Why is life
so damn complicated? Dad's car

is gone, but when I go inside the house,
I hear someone moving around

down the hall in one of the bedrooms.
I exit quietly, go to my truck, retrieve

the Glock. Hoping the intruder
isn't a better shot, I move stealthily

toward the noise, which is coming
from Luke's room. I hold the gun

in front of me, release the safety.
One. Two. Three. I rush through

the door. "Stop what you're doing,
or I will shoot. Do. Not. Move."

The woman screams, but freezes.
It's Lorelei. When I lower the gun,

I notice my hands are shaking.
"What are you doing in here?"

But once I get the chance to study
the room, it becomes obvious.

> *Sorry I freaked you out. I'm just*
> *packing up your brother's stuff.*

"No you're not. You have no right.
In fact, get the fuck out right now."

> *Listen. Your dad and I discussed*
> *this and he told me to go ahead.*

Adrenaline

And more than a weak shot
of anger have skyrocketed
my heart rate. "My dad? Why?
And where is he?" Before
she can answer, it hits me full-bore.

"I could have shot you,
you know. Somebody else
with his finger on this trigger,
you might be dead. What the fuck
were you thinking?

What the fuck was *Dad* thinking?
Why would he leave you alone
here? And why are you messing
with Luke's stuff?"

I lift the Glock and her eyes
go wide. "Don't be ridiculous.
I'm putting the safety on."

> *Take a deep breath, okay?*
> *You're hyperventilating.*
> *Your dad should have told*
> *you already. . . .*

Déjà vu.

Apparently

Lorelei is moving in.

> Her husband got their house.
> She's been living in an apartment.
> She and Dad feel ready to cohabitate.

Luke's room is a shrine.

> Everything in it is a reminder.
> No one can move on like this.
> Luke would want us to stop grieving.

Lorelei needs an office.

> She's a medical transcriptionist.
> She works from home, so, yippee!
> She'll be here most of the time.

Dad went into Eugene.

> To get more packing boxes.
> To buy paint, rollers, and brushes.
> He should be back any minute.

Lorelei can't stand mauve.

My Good Day

Disintegrates like dry manure.
She has already boxed most
of the clothes from Luke's closet.

But the bed is intact, still made
up with the same sheets it had
on the day he died. The clock

on the wall blows its whistle.
Six o'clock. "Will you leave
the rest until tomorrow? I want

to sleep in here tonight." I need
to say a final goodbye whether
or not any specter of him is here.

> She actually lowers her eyes,
> a renegade wolf seeking her place
> in a new pack. *Of course. Did*
>
> *you have dinner? I can fix you*
> *something. I'm a decent cook.*
> *Your dad bought groceries.*

"Yeah, I know. I happen to live
here." At least, for the time being.
"Look, Lorelei—"

Call me Lori. Everyone does.
Lorelei is such a mouthful.
Three syllables are a mouthful.

"Please don't interrupt me.
I'm going to tell you the truth,
Lorelei. I think your relationship

with Dad is contemptible. I know
the whole story, or at least enough
of it to understand your reasons,

so no use arguing them. I'd like
to say I feel this way because
my mom and I are close, but that

isn't the truth. Nor can I say moral
bankruptcy doesn't run in this
family. But I am highly offended

that my father decided to move
you in here so soon after Mom left,
and completely pissed that you chose

to make your first official act
as woman of the house erasing
my brother's presence completely."

She Opens Her Mouth

Wisely closes it again.
We have nothing to say
to each other right now.
"I'm going to make myself
a sandwich. I'll eat in here. Alone."

First I return the Glock
to the safety of its lockbox,
then I go slap peanut butter
and jam on a slice of bread.
Grab a couple of beers,
which slims a six-pack
to four. Screw it. Maybe Dad
will think Lorelei is a lush.
If not, whatever. He owes me.

The sandwich goes down
in four short bites, a can of brew
in three long swallows.
My stomach is full, the rest
of me hollow. I sit on Luke's bed,
watching *Batman Forever*
on my laptop. Val Kilmer
as the sad, dark superhero.
Like me, minus the superhero.

About the Time

Batman and Robin reach Claw
Island, I hear a very loud voice
at the far end of the house.
It's so loud, in fact, that it rises
above the noise of the movie.
I take it Dad's home. I brace
for confrontation in:
Three. Two. One.

Bam! The door slams against
the wall. *What the hell got into
you? I bought you that gun for
target practice, not to go running
around playing vigilante. You
could have killed Lori!*

"Uh, yeah, Dad, that's what
I told her. On the bright side,
I didn't shoot. She isn't dead.
And things are looking up for Batman."

He crosses the room in two long
strides. *Turn that fucking thing
off. This is a serious matter,
smart-ass. Where's the Glock?*

I shut down the laptop. Stand,
to feel less vulnerable. "I'm not
giving up the gun, Dad. I think
my reaction was totally reasonable,
considering I came home to what
I thought was an intruder."

        You realize an actual intruder
        might have had his own gun?
        Or might have taken yours away
        from you and used it himself?
        Barring all that, how would
        you feel if you actually shot
        and killed someone, either
        purposely or by accident?

"Excellent questions, Dad, and
I promise to think them over.
But they would be moot if only
you would've bothered to communicate
the fact that you were moving
your girlfriend into my home.
Not to mention sanctioning
turning this room into her office."

        Better that than a shrine.

Tension Bleeds

From his shoulders and neck
and he starts to turn away.
Confrontation over? What if
I don't want it to be?

> *It's time to move on.*

I notice Lorelei standing just
across the threshold. "You certainly
don't seem to have a problem
with that, Dad. You moved on before
this room became a shrine."

He starts to turn back, but Lorelei
gestures for him to really, truly move
on. He goes over, kisses her softly.
The door is still open when she says,

> *It's a lot to drop in his lap*
> *all at once. Give him some*
> *time. He'll come around.*

At least she stopped what might
have turned ugly. At least he isn't
bitching about me drinking his beer.

Slipping into Sleep

I notice Luke's scent
has faded from the pillow,
which now smells a lot
more like me. When
Luke's clothes are in
boxes, and these sheets

are washed and this bed
is gone, every vestige
of Luke will have vanished;
the only thing left, memories.
I reach into my recollection,
find us again in the shade

of that bridge discussing
alternate evolutions. He
was ever so much older
than the sum of his birthdays.
Maybe he was an alien
after all. Maybe he did
find his magic, and then
he was ready to go.

The Alarm

Wakes me at seven thirty.
I've kicked off the covers
during the night, and I shiver
beneath a pale sheet of light.
I will never come into this
room again. "Goodbye, Luke."

No point in making the bed,
I leave it in disarray. I dress
in the same clothes I had on
yesterday, not bothering to
shower. I circle the room once,
touching the walls, which will

likely be some awful neutral
shade by the time I return home.
I look for proper mementos of
my brother, choose the clock
and a picture of the two of us
that is sitting on the nightstand.

I put those in my room, along
with my laptop. Then the Glock
and I head over to the range.
I've got a job, and the thought
of making a few extra bucks cheers
me a little. I might need the cash.

On the Way Over

I come to a decision. When I arrive,
Uncle Jessie is just unlocking the door.

I bring the Glock in with me. "Do
you happen to have a locker available?"

I should know this information,
anyway. Some people prefer to keep

their weapons at the range, so Uncle
Jessie has a storage area, complete

>   with lockers. *Sure. I've got three*
>   *open. Why? You want to use one?*

"Yeah. Since I'll be out more often,
I might as well keep my pistol here.

There've been some burglaries in
the neighborhood. Better safe than sorry."

That's a lie, but I don't really want to
tell him I came damn close to taking

out my future stepmother. I only want
to shoot targets. I don't want to be sorry.

It's a Slow Afternoon

Uncle Jessie and I spend
most of it sitting side by side,
shooting the breeze, which
isn't quite as exciting as
the target shooting I did
earlier in the day. I even

got paid for that time since
I was helping an older lady
learn how to hit what she
pointed her gun at. But now,
two members out back and
the office empty, talk turns

to Dad, and how I came
home yesterday to find out
he's moving his girlfriend in.
I omit the part about almost
shooting her. "I found Lorelei
dismantling Luke's room."

> *Lorelei? Not the same one*
> *he used to go with, is it?*
> When I say yes, he shakes
> his head. *My, my, my. Last time*
> *I saw her was right before I deployed.*
> *She was about ready to pop.*

Pop?

"You mean 'pop' as in have
a baby?" Something else no
one bothered to tell me?

> Well, yeah. Looked like she
> swallowed a basketball.
> Had a little girl with her, too.

Holy crap. She's got *kids*?
I'm getting sick of surprises. "You
deployed ten years ago, yeah?"

> Hell, yeah. Fallujah or bust.
> Don't know what I was thinking,
> joining up. No one's a hero in war.

He goes on to tell Iraq stories.
Some I've heard, others are new,
but I'm not really paying attention.

I nod and grunt, toss out
a comment or two when something
he says sinks in. But mostly,

I'm stewing about Dad, his woman,
and her children, damn them all.
The last thing I want is new siblings.

When I Get Home

Dad and Lorelei are eating
dinner. I slam the front door,
stomp into the kitchen. Dad
gives me his pissed expression;
she just looks hopeful.

> He: *Where the hell have you been?*
> She: *Hey, Matt. Join us? I made—*

"No, thanks. I'm not hungry."
Total lie. "And I was at work.
Sorry, I forgot to tell you Uncle
Jessie gave me a job. Weekends
and holidays, ten bucks an hour."

> She: *I think that's great!*
> He: *What happened to discussion?*

I go to the fridge, grab a beer, pop
the tab. "You mean, like discussing
moving *her* in? I don't remember
that discussion. Or was there one about
scrubbing Luke's room free of him?

Or wait. Is there, perhaps, a pending
discussion about her kids?"

Dad Tells Me to Stop

Drinking his beer,
stop drinking his Jack,
stop drinking, period,
or he'll put me in rehab,
I just might have a little problem.

(Dare you to try it, pot-who-calls-the-kettle-black.)

She tells me she's got
a daughter who's twelve,
and a son who's ten,
both of whom will live
with their father so they
don't have to change schools,
don't have to lose friends.

(All they have to lose is their mother.)

He says they'll come to visit
some weekends, and over
the summer. She says not
to worry, they have sleeping
bags and love to pretend
they're camping out
when they sleep on the floor.

(Wonder how long before they'll have my room.)

Monday Morning

English class is all abuzz
as Ms. Hannity collects
her five classroom copies of
The Perks of Being a Wallflower.

> *Just until the school board meets,*
> she promises. *I'm positive they'll*
> *retain the book. It's a necessary story.*

It seems some parent challenged
it due to offensive content.
The review committee voted
to keep the book without restrictions.

That angered this parent, who
accused the committee, our librarian,
and the English teachers who offer
Perks as independent reading,

of "promoting the homosexual
agenda." He organized a campaign
within his church to insist on a vote
by the school board, and until

that happens, the books are being
removed from the library and classrooms.
Said parent happens to be Hayden's dad.

I Know That

Because Frank DeLucca's
letter to the editor is circulating.
Excerpt:

How can any teacher, in good conscience, place
pornography on a sanctioned reading list? This
book contains graphic descriptions of masturbation,
intercourse, rape, and homosexual sodomy. It, in
fact, seeks to legitimize the homosexual lifestyle,
and if a review committee votes to retain this book,
it is promoting the homosexual agenda. Ditto any
librarian who displays this book in her library or
teachers who recommend it to their students.

Oh, it gets better:

It is not enough to say leave it to the individual
parent to decide what his child may read. Too
many parents don't have the time or inclination
to observe what their children are reading, and far
too many parents don't raise their children to respect
their decisions. That is why we, as a community,
must assure that every book our children can access
meets high moral standards. This is what God
would have us do.

Apparently, God's into banning books.
Plenty of sex in the Bible. Would he ban that, too?

DeLucca, Raging Jerk

"High moral standards," meaning
his own. How many decent books
could meet them? How many
decent people could? And what,
exactly, is *his* agenda? Why so
publicly take this to the extreme?

> Ms. Hannity vows to soldier on.
> *My colleagues and I will speak*
> *before the school board. We don't*
> *believe in censorship, but there's*
> *more. Some young people have no*
> *one to speak for them. Charlie does.*

Charlie, the main character
in *Perks*, could have spoken
for Luke when nobody else did.
Ms. Hannity has just soared in
my estimation, even with her fake
Southern accent. Frank DeLucca,

on the other hand, has plummeted
quite near the gates of hell. Now
I remember, not long ago, Hayden
reading *Perks*. Surely she's not
involved in this, she and her youth
ministry minions? Dare I ask?

I Catch Her at Lunch

Because I can't let it go,
and also because I miss her.
Lucky me, I even manage to
find her before she can reach

her friends. "Hey." I offer
my warmest, most genuine
smile. "Can I talk to you for
a minute? How are your feet?"

She looks confused. *My feet?*

"Never mind." Sometimes
I need to rein in my stupid
sophomoric humor. "Actually,
what I wanted to ask was about
this book challenge thing."

She goes chill. *That's my father.*

"I know. I saw his letter. But
I was wondering if you agree.
I mean, I thought you liked
Perks. You're not supporting
this craziness, are you?" Say no.

The Bible tells me to honor my father.

Good Luck with That

She keeps glancing over
my shoulder, so, "I know
you want to join your friends,

but can you tell me one thing?
Whatever happened to brave,
independent Hayden, the girl

I fell in love with? The one
who fell in love with me, too,
despite what her father had to say?

Where is the determined girl
who was willing to risk eternal
damnation to spend time with me?"

>   She turns those killer eyes up
>   to meet mine. *That girl lost her way.*
>   *She forgot to put God first, always.*
>
>   *This girl found her way back.*
>   *People change, Matt. I'm sorry*
>   *you have a hard time accepting it.*

She Gets the Last Word

But then, she always did,
except, maybe, with her father.

Anyway, she's right. I don't
like change. I prefer a nice,

solid status quo—too bad,
so sad for me. When Hayden

goes, she takes my appetite
with her, so I start toward

Mr. Wells's room. I can sit
outside the door until he unlocks

it, calls class to order. Almost
there, I notice Vince not far

ahead of me. Engage? Pull back?
Screw it, what *do* I have to lose?

I quicken my step until his arm
is in reach. "Hey, Vince?" I say

as my hand closes on his bicep,
which is boulder strong and

I really hope he doesn't decide
I'm being aggressive. He stops

        without turning around.
        What do you want, Turner?

I maneuver around him,
noticing how people scoot

wide of the possible conflict.
"I just want . . . Look, this is hard,

and I don't expect you to forgive
me, but I hope you'll at least

consider it. I'm sorry I didn't
believe you about not outing

Luke. Hayden told me what
really happened and . . . Shit, man.

I should have listened to you,
should have known you better."

        He doesn't punch me, but neither
        does he offer to shake my hand.

He Says

Yeah, dude, you should have.

Then he walks away.
I'm not sure how to
rate the encounter.
Hopeful?
Hopeless?
A big fat question mark?

You tried, and that's what counts.
It's Alexa, standing behind me.

When I turn to face her,
she insinuates herself under
my arm, slides her hand
around my waist. As surprised
as I am, I accept her presence.

Anyway, give him some time.
I bet he'll come around.

"Maybe." People are checking
us out, no doubt wondering
what we've got going on.
That includes Hayden and
the Biblettes, who've vacated
the lunchroom. That makes me smile.

In American Culture

Mr. Wells decides to take
a break from fifties advertising,
in favor of a discussion
of book censorship in America.

> *Some of the most challenged books*
> *are also considered "must read."*
> *These include classics like* Of Mice
> and Men, To Kill a Mockingbird,
> *and* Slaughterhouse-Five. *Can*
> *anyone tell me some more modern*
> *books that are regularly challenged?*

Hands go up and titles are
offered up:

The Perks of Being a Wallflower
I Know Why the Caged Bird Sings
The Color Purple
The Catcher in the Rye
The Kite Runner

> *All regularly challenged,* agrees
> Mr. Wells. *Also* Harry Potter, Junie
> B. Jones, *and* Captain Underpants.
> *Don't groan. Some parents think Junie*
> *and the Captain are poor role models.*

Let the Discussion Begin

It's a good one, revolving
around reasons for challenges,
outcomes, the First Amendment,
and parental involvement.
The last because of DeLucca's
published opinions.

> As the period winds down,
> Mr. Wells gives an assignment.
> *I want you to write a letter*
> *to the school board. I don't care*
> *which side you come down on,*
> *but address the current book*
> *challenge in this school. Please*
> *write to convince. At least three*
> *full paragraphs, single-spaced,*
> *business letter formatting.*
>
> *Many of you are in my senior*
> *seminar classes. We've already*
> *looked at local government and*
> *how it works, so you understand*
> *that your voices can count. If*
> *you're not in those classes, you*
> *will be next year, so you're just*
> *getting an early start. Make your*
> *voice heard, whatever your opinion.*

After School

I text Alexa, see if she wants
to get food with me. My appetite
has returned with a vengeance.
She meets me at the truck.
"El Tapatio okay? I'm in the mood
for a massive burrito."

> *Whatever you want.*
> *You're driving.*

We are seated, with our order
in—à la carte chicken taco
for her, steak burrito for me—
when she comments,

> *You're going to spoil*
> *your dinner.*

"This totally *is* my dinner.
It's this or dine with my dad
and his girlfriend. I don't care
how great she cooks. I'm not
going to share their table."

> *Oh.*

That's It?

"Oh? Is that all
you've got to say?"

> She shrugs. *It's not really
> any of my business, but . . .*

"But what? You can't leave
me dangling here."

The food comes just as
she opens her mouth
to say something. Instead,
she takes a bite of taco.

> After she swallows,
> she ventures, *I was just
> wondering how long it will
> take you to forgive them.
> I don't think forgiveness
> is your strongest attribute.*

"Maybe you're right. But why
should I forgive them?"
They've flipped me bass-ackwards.

> *You just asked Vince for forgiveness.
> Maybe the price is giving it.*

I Haven't Managed It

By the time I get home. Man,
not sure I can fall for a girl
who can out-philosophize me.
How annoying, although, in
retrospect, sort of lovable, too.

I'm softening a little, but then
I walk past Luke's room, where
the open door leaks the scent
of new paint. I peek in. Khaki,
aka baby shit green. Lovely.

How am I supposed to forgive
that, not that it surprises me.
Lorelei will forevermore be
synonymous with baby shit green.
That must mean her kids are little

shits. Ha! I will take amusement
where I can find it in this mess.
Speaking of messes, the one that
was my room this morning has
been straightened away. I am not

amused at that. "Hey, Lorelei,
wherever you are!" I yell. "Leave
my messes alone! They're mine!"

I Lock Myself In

My artificially clean room,
mess up the bed, just because,
and when I peel back the quilt,

I notice she's changed the sheets.
These smell of some unfamiliar
detergent. It probably has a name

like "Garden of Clean" or "Rain
on Apple Trees." Too feminine,
and I bet it makes me itch.

I give the sheets time to air out,
go to my desk, and turn on
my laptop, start writing a letter

to the school board in my head.
It would be easy to let emotions
interfere with stating what should

be obvious to any thinking person
in a clear way. I remind myself
not to use obscene language; not
easy when it comes to Mr. DeLucca.

Finally, I Type

Dear Lane County School Board Members:

I am writing to urge you to retain the book
The Perks of Being a Wallflower in Lane
County High School libraries and classrooms.
This book is an honest representation of issues
every young person is faced with, offering
the necessary perspective teen readers need
to make informed choices.

Frank DeLucca, the man who is spearheading
this challenge, wrote in a recent letter to
the editor that many parents aren't involved
enough in their children's lives. I agree with
him there, and nowhere is this more apparent
than when it comes to frank (excuse the pun)
discussions about sex and sexuality. However,
his assertion that dialogues about masturbation
or rape somehow equate to pornography makes
me worry a little about what arouses the man.

That he chose to involve other members of his
church and insinuate God into the conversation
is likewise alarming. From what I've observed,
"high moral standards" are not the exclusive
domain of Christians, and the phrase itself is
obscure. Who gets to define it or decide which
literature fits that definition? I don't know

that much about the Bible, other than it was
written thousands of years ago, which dilutes
its relevance. However, I know its faithful
followers tend to cherry-pick verses to suit
their needs, the same way they cherry-pick
words or scenes from other books to label
obscene. It's all about context, and if you don't
read a book in its entirety, there is no context.
Have these people who are challenging Perks
actually read it, or are they relying on Internet
research to find objectionable material?

Finally, I must address the "homosexual agenda"
accusation. First of all, what agenda, exactly,
is that? Demanding the equal rights promised by
the Constitution, rights already afforded them
by the Supreme Court of the United States?
Second, what's next? Removing books with Muslim
characters, because these somehow promote
Sharia law? Banning books with Latino characters
because they might make readers sympathetic
to immigration reform?

In discussing the challenge, my English teacher,
Ms. Hannity, said some kids have no one to speak
for them. My little brother was one of those kids. Luke
was gay, and nobody spoke for him. If he were here
today, I'd make sure to give him books like Perks, with

characters who could speak for him, so he'd know
he wasn't alone and that he'd find his way eventually.

But Luke isn't here. He took his own life, a victim
of intolerance. Maybe if the kids who drove him
over the brink had read the right books, they
would've understood that being gay doesn't make
you bad or even different. It's an intrinsic
element of who you are. Maybe they would have
shown the tolerance their parents and ministers
never taught them.

There are young people who need books to speak
for them. And there are others who need books
to speak to them. Perks is a necessary book for
all. Please keep it on our bookshelves, with
unrestricted access. And please don't allow a
clearly prejudiced few to decide for the rest of
this community what we may or may not read.

When I Finish

I go back, insert business
letter headers and the date,
clean up spelling

and grammar, clarify
meaning. Sign my name
at the bottom.

The content satisfies
me, but in writing
it, one thing crystallized.

I was Luke's big brother.
It was my job to be his voice,
and I failed miserably.

I never told anyone about
him being depressed or
taking Mom's pills.

Both probably contributed
to his decision. And I didn't say
a word. Not even a hint.

Neither did I confront those
jerkwads, tell them to back off
or face imminent destruction.

No, I, in my infinite wisdom,
decided the best way
to proceed was to do nothing,

to let it all blow away like wildfire
smoke, and that's what I told
Luke to do, too. "It will get

better, just like everyone says."
Was it because I believed
the counsel or because it was

the easier route? Even before
all the shit stirred up,
when Luke first came out to me

I begged him to stay quiet.
I'm just as guilty of intolerance
as anyone else.

I was his brother.
I should have been his voice.
Instead, I was his censor.

It's a Two Pills to Sleep

Kind of night. No booze
chaser. Don't want to emerge
from my room, nor risk
confrontation.
I settle into my
strange-smelling bed,
think about firing up my music.

Instead, for some
inexplicable reason,
I call Alexa, who is surprised,
and pleased, that my churning
brain chose to dial her number.

The problem with pills
is they make you want to spill
your guts, but your tongue
grows thick and your stream
of thought slows to a trickle.

Still, after two or three
sentences of minuscule talk,
and a couple of false starts,
I manage to come clean
about both the pills
and what's bothering me.

"I sucked as a brother.
If only . . . I mean . . . ah,
Jesus. I can't fix any of this.
I can't bring him back.
And no one but me
gives a shit, you know?"

> *I do.* Her voice is a gentle
> wave lapping against
> my ear. *No one can bring
> him back, Matt, and there's
> more than enough guilt
> to go around. Get some
> sleep. We'll talk tomorrow.*

I think she'll hang up,
but instead she starts singing
in a clear, beautiful alto,
Linkin Park's "What I've Done."
The lyrics swallow me.

Will mercy ever come and
wash away what I've done?

Or maybe, more accurately,
what I didn't do.

When I Turn In

My letter, Mr. Wells reads
it on the spot, along with
several others. He observes,

> Looks like we're coming
> down around five to one
> in favor of keeping the book
> available. Does anyone care
> to share what they wrote?

Hands go up. Mine is not
among them. I have no desire
to share. At least, not until one
of the Biblettes, Kerri Cook,
decides to read hers. The highlights
(although "high" is an incorrect
reference) come straight from
the Frank DeLucca Handbook:

- *Community standards . . .*
- *Impressionable children . . .*
- *Easy access to pornography . . .*
- *Doing battle for the Lord . . .*

As She Reads

I do a little Web search on
my phone, and when she finishes
I blurt out, "Do you even know
the definition of pornography?"

> *Well . . . not exactly,* she admits.
> *Dirty books and pictures?*

"Dirty? You mean, like,
they need a bath? But no,
as per the *World English
Dictionary*, pornography
is 'words, pictures, films,
etc. designed to stimulate
sexual excitement.' Do you
believe that's what Stephen
Chbosky was trying to do
when he wrote *Perks*?"

> *Um, probably not, but what if
> that's an unintended side effect?*

"Does reading about rape
turn you on? Because if it
does, you might as well stop
battling for the Lord. You've
already lost the war."

Gasps and Whistles

Send Kerri back to her seat,
beet-faced. Mr. Wells does
his best to rein in the noise.

> *Okay. That's enough. Can we*
> *show a little respect for opinions*
> *that differ from our own, please?*
>
> *I really think you ought to read*
> *what you wrote, Matt, since*
> *you're clearly on opposite sides.*

He offers my letter and I reach
out to take it. "I guess. Whatever."
I'm usually not big on standing

up in front of a bunch of people
and sharing my opinion verbally.
I much prefer writing my thoughts

down on paper. Fortunately, I have
that in front of me, and when I finish,
most everyone, with obvious exceptions,

joins a chorus of approval—*right on*s,
and *yeah*s and a *no shit* or two. Poor
Kerri can only cross her arms and frown.

Finally, Mr. Wells breaks it up.
Ahem. Okay. Thank you for
the well-organized and thoughtful

way you pleaded your case, Matt.
You, too, Kerri. I'd like both of you—
no, all of you—to consider attending

the school board meeting. I'm happy
to send these letters ahead, but
showing up in person and asking

to be heard is much more powerful.
It's important for the board to understand
the impact their decision will have.

The meeting is next Thursday evening
at seven o'clock, here in the cafetorium.
Come see how government works.

When Class Breaks Up

And I start toward the door,
Mr. Wells catches me.

> *One second, Matt. I really
> do hope you'll come to that
> meeting. I'm afraid the other
> side is going to be quite well
> represented. They're very*
>
> *organized. There needs to be
> a strong contingent speaking
> out against censorship, and
> your letter is a compelling
> argument. You'd be a great help.*

"Thanks, Mr. Wells, but I'm
not sure the school board would
care about hearing from me."
The classroom has emptied,
a fact he confirms before he

> *adds, I hear Frank DeLucca
> is running for a school board
> position. I think this is a grand-
> stand play to get his name out
> there. If he manages to sway*

the current board, it would
definitely position him well.
The last thing we need are zealots
in charge of our schools, yeah?
Please think about attending.

DeLucca's decisions probably
wouldn't affect me, but he's got
a point. "I'll try to be there. And, hey,
maybe I should run for the school
board!" It's supposed to be a joke.

So why does he say, *Maybe*
you should. Are you a registered
voter? That's the main requirement,
and living in the district you run in.
Of course, you might have a better

chance of winning in a year or two.
But as I told you, I really think you
should consider politics, and school
board is a good place to get your feet
wet. And maybe major in poli-sci?

The Dude Is Relentless

"Thanks, Mr. Wells. I'll keep
that on my radar." Me, a politician?

Don't you have to be morally
bankrupt and heavily connected

to old guys with vaults full of
money to burn? I don't know

many of those, but even if I did,
I'd probably try to get them to buy

me something better than a school
board position. Still, I just might

attend that meeting. It would be
fun to go full throttle up against

Hayden's Peeping Tom father.
That thought stays with me the rest

of the day, and people probably
think the big-ass grin I'm wearing

is indicative of an impending mental
breakdown. Can't wait, Mr. DeLucca.

Alexa Catches Up

With me after school.
I have to admit it's kind of nice
having someone—anyone—come
looking for me who doesn't have
an ulterior motive. Or does she?

> *Are you busy this afternoon?*
> *Have time to drive me home?*

Okay, not the worst ulterior
motive and I don't have anything
to do but homework. "Not busy.
Happy to drive you home."
We are barely out of the parking

> lot when she says, *Any chance*
> *we can go somewhere and talk?*

Shazam! I hear Martha tell me,
Communication is key to any
relationship. I suppose Alexa and
I do have a relationship of some kind.
"Do you have someplace in mind?"

> *Anywhere, really. I just have*
> *something I need to tell you.*

Something She Needs to Tell Me?

Crap! No, it can't be that. She swore . . .
Wait. How effective *is* the pill?
Ninety-eight percent, yeah? "Okay,
but can you give me a little hint?"

> *Just please take me somewhere*
> *we can talk privately? Somewhere*
> *I can walk home from in Steve*
> *Maddens if I must.* It's a joke,

and she smiles, but doesn't offer
another word, and, disturbed
only by the metronome rhythm
of the windshield wipers, the silence

swells with uneasy anticipation
until we reach one of my favorite
contemplation spots next to the river.
"This okay?" She nods, then withdraws

> again for several long minutes.
> Finally, *I'm not good at keeping*
> *my feelings stashed inside, so please*
> *forgive me if I make you uncomfortable. . . .*

She Tells Me

She realizes Hayden
is still a ragged wound,
that this isn't a demand

for commitment, or for
me to hurry and make up
my confused mind.

(Okay, the "confused"
is my interpretation of
the tone of her voice.)

> *I just need to know*
> *if there's any chance*
> *of an "us." I feel like*
>
> *there might be. When*
> *we're together, we have*
> *fun, and there was that night,*
>
> *which was spectacular*
> *and . . . I mean, I don't*
> *mind waiting, as long as . . .*

She's so adorable and
genuine and anxious,
I can't help myself.

I Reach Across

The seat, pull her to me, and
before my lips can even find
hers, she offers her tongue.
I suck it into my mouth,
and the slippery dance begins.

Her lips taste of berry gloss,
too subtle to be seen, but delicious
to savor. Her dark hair is a silky
cape down the length of her back,
and when I thread my fingers
through it, the luscious perfume
of her shampoo envelops me.

We kiss without pause for a very
long time, and when she pulls back
to take in air, I kiss down her neck,
back up her jawline to her ear.
My tongue explores there, lobe
and creases, and an earnest moan
escapes her lips, and I am instantly

erect. This could go further, could
easily go all the way, and while
I would immensely enjoy that, I'm
kind of glad there's a steering wheel
in the way. "I want you," I rasp.

"But not like this. Not here, not
now. I don't want to take advantage
of you, or taint what we might
become. I like you a lot, Alexa.
Could I love you? I think I could,
and I don't want that to happen
because we have great sex. I want
great sex to grow from love."

She kisses me gently. *Okay.
But tell me, is that ghost of
Hayden you talked about once
still standing in your way?*

"Probably. But she's fading fast.
And, hey, on the bright side,
I'm definitely not gay!" I offer
as proof another round of sizzling
hot making out. When we turn
the burners to low, I ask, "So,
did I answer your question?"

She smiles. *I think you did.*

I think I did, too.

We Spend the Next Week

Attempting connection, at school
and after. It's a slow, but obvious,
build of affection, and sometimes

when we walk knotted together
along the corridors, I feel like
we're on display, especially if

we happen to encounter Hayden
or Jocelyn, who, of course, will spill
anything and everything she observes

to her gaggle. Hayden tends to look
away, but the few times she has met
my eyes, I saw a couple of things.

One: hurt, which I don't understand.
(Was I supposed to remain single
for the rest of my life, or even this year?)

And two: something resembling
self-congratulations, like, "I knew it
all along." Whatever. I don't need

to please Hayden DeLucca,
beautiful, backstabbing
wood nymph, anymore.

Alexa and I Do Try

To expand our little dotted line
into a wider circle, or at least a

bigger box, and on Friday
she springs a surprise.

> *Marshall's parents are out*
> *of town this weekend. We're*

> *going to a poker night at his*
> *house. Ten-buck buy-in.*

I have a lot to learn about
this girl. "You play poker?"

> *Uh, yeah. For years. Do you?*
> *If not, I'll teach you how.*

Which makes me smile. Alexa
makes me smile pretty damn

often. "I think I can remember
how, but thanks for your offer."

> She winks. *Anything I can do*
> *to entertain you, my dear.*

We Arrive at Eight

I expect a foursome, but there's
a bigger surprise. In addition to
Holly, Lainie and Vince will be
sharing the table. "What are you?"
I whisper to Alexa. "A sorceress?"

> *Would a sorceress admit*
> *that's what she is? Witches*
> *are craftier than that. No,*
> *Lainie and I decided it was time*
> *for you two to get over yourselves.*

It doesn't happen immediately.
We nod a curt greeting and when
we sit at the table, Vince looks
every bit as tense as I feel.

The girls chatter on about nothing,
relatively, as Marshall counts
out chips and we ante up.
They're going to get creamed.

You have to pay attention when
you play poker, and I do my best
to concentrate. The problem is,
between the beer, which Vince
supplied, and the inane girl talk,

my attention span is pretty darn
short. Not only that, but it's been
quite a while since I've attempted
this game. And if I thought luck
was going to help me out, it was

wishful thinking. I'm the one who
gets creamed, but the weird thing
is, I don't really care. It's fun, just
shooting the shit. Eventually, both
Vince and I loosen up, and

when he steps outside for a smoke,
I invite myself along. He lights up,
takes a big drag, and I watch his
exhale disappear into the mist.

"I know I already told you this, but
I apologize for being such a dick.
Not that I'm not still pretty much
a dick, but I'm working on it."

He inhales slowly. *I'm not totally
guiltless, and that's something
I can't shake off. I liked Luke.
I'm sorry as hell about everything.*

Strange

Somehow I never considered
he might be clinging to guilt
himself. It just never occurred
to me that any of the people
involved might give half a damn
about my brother. Pretty sure

he's the only one, though. I ask
about his parents; he says they're
plugging along. I tell him the news
about mine, and the woman who
has moved into my home, usurping
my mother's place. I expect surprise,

> or at least sympathy. Instead,
> he says, *I saw that coming years
> ago, dude. Your mom and dad
> only shared the same room
> when they had to. I can't believe
> they stayed together this long.*

He stubs out his cigarette,
goes inside. I hang back
for a second, enveloped by cool
rain-infused air. What else do
other people see that I manage
to close my eyes to?

Holly Winds Up

The evening's big winner, which
is irritating because she claims
it's beginner's luck, and I believe
that. She was totally clueless,

yet fate smiled on her anyway.
She and Marshall surreptitiously
wander down the hall to one bedroom.
Lainie and Vince go off in search

of another. Alexa and I take the sofa,
and I pull her into my lap, tip her
cheek against the hollow of my chest.
"Thank you," I whisper into her ear.

        For what?

"Just everything." We kiss, and I think:
For trying to repair relationships
I deemed hopeless. For attempting
to soothe my anger, assuage my guilt,

silence my ghosts. For doing your
level best to make me whole again.
Desire floods through me, scorching
and beating wildly, like my heart.

I can feel the flush of Alexa's
own heat where the V of her jeans
straddles my thighs. She works
at the buttons of my shirt, kisses

the skin she exposes with lips
wet from my own, down my chest
and over my belly. "You'd better
stop, or I won't be able to."

Instead, she drops to the floor
on her knees, opens the zipper
of my fly with delicate fingers.
I start to protest, but she pushes

      back. *Let me. I want to.*

If there's a paradise, this must be
it—the slow, sure slide of tongue
and mouth, the urgent coax of
spit-slicked hands, the gentle brush

of silken hair, all lifting me up, up.
Faster. Stronger. Higher. No way
to stop, I give myself up to pulse
upon pulse of pleasure. And I almost say . . .

I Love You

Except somewhere
in the hall a door opens,
and we hurry to disguise
the evidence of my
near-nirvana experience.

Vince comes stomping
into the room. *Freaking
girls and their periods.*

He takes one look at my
still open shirt, the guilt
implicit in our body
language, not to mention
my satisfied expression.

*Oh. Please excuse
the interruption, you lucky
sonofabitch. Carry on.*

He grabs a brew, returns
to Lainie, and Alexa curls
up next to me on the couch.
And I'm glad I didn't spout
those words because I'm still
not sure if I truly love her,
or if I just love *it*.

The Next Morning

I'm still processing. I asked her
for space over the weekend—
well, I blamed it on work and
parental interference, both valid

excuses. I suppose she could have
come out to the range, which is eerily
quiet most of the day, at least until
an obviously inebriated Gus slams

> through the door. *G'day, boys!*
> *I'm here. Ain't that queer? Heh heh.*
> *Get it? Here. Queer. Give this poet*
> *a gun. I think I can shoot straight.*

Uncle Jessie isn't about to let
him handle a weapon. *Now, Gus,*
you know you're in no condition
to be messing with a pistol.

> Gus bristles. Yeah, that's the word.
> His blood pressure shoots through
> the roof—you can see it in the way
> his face turns red. *What you sayin'?*

I'm just looking out for you,
buddy. A liquid breakfast isn't
the right fuel for shooting guns.
What's up with you, anyway?

Uncle Jessie is good at damage
control. Gus's face returns to ruddy.
Is jus' ah'm nervous. Gon' see
that lawyer Monday about cus'dy.

He's taking my rent money, but
that's okay, long as he knows his shit.
Bitch wan's give my babies a new
daddy, and I ain't good with that.

Now he breaks down, in that way
drunk people do—a complete
body shudder, followed by
immense, gut-wrenching sobs.

Uncle Jessie gives him a minute,
then goes over, puts his arm
around Gus's shoulder. *Let's take*
you up to the house for a while.

He Leaves Me

To mind the place while he tries
to help Gus sober up enough to

drive home. It takes several hours,
and when Gus finally gets in his car,

Uncle Jessie comes in, concern
etched on his face. *I'm worried*

about Gus. Don't think I've ever
seen a man near so angry with

the world, or quite so unsure
about his legit place in it. I hope

that attorney is good, or that
his ex's sucks, because any judge

worth his beans is gonna see
Gus is a walking, talking IED.

Not his fault, not at all. Goddamn
government can pay for bombs

and tanks and drones, but can't find
enough money to fix their triggermen.

The Parental Element

Of my "see you Monday"
equation is Mom, who shows
up at home, announced to me,
but not to Dad and Lorelei.
I actually have a little fun with that.
Hey, not my place to interfere.

She walks through the door
(which, officially, is still half hers)
just about the time her not-quite-ex
and his girlfriend sit down to dinner
at (still officially half hers) kitchen table.
I have to admit I enjoy watching.

> Mom, I think, shows great restraint.
> *Oh. I guess I didn't realize we were*
> *playing Wife Swap tonight, only*
> *I don't see my swap partner here.*
> *By the way, not sure you know*
> *this, Wyatt, but our bed? You might*
>
> *want to get it fumigated. Before I*
> *left, I was noticing these strange*
> *bites. I researched. Might be bedbugs.*
> *You two aren't itchy, are you?*
> Score, Mom. Why does that warped
> brand of humor seem familiar?

Mom Has Come

To collect the last of her personal
possessions.

Summer clothes—
shorts and tank tops, swimsuits
and lacy cover-ups.

Books, including the Bible
awarded her in second-grade
Sunday school.

Framed photographs,
excepting those where Dad
shared the shots.

Souvenirs and knick-
knacks she collected
over the years.
Anything that bore her stamp.

She has come with containers,
expecting to pack them up.
This surprise is on her.

Lorelei has already boxed
them and put them in the garage,
stacked on top of Luke's.

As I Help Load

Boxes into the back of Mom's Xterra,
I can't help but notice something.
"Hey, Mom. Did you quit smoking?"
Her clothing and hair always reeked
before. But she smells neutral.

> *You can tell?* She totally beams.
> *It wasn't easy. I picked up that habit*
> *in high school. But Sophie insisted*
> *no boutique anyone wants to frequent*
> *can smell like used tobacco.*

"Wow. That's awesome. Guess
you don't need this, then." I hold up
one of her old ashtrays, spilling
butts and stink. "I can't believe
Lorelei hasn't already sterilized it."

I dump the whole mess in a trash
can outside the garage door.
"What's it like, living with hippies?
Are you eating vegan and running
around through the woods naked?"

She laughs. *Vegetarian, not vegan,*
and I sneak cheeseburgers whenever
I'm in town. No nakedness. Ew. Ugly
thought. But we're talking about selling
hemp clothing and such in our boutique.

"All natural. I'm sure your Heavenly
Guru would approve." Probably a lot
more than Mom approved of my little
joke. Subject change in order. "So,
you're going through with the boutique?"

Yep. We're looking at storefronts
right now, in fact, as well as suppliers.
We hope to open by midsummer.
We've got a lot of work ahead of us,
but the positive energy is flowing.

"Positive energy? You're definitely
skewing toward hippie. You didn't
trade tobacco for weed, by any chance,
did you?" Ridiculous, although it could
explain the upswing in her mood.

She Actually Winks

When was the last time
she winked at me?

> *I'm taking the fifth. But I will*
> *say sometimes the place smells*
> *pretty darn* green, *if you catch*
> *my drift. Not that I'd indulge.*

Wowza! I think she might.
Guess it's better than naked.
"Sort of weird, the way Sophie
turned out, considering the way
she was raised, don't you think?"

> *She always did lean more*
> *toward the spiritual than*
> *the biblical. Used to piss off*
> *Mom and Dad that she thought*
> *animals had souls and deserved*
> *heaven more than some people.*

"Explains her going vegetarian,
and if I believed in souls, I'd say
she was absolutely right. You
still going to church regularly?"

I'm down to once in a while,
actually. Don't give me that
look. I'm still a believer, but
I don't like the politics. Maybe
my sister is rubbing off on me.
What's going on in your life?

I tell her about school, the book
challenge, my attempt at swaying
the school board. I mention breaking
up with Hayden, and I tell her why.

You can bust your behind
trying to build a relationship
on attraction, but if you want
it to last, you'd better share
common interests. Believe me,
your dad and I are poster children.

We stuff the back of the Nissan,
but there's no way we can fit
everything in. Not even close.

Any chance you could deliver
the rest? Luke's stuff, too. You haven't
visited your grandparents in a while,
and Sophie would love to see you.

I Promise

I'll find the time, and I probably
will. Not like I'm overcommitted.

And when I do, I'm happy to stop in
and say hey to Aunt Sophie and Uncle

Shawn, but I'll probably find an excuse
to skip the Creswell GPs. The old

coots would probably force-feed
the Old Testament to me. I'm tired

of people worried about picking up
the remnants of my unsalvageable

soul. Yes, they're getting up there,
and if they drop dead tomorrow,

I'm sure I'll regret not seeing them
more. But maybe not. And anyway,

I figure they've got a few years left.
That might change if they decide

their mission on earth has been satisfied.
Hey, I could be the key to their longevity.

Getting Ready for Bed

I think about Mom laughing again
and fall into flashback, where I store
snapshots of our past in obscure

folders. I find images of Luke
and me giggling like idiots over
absurd jokes Mom told. One

or two of those black-and-white
photographs even record Dad
laughing along with the rest of us.

Why does time erode relationships?
Is there a way to avoid its relentless
lapping? Is any love strong enough

to withstand the chipping away?
After witnessing the total corrosion
of my parents' marriage, watching

my private foundation crumble,
it's probably not so strange that
I clutched my love for Hayden far

longer than I should have, nor
that it's such a struggle to chance
falling in love again.

By Thursday

News of the Cottage Grove,
Oregon, book challenge has
spread beyond the city limits,
and over the state lines. The AP

picked up the story from a local
newspaper and ran with it.
Variations have appeared in
the *Huffington Post*, *UK Guardian*,

and *School Library Journal*.
Mr. DeLucca has, in fact, positioned
himself very well, at least if name
recognition can get you elected

to the local school board. Here,
no doubt it can, and will, unless
that name spurs a negative association,
and that has become my own mission

on earth, at least for this week.
Looks like I'll be attending my first
school board meeting tonight,
and not only that, but address

its members. Alexa has been
rounding up friends, and friends
of friends, to help stack the audience
a little more fairly. DeLucca's faction

will arrive in full force, and if it
comes down to a handful of First
Amendment proponents versus them,
their voices are going to be louder.

Come to think of it, Alexa has been
amazing—a regular little firebrand,
stirring up the student body. I could
do worse (and have!) than this girl.

That's what I'm thinking after school
as I put on decentish clothes (khaki
pants, a *clean* button-down shirt, scented
Rainforest Chic or some such garbage).

"Dress to impress," the saying goes,
and I'm giving that my best shot.
Of course DeLucca et al. will
probably turn up in tuxes and gowns.

Somewhere in the House

A telephone rings.
So strange, hearing
that sound. Before
Lorelei, it hardly
ever rang. But now,
apparently, she needs
it for her business.

I can't believe how
easily she assimilated,
requisitioned Luke's
room and the phone
and the kitchen. I'd like
to quit being offended,
stop feeling like I don't

belong in the home I
grew up in and lived
in my entire life. Yeah,
I know at eighteen I
should be thinking
about moving out,
moving on. Would I

be more willing to do
just that if it didn't seem
like I'm being pushed out?

Someone Knocks

On my door rather urgently.
"Hold on. Let me zip up."
When I open it, the Lorelei
on the far side looks one
notch beyond concerned.

That was your aunt on the phone.

"Aunt Sophie?" Why would
she call, unless, "Did something
happen to my mom?"

No, not Sophie. Uh . . . Quin?
She's at the ER with your uncle
and would like you and your dad
at the hospital as soon as possible.

"Uncle Jessie? What's wrong?"

Apparently he's had a heart attack.
He's undergoing angioplasty now.

"So, everything's under control,
then?" This can't be that bad, with
modern medicine and everything, right?

It sounds pretty serious. I'd go now.

Not Serious

As in "could die" serious, surely.
I just saw him a couple of days ago
and he looked . . . not great. He hasn't
looked great, in fact, for weeks. Shit.
There goes my first school board
meeting. Oh, well. At least I'll be dressed

handsomely in case I run into any cute
nurses. Oh man. I hate hospitals. I take
the time to call Alexa, let her know
where I'm going. "You speak for me,
okay?" If anyone can hold her own
against Frank DeLucca, it's Alexa.

>   *Do you want me to meet you*
>   *at the hospital?* she asks.

"You don't have to do that. Hospitals
suck. The meeting will be a whole lot more
interesting than sitting around a waiting
room, tracing cracks in the ceiling
with your eyes. I'm sure he'll be fine."

>   *Give Quin a hug for me, okay?*
>   *And, just so you know, I love you.*

"I know."

Lorelei

Catches me at the front door.

> *Would you mind giving me*
> *a ride? I caught your dad*
> *in a meeting. He's on his way*
> *to the hospital, and I'd like*
> *to be there to support him.*

The last thing I want to do
is give this woman a ride,
but in the seconds I have
to decide, I can't find a good
excuse to say no. "I guess."

The drive is what you might
call awkward. Especially when

> she feels the need to say,
> *I know we've dropped a lot*
> *in your lap very quickly, so*
> *I understand how you might*
> *resent me—*

"You?" I interrupt. "You give
yourself an awful lot of credit.
I don't resent *you*. It's *him*."

Him

My father, and there's a litany
of things to resent him for.
I go ahead and list them:

One:
fucking off on her in
the first place, resulting in

Two:
the pretense of a marriage
and a couple of unnecessary,
unplanned, unwanted children, who

Three:
he disrespected, neglected,
ultimately rejected, and, once in
a while, terrified, which led to

Four:
his wife's alcoholism,
and my own anxiety, especially
after his younger child's suicide.

"All any of us wanted was his love.
But he always reserved that for you."

She Chews on That

For a couple of minutes,
but if I believe I've carved
channels of doubt into
her marble heart, I'm wrong.

> *You make him sound evil.*
> *He's not. Conflicted, certainly,*
> *and not very good at showing*
> *emotion, but I can tell you*

> *he loves you, and he loved*
> *Luke, despite how it might*
> *have seemed. After . . . After*
> *it happened, he changed.*

"How can you defend him?"
A mad jolt of rage buzzes
in my ears. "He was half to
blame for what Luke did!

He called him a fag, a waste.
His own son! And he called him
a pussy! How can you say
he loved him? He never
once stood up for him!"

> *Did you?*

The Buzz Intensifies

"Of course!" (Lie, lie, lie.)

I'm sorry, Matt. I didn't mean
to be so blunt. But there's one
thing I want you to know.

After Luke's suicide, your father
would have left me, gone back
to his family, I think for good.

He was broken, and looking
for you to glue him back together.
Instead, you pushed him away.

Blame is a venomous thing.
Your mother was in pain,
and withdrew. You were in

pain, and lashed out, when
he desperately needed comfort.
You gave him back to me.

I can't make you forgive him,
but I can help him forgive himself.
Can someone do that for you?

Dislike Swells

Like a sun-baked corpse,
into something close to hate.

I really have no proper response,
so I settle for silent introspection
until we turn into the parking lot.

Here's another thing I resent:
that this stranger knows—

or intuits—so much about me.
Or maybe she's just an exceptional
guesser, like one of those pretend

clairvoyants you see on talk shows who
can pull a person cold from the audience,

read the shadow of a missing
wedding ring, and wow the crowd
by postulating that person is recently

divorced. Then again, some of those
pseudopsychics are privy to inside

information gleaned from pretaping
interviews. Lorelei has access to plenty
of inside dope about me, too.

Dad Meets Us

In the lobby.
Hope Lorelei's glue
is in good supply
because the chinks
in Dad's shellac are obvious.

"He's going to be okay, isn't he?"

> *It's touch-and-go, I hear.*

Way too much forced bravado,
Dad. "But what happened?"

> *He had a massive arterial*
> *blockage. He came through*
> *the angioplasty okay, but*
> *he's not rallying as quickly*
> *as they'd like. They just moved*
> *him to ICU. We can wait there.*

Lorelei gets directions
to the intensive care unit
from a volunteer manning
the information desk and when
she returns, Dad slides his arm
around her shoulders, tilts against
them, slight support to lean on.

I Follow Them

Two steps behind, watching
the way he's relying on her.
Screw it. Maybe that's not
totally bad. Suddenly, I wish

I would've encouraged Alexa
to meet me here after all. I want
a strong woman to lean on. Instead,
I throw my shoulders back, tilt

my chin toward the ugly ceiling,
with cracks I'll be counting soon.
No use getting a backache from
poor posture. Ache. That word

punctures my own forced bravado.
Why didn't I make Uncle Jessie
go see a doctor? I knew those aches
of his signaled something more

important. Damn. I seriously let
every single person in my life down,
and once again, my failure might
cost someone I care about—no, wait,

someone I love—his life. Hell
has a place reserved for me.

Waiting Sucks

Especially when relying
On a fifteen-inch TV to disturb
the monotony of sitting
on varicose-veined
faux leather

(mind wandering to random
places, like who sat here
before and who was that
person waiting for news about)

listening to the scripted
rants of pundits,
right and left, the only real
difference between them
a yay or no-way
about whatever
they're "reporting."

We're not the only ones
here simultaneously hoping
for and dreading news.
Every movement
in the corridor
elicits reaction—
heads turn, postures stiffen.

There are those
who deal with stress
by supporting Big Tobacco.
They leave, for varying lengths
of time determined, I'm sure,
by the depth of their habit.
Then they return, steeped
in nicotene.

I've never tasted tobacco.
Some of my friends smoke,
but Mom's stench always
turned me away, cold.
So why do I semi-crave
a cigarette now?
Must be something to do
with the satisfied smiles
on the faces of those who
embrace the habit.

If I'm willing to immerse
myself in stink,
would I be able to grin
like that, despite knowing
whoever it is I'm waiting on
news about might disappear
from my life forever?

Three Hours In

I'm fighting the nod
that signals the need for sleep
(or boredom) has won.

I jerk into awareness,
notice Dad and Lorelei have
given in. They're dozing,

attached, cheek to chest.
A nurse happens by and notices
the three of us, now the only

> ones in the waiting room.
> Where did everyone else go?
> *Who are you here for?* she asks,

then goes to consult her charts.
When she returns, I notice the name
on her badge. Meri Valencia. Nice.

> *Mr. Turner's resting comfortably.*
> *Why don't you all go on home*
> *and come back in the morning?*

"Okay. But can I talk to Quin
first?" Nurse Meri looks totally
confused. "You know, his . . . wife?"

Her eyes flash understanding.
Oh. He's not married, you know,
but if you're referring to his fiancée

she's in the chapel. She's been there
for hours. She lowers her voice.
I made sure she got some food.

She was pretty upset when they
came in, especially when she wasn't
allowed to stay with him.

I don't blame her, of course, but
they haven't even registered as
domestic partners, and he was in

no shape to sign papers allowing her
in ICU. They can fix that tomorrow,
assuming he's well enough to write.

"Thanks, Meri. Has anyone ever
mentioned how ironic your name
is, considering your profession?"

She rolls her eyes. *Pretty much*
everyone. The irony of that is,
I'm really a cheerful person. See you.

I Nudge

Dad and Lorelei awake, repeat
what the nice, progressive
nurse told me—"Go home,
come back in the morning.
He's resting comfortably."

Which could be code
for "be ready to say goodbye
in the morning" or might
just possibly be good news.
I doubt she's a bullshitter.

As Dad reluctantly leaves,
I check messages to find,
of course, a short one from
Alexa. *SOME PEOPLE ARE
ASSHATS. YOU'RE LUCKY YOU*

*MISSED GETTING THIS ASSHAT
FOR A FATHER-IN-LAW. FILL
YOU IN LATER. KEEP ME POSTED,
OKAY? LOVE YOU LOTS. CALL IF
YOU WANT TO TALK.* One thing,

at least, I definitely love about
this girl is her ability to know
exactly how much, or little,
to say. That is a noteworthy talent.

Before I Go on Home

I find my way to the chapel,
which is dark and claustrophobic
and scented with some exotic
incense. Quin is easy to spot.
She's the only one here.

She sits leaning forward, and
very still, forehead against
the chair in front of her. I'm not
sure if she's awake and I don't
want to startle her. Softly, "Quin?"

>Her head lifts immediately.
>Was she praying? Without turning,
>she says, *Matt. I'm so glad you came.*
>*Is everything okay? Any news?*

I wander down the short aisle,
scoot into a chair beside her.
"Last I heard from the cheerful
Nurse Meri, he's resting comfortably.
What about you? You holding up okay?"

>*I'm stellar. I mean, I'm not the one*
>*who had the heart attack. It's just*
>*such a shock, you know?*

"It definitely threw me, but looking
back at how he's been feeling
lately, I think the symptoms were
there all along. I tried to talk him
into seeing a doctor, but that is
so not Uncle Jessie's thing."

*Is your dad here? Did he get to
see Jessie? They wouldn't let me
in, did you know that? I'm not
legally attached to the man.*

"They wouldn't let Dad see him,
either. But he did come. Nurse Meri
just chased us all out of the waiting
room and told us to come back
in the morning. Cheerfully, of course."

That rates a smile, or at least
a half smile, but her mind has
wandered. *We always meant
to fill out the proper paperwork
to legitimize our partnership,
but it was never a priority.
We were stupid. We were
sure we had plenty of time.*

Priorities

Are hard to prioritize,
even at my age, when
my options are relatively
limited. Being an adult
must suck because then you
can't use excuses like,
Yeah, but I'm just a kid.

"Everything's going to be
all right, Quin. And no
worries. If you and
Uncle Jessie don't put
filing necessary paperwork
at the top of your list, I'm
just the guy to remind you.

Let me drive you home.
I'll stay over tonight
so you won't be alone
out there. In the morning,
you can get all beautiful
before I bring you back.
I'm skipping school
tomorrow, regardless."

I'm Almost Surprised

When she says okay, but then
what choice does she have?
Dozing in a hard wooden chair
in a room reeking of sandalwood?

She follows me to my truck and
I open the passenger door for her.
Before she climbs up inside,
she rewards me with a weak hug.

> *I just want to tell you thanks*
> *for all you do for Jessie and me.*
> *He talks about you all the time,*
> *you know. I'm glad you're close.*

Part of me wants to protest.
I am close to no one, really.
But then again, I guess the people
I'm closest to at this point in

my life are Uncle Jessie and
Alexa, not necessarily in that
order. And after those two,
unbelievably, I'd have to rank

my mother.

When We Get to the House

Larry, Mo, and Curly are freaking
out. Hungry, yes, but more. It's like
they intuit their "dad" is in trouble.

They sniff around the truck, then
nudge Quin, one after the other,
as if asking, *Where did he go?*

I help divvy up kibble, and after
the dogs eat, take them out for a pre-bed
sniff and piss. When the four of us return,

Quin has made up the couch for me.
It's late, but she sits in the rocking chair
for a few minutes, drinking a hot

toddy. She doesn't offer one to me,
but I'm good with that. Sleep won't
elude me tonight. In fact, I'm dozing

when my mouth opens up and words
hiccup out. "Hey, Quin. In the chapel?
You weren't, like, praying, were you?"

> Slip-slip-slipping away, but some
> small piece of me hears, *Would it
> disappoint you if I confess I was?*

Adrift

In the narrow pewter space
between the gray of consciousness
and the obsidian where dreams ebb
and flow, I am drawn to the sound
of Quin's voice, gentle in prayer.

She doesn't plead. Doesn't demand.
It's more like she's having a regular
conversation with somebody just out
of sight. *Jessie isn't a perfect man,
like I have to tell you that. But he's*

*a good man, and special to me. If you
can see your way clear to help him
get well, I'll work real hard to pay
you back. Just tell me what you want
me to do.* Now she's quiet. Can she hear

something lost to me? *One more thing.
Jessie's probably scared. Since I can't
be there to shore him up, could you please
send him peace of mind and a little love
from me? In your name. Amen.*

So much pain, and yet hope, too.
And something else, something deeper—
wonder, I think, as if she's tapped into
something marvelous, and well beyond
this world. What does it take to find that?

Can you randomly discover it, or does
it require faith? Can faith be as simple
as tossing questions toward the Great
Unknown, then listening for answers?
But what if you never receive them?

Alexa once asked if I wouldn't feel
better knowing some piece of Luke
still existed somewhere. "Hey, little man,
you there? Can you hear me? Throwing
this out there, just in case. Any way

you can put in a good word for Uncle
Jessie? We sure don't want to lose him
just yet. You can wait a while for his
company, can't you?" Wow. Did I say
that out loud? And was it a prayer?

A Strange Slant of Light

Pulls me from sleep toward morning,
and when I open my eyes Curly
is standing there, staring at me.
He gives me a big old doggy tongue
right across my mouth. "Ew! Gross!"

> Quin comes out of the kitchen.
> *Ha-ha. No alarm clocks necessary*
> *in this house, that's for sure.*
> Her hair is knotted in a single
> long braid down her back, and

she's wearing an ankle-length
blue polka-dotted dress in place
of her usual jeans. I offer her
a wolf whistle. "Wow. Hope
Uncle Jessie is appreciative."

> *Probably more grouchy than*
> *appreciative, but he's got every*
> *reason to be grouchy. Coffee's*
> *ready, and I can fix you some eggs*
> *if you're hungry. Then we should go.*

I Decline the Eggs

Accept the coffee in a to-go cup,
and as we pass the office on our way
out, I stop long enough to hang
a note on the door: *Closed Due to
Unexpected Circumstances. Check
Back.* I make a mental note to record

some information on the answering
machine, once I have the info myself.
By the time we reach the hospital,
right around nine, Uncle Jessie has
already signed the necessary document
to allow Quin into his room. We both

start that way, but are halted by a not-
so-Meri nurse outside the door. *Two
visitors max at a time, please. You'll
have to ask the two who are in there
to step outside for a few minutes.
He's in no condition for a party.*

The Hulk-like woman waits for us
to nod understanding before stomping
away. "Charming." Quin and I trade
places with Lorelei and Dad, who's
tousled. Lose a little sleep, Dad?
Guilt, or an extended roll in the hay?

As We Pass

He stops me briefly. *We're going*
to get some breakfast, but we'll be

back. So you know, I got hold of
my parents, and they're driving down

from Portland tomorrow. I'd like to
offer them your bedroom, if that's okay.

They'll probably stay a week. Barring
unexpected complications, Jessie will

move to a regular room later today,
and hopefully be out of here Monday

or Tuesday. He's got a crazy idea
in his head, and unless Quin disagrees,

looks like there might be a wedding
next week. He won't even wait until

he heals up, says he wants to be sure
she's taken care of if his ticker decides

it's had enough. Too bad it takes something
like this to make a person see the light.

Too Bad It Takes

Something like this to make
a man visit his brother, too,
but I'm pretty sure I don't need
to voice that opinion. I'm guessing
guilt has steamrolled right over him.

"It's fine for Gram and Gramps
to take my room. I can stay out
with Quin over the weekend,
then crash on an airbed in Luke's
room." I shoot Lorelei a wicked
glare. "As long as it's okay with you."

> *Of course. I don't think I'll get*
> *a lot of work done for the next*
> *few days anyway, so no worries.*

I kind of hate how she's so
accommodating. Actually, more
than kind of. Off they go in search
of pancakes, and I watch just long
enough to see Dad snake his hand
around her narrow hip, coax her closer.
I hear Alexa urging forgiveness,
but clinging to resentment
is much easier.

In the Short Span of Time

It took for that exchange, Jessie
has already sprung his surprise
on Quin, who sits on a chair
very close to the bed,
eyes shining tears.

> *Look at her,* he purrs to me.
> *Isn't she just about the most
> beautiful woman in all the world?*

He's lying flat, without even
a pillow, tubes running into his arm
and nostrils. Regardless, happiness
illuminates his face.

> *Never saw the need to tie the knot
> before,* he wheezes. *But this li'l
> experience opened my eyes.
> We shoulda done it long time ago.
> Guess I'm lucky she di'n' run.*

Definitely some decent drugs
being piped into his veins. "Duh,
dude! But wait. What did Quin say?"

> *I'm kin' messed up, but I think
> she said yes. Din' you, Quin?*

She Did

Whoopee! We're going to have
a wedding, and that allows joy
to temper the overriding fear
that Jessie's time could be short.

"So I guess we should look for
a cake that's fat and sugar-free,
yeah? I mean, you'll have to
watch your diet now, right?"

> *Smart-ass. I wouldn't be too*
> *cocksure of yourself, though.*
> *Heart disease tends to run*
> *in families. Tol' your dad*

> *the same damn thing, not that*
> *he ever listens to anything*
> *I advise. Can' believe how pretty*
> *that li'l Lori still is, ya know?*

Do. Not. Argue. "Careful,
now, or you'll make Quin
jealous. Still plenty of time
for her to run. Right, Quin?"

She smiles right past her tears.
Way too late for that, Matt.
Anyway, I'm not the jealous
type, and at the moment I've got

more important things on
my mind than Jessie Turner's
wandering eye. I'm just glad
he's still around to let it wander.

"Yeah, well, I'd be concerned
if I were you. If he thinks Lorelei
is good-looking, he probably
thinks Nursezilla is pretty, too,

and you never know where she
might decide to put her hands."
In my best "large woman" voice,
I say, "Sponge bath, Mr. Turner?"

Quin laughs, then retorts,
Better her *giving him a sponge*
bath than me. Now if you'll excuse
me, I need to visit the ladies' room.

When She's Gone

I scoot into the vacant chair.
"I'm glad you're going to marry
her. It's a damn good decision."

> His eyes close and he whispers,
> *Funny how your mind works*
> *when you believe you're dying.*
>
> *First you recycle regrets. Should*
> *have. Could have. Why didn't I?*
> *I had a pretty long list there, and*
>
> *right at the top was Quin. That*
> *would be one hell of a reward*
> *for putting up with me all these*
>
> *years, huh? Debt. Her home and*
> *property in my name, and no will*
> *to say where it should rightly go*
>
> *when I die. She's listed as beneficiary*
> *on my pitiful life insurance, but that*
> *wouldn't take her very far. I got*
>
> *the chance to make it right, and*
> *by God, I'm gonna do exactly that,*
> *just as soon as I get out of this place.*

He goes quiet, except for pulling
breath, and I think he's fallen
asleep. But when I start to get up,

he puts out a hand. *Something
else. I really thought I was checking
on out of this world. After regretting*

*came a big rush of fear. I was soul-
deep scared that the crazy pain
in my chest was all I was getting*

*before everything went black.
The end. Finis. Nothing more.
I yelled, "Help!" and I know*

*those people working on me thought
I was talking to them, but I wasn't,
you know? I was calling out to*

*the universe and all of a sudden . . .
I don't know how else to say it,
but I wasn't scared anymore.*

*And I have no idea what that means,
only if there is something after this
lifetime, I want to learn what it is.*

All That Talking

Combined with his morphine drip
has wiped him out. He slips down
into a sea of sleep, much too deep
for dreams to find him. I've never
considered what it's like to come
face-to-face with death. Would I

be "soul-deep scared" of everything
going black? Does it happen all at
once, or does the light fade slowly—
gray, grayer, pewter, coal, obsidian?
If I had that time, would I recycle
regrets? I haven't lived very long,

relatively speaking, but I've managed
to collect quite a few. Do small regrets
flicker, huge ones flash, or are they
more like weights, stacked one by one
until they crush you into oblivion?
Would my very last flashback

be Hayden and me getting hot on
a blanket, segue to a funeral
on a sweltering summer day?
It's just not fucking fair that Uncle
Jessie has the chance to make good
his biggest regret, but I never can.

The Whisper of a Skirt

Tells me Quin has returned.
I stand to give her the chair
by the bed. Not a whole
lot for me to do here. I almost
wish I'd gone to school after all.

"Dad wants me to let Gram
and Gramps have my bedroom,
so if it's okay, I'll stay with you
over the weekend. That way
I can mind the range if you want."
At least I'll have something to do
besides sitting here thinking
about stuff I'd rather not consider.

> *Sounds good. I'll probably*
> *hang around here until*
> *they kick me out. Take the keys.*
> *And you'll feed the dogs for me?*

"It's the least I can do in return
for the room and board. I'll stop
by the house for some clean
clothes. Let me know if you need
anything while I'm still in town."
I start to leave, but she stops me.

Hold on just a minute. I know
you're pissed at your father
and his girlfriend, but I hope
you can find a way to reconcile
your relationship with them.
That old saying "life is too short"
has taken on new meaning.
I think we all need to allow
ourselves some healing now.

"I wish I could, Quin,
but I'm not really sure how.
I promise to work on it, though."
I give her a hint of a hug.
"You're okay driving
yourself home, right?"

Of course. I think the drama
has subsided, at least for now.
Leave the lights on, but
don't wait up for me. Not sure
what time I'll get there.

There's Nobody Home

When I get there, and that's all
good with me. I straighten my room,
strip the sheets from the bed, empty

my clothes hamper, and take the dirties
to the laundry room. No use grossing
out the grandparents with the smell

of used underwear and socks, and
anyway, I haven't stroked my OCD
tendencies in a while. I prefer neat

to train wreck. I go ahead and clean
up, and, man, does it feel great to brush
my teeth, something I haven't done since

yesterday. I'll take my toothbrush with
me, along with two changes of clothes.
It strikes me that sometimes the little

things can mean a whole lot. Maybe if
I focus on those for a while the big stuff
will rectify itself. Okay, maybe not, but

it's better than stressing over crap
beyond my ability to change. I grab
my cell phone charger and laptop, too.

I might need some entertainment
if things happen to be slow. On my way
out of town, I stop by the grocery store,

grab a frozen pizza, some lunch meat,
and bread. Self-sufficient, that's what I am,
not to mention suddenly ravenous.

I happen to arrive at the range just
behind a UPS truck, which pulls right up
to the office door. The driver waits

for me to meet him and sign for the long
narrow package. There's a rifle inside,
that much is obvious. Turns out it's Gus's

old gun—Fiona!—returned from the smith,
almost as good as new. He'll be one happy
camper when he sees it again, that much

I know. I lock it in the rifle cabinet,
close up the office, and head to the house
to feed my aching belly. While the pizza

bakes, I call Alexa, who's already home
from school. The sound of her voice stirs
something inside. I really want to see her.

We Talk

Until the pizza browns, while
it cools, while I wolf it down.
I tell her Uncle Jessie should
pull through fine, about
the likely upcoming wedding.
"You're invited, of course."

> You'd better be careful. Weddings
> tend to bring out the romance
> in people. Then again, I'd kind
> of like to see you romantic.

Good thing she can't see me
blushing. "What do you mean?
I am the most romantic guy
I know. You just wait.
I'll show you romantic."

> She laughs that deep, husky
> laugh of hers. *Awesome. It's a date.*
> *Hey. I've got some news for you.*
> *The school board voted to retain*
> Perks. *Mr. DeLucca is livid and*
> *vowed to reopen the challenge*
> *when he's elected. Dictator.*

We extend the conversation
for almost an hour, talking about
everything from books to our families
to guns to politics—most of which
we happen to agree on, thankfully.
I really don't want to argue with her,
or anyone, and she makes that easy.
The few things we don't see eye
to eye on matter hardly at all.

Eventually, she gets called
to dinner, and I'm sorry we have
to sign off. "Unless Uncle Jessie
happens to take a turn for the worse,
I'll be out here all day tomorrow.
Come out, I'll let you touch my weapon."

More lovely laughter. *Excellent.*
Practice makes perfect, I hear.
Hey, Matt? I love you.

As soon as I hear the click,
I say, "Hey, Alexa? I love you, too."
Because I realize I do.

In True OCD Fashion

I clean up the kitchen.
Quin should be very pleased.
Then I fill the dog bowls.
Where are those mutts, anyway?
They're usually waiting
on the step come dinnertime.

But when I open the door
to call them, I hear furious
barking in the distance.
I step out into the yard to try
and tune in to their location.
I think they're down by the office.

There's a thin, sharp *crack*.
Gunshot? No doubt. I start
toward the truck. Change my mind,
go inside, grab my phone, dial 9-1-1.
Then I head downhill on foot.
When the parking area comes
into view, I recognize the car.

It belongs to Gus. Neither he
nor the dogs are anywhere in sight,
but when I circle to the front
of the building, I can see
he's broken his way inside.

An Intelligent Person

Would stay put.
Wait for the cops.
But like an idiot,
I push through the door.
The lights are on—did he stop
to turn them on or did I leave
them on before? "Gus?
That you? What are you
doing here? We're closed."

Don't want to startle the fool,
who's rummaging around
in the gun locker room.

> 'Course it's me, asshole.
> But don't you fucking
> come back here! I mean
> it! I'm gonna do this.
> But first I want Fiona.
> She's mine, goddamn it.
> Come 'ere, you bitch!

He's totally out of his mind
wasted. Uncle Jessie could talk
him down. Not sure I can.
But for some odd reason,
I think I should try.

"Hey, Gus. If you chill,
I'll open the rifle cabinet for you.
I've got the key right here."
He stops his thrashing,
and the sudden silence is eerie.

> All right then. 'S only fair.
> 'S my grandpa's gun an' I want
> her. That damn Jessie thinks
> he can keep Fiona, I'll kill him.
> Where is that fucker, anyway?

I make my way cautiously
to the locker room door.
"I'm coming in, okay?
Uncle Jessie's in the hospital.
He had a heart attack."

Gus, whose attention
has been directed toward
the rifle cabinet, turns
to face me. They say certain
sights make your blood run
cold. Mine freezes solid.
I force my voice steady.
"What are you doing, Gus?"

He's Wearing a Vest

And strapped to it are what
appear to be explosives. On his hip
is a holstered gun. He smiles,
his eyes fill with crazy, and
suddenly I can't breathe.

> *Hey, Junior. Didn' you know*
> *I'm a dee-mo-lition expert?*
> *Goddamn army taught me a thing*
> *or two. Goin' blow this place*
> *to kingdom come, and I'm goin'*
> *along for the ride. Ain't nothing*
> *left to hang on for anymore.*

Think, think, think. Where are
those damn cops? "Take it easy,
okay? Why this place, Gus?
I thought you liked it out here."

> *I thought I did, too. Thought I liked*
> *that sonofabitch Jessie. Then he went*
> *and sold me out to that lawyer.*
> *Bastard took all my money. Every*
> *red cent. Then he tells me he don'*
> *think he can help me. That whore's*
> *gonna take away my kids forever.*

Just talking about it starts him
twitching. He lifts up and down
on his toes, his hand moves
toward his pocket, and one word
comes to mind. Trigger.

Inhale. Exhale. Palms up, palms
down won't help me now.
"Come on, Gus. There are other
lawyers. If it's money, maybe
we can hel—"

> *No! No more lawyers. No more*
> *money. No one can help me now,*
> *so I'm going out with a bang. Ha-*
> *ha. Bang, get it? My only regret*
> *is your uncle isn't catching*
> *this freight train with us.*

Us? Holy shit. He means to take
me with him! I start backing up
slowly, but when I see his hand
move again toward his pocket,
I turn and run and

Where Am I?

I'm awake,
at least I think I am.
Everything's dark.
Everything's silent.
Dead silent. Dead.
Wait. Am I dead?

The last thing I remember was . . .

Percussion! An incredible
blast of noise and a mad
thrust of energy. It was . . .
Gus. I must be dead.

But I can't be dead.
I'm conscious.
Concentrate.
I'm lying on something.
Firm, not hard.
Not the ground.
Bed?

Try to move.
Can't, not much, but now
I'm aware of my hands.
I can feel my fingers.
Pretty sure they're all there.

I'm breathing. Yes. Inhale.
There's a smell, familiar,
but not of home. Antiseptic.
Bleach. The odd scent
of oxygen. Hospital.
That's it! I'm in the hospital.

Awake. Aware. In the hospital.
I can feel. I can think.
So why can't I see?
Am I blind? Oh, God,
did he make me blind?

And why can't I hear?
No chatter. No footsteps.
No *whoosh* of machines.
No squeak of bedsprings.
What else did he take from me?

I try to move again,
but I must be strapped down.
Either that or all that's left
of me is my fingers. No pain.
That's good. I can unhinge
my jaw. But when I open
my mouth, no sound comes out.

At Least, I Don't Think

Any sound came out, because now
there's movement around me.
Someone touches my hand,
and I know it's Mom, the feel
of her skin so familiar, plucked
from recollection. "Help me,"
I want to say, and maybe I do.

But I can't hear my voice,
can't see Mom's face. I'm desperate
to know what's wrong with me,
but all she can do is stroke my arm,
and I imagine her talking to me,
telling me everything will be okay,
be calm. And I try. For her.

But I'm scared. So scared.
Do I have legs? I work real hard,
and my right foot jerks.
Oh my God, is there a left one?
"Help me, Mama." Instead,
I feel her move away, replaced
by someone else, and now
comes a rush of contentment.
Not quite pleasure, but close.
At least they've got good drugs
in here. Going, going . . .

Time Has No Meaning

Not in this place.
I rise up into soundless,
sightless consciousness.
Have no clue how long
I've been in suspended
animation. I find I can lift
my hands and I bring them
to my face, most of which

seems to be covered with
gauze. Bandages swaddle
my head, cover my eyes.
Maybe I won't be blind
when those are removed.
Or maybe I'm still going to die.

I lie as motionless as possible
so they don't put me back
under. I swear if I make it,
the first thing I'm going to do
is tell Alexa I love her.
I think she's been here.
I can smell her perfume
afloat the antiseptic.
Will I ever see her face
again? Damn. Popped

my own bubble. Why would
I think Alexa—or any girl—
would want a sightless me?

I consider life minus eyes.
I could never drive again,
never shoot, never ride
my bike along the river.
And that makes me think
of Hayden on a blanket . . .
No. Not Hayden. Alexa.

My sweetest Alexa, hot and
luscious in my bed. I'm crazy
with need for her. Kissing
her face, her neck, down
over her belly, close to that
special spot between those
beautiful legs, and almost there

when "Back in Black" interrupts
us. Now it's Luke I see and
always will, with or without
functioning eyes, his own eyes
forever sightless, and I know
redemption is lost to me. . . .

And I Ascend

From the depths again.
Up, up, into awareness.
But there's something
different this time,
somewhere in the darkness.
Sound. A slight vibration.

a-a-a-a

I focus, give it my complete
attention, and it grows into
a low rumble.

A-a-a-a.

It's the first sound of any
kind I've heard since . . .
whenever, and I rejoice.

A-A-A-A.

What is it? Not mechanical,
I don't think. More vocal.
"Hello? Is someone there?"
Can you hear me if you are?

A-A-A-I

I wish I could see. "Can you
come closer?" I do think
the rumble is a voice. A man's?

A-A-A-l-l-f

Low. Familiar. I know it.
Dad? No. Uncle Jessie? No.
Younger.

A-A-l-l-f-f-a

And suddenly it sinks in.
"Luke?" I've either gone crazy
or they're upping my meds.

Alphatryptonites

It can't be! "Luke? Where
are you? I can't see you.
It's too dark. Luke! What
is it? What do you want?"
Everything falls completely
silent again. "No! Don't go!"

Comes a whisper,
Alphatryptonites forgive.

Stunned

I can only pretend to process
what just occurred—or didn't.

I don't believe in otherworldly
anythings. There was no Luke.

So why did I call out to him?
I've got some major shit embedded

in my psyche, that's for sure.
Who knows what opiates might

dislodge? On the other hand,
a low haze of pain shimmers.

When was the last time they gave
me anything? I need answers,

damn it, not hallucinations. "Luke?"
But of course, no answer will come.

Whatever that was has deserted me.
Although, wait. If that was, indeed,

a piece of my psyche, I hope it left
the good stuff behind. Is there good stuff?

As I lie here, surrounded by suffocating
darkness digesting possibilities,

I may not be able to see, but a couple
of things have become very clear.

I can hear something, and not some
inexplicable thing, but some external

corporeal noise. It's muffled, almost
a whisper of conversation or maybe

a television. I've exited the well
of total silence. The other thing is

even more important. No, it's vital.
Either some ghost of my little brother

just traveled light-years, traversing
the wilderness of death to forgive me,

or I have forgiven myself.

After

It's been three months since Augustus
Lee Swanson went out to the Turner
Shooting Range looking for some
warped form of justice. Experts have

profiled him, and while they might
have argued exactly what set him off,
they all agreed post-traumatic stress
disorder was a contributing factor.

I could've told them that. What
saved most of the building—and me—
was his triggering the device while
still inside the locker room, containing

most of the shrapnel and much of
the explosion's force. Had I not chosen
to run in the opposite direction, well,
who knows? That's the good news.

Not so good? Major mistake, and
one I'll remember in case I'm ever
again hauling ass away from a bomb,
was glancing back over my shoulder

just about the exact second everything
blew. I remember none of this, of course,
but when shards of wood and metal
went flying, my face became a target.

Small splinters hit my left eye, while
a larger projectile punctured my right
cornea. With a transplant, my vision
will improve immensely, at least

that's the promise. Right now, it's like
peering through sheer dark curtains.
As for my hearing, I'm not completely
deaf. I mean, if you shout at the top

of your lungs, I can pick out a few
key phrases. It may get better with time,
but maybe not. But, hey, technology
has done wonders with hearing aids.

So what if I look like a decrepit old man
when I'm barely old enough to vote?
I'm slowly getting used to the idea
that I'll never exactly be normal again.

But Maybe Normal Is Overrated

Because abnormal me
has discovered that I've got
a lot to live for. My family—
near and extended—has rallied
around me. As I recovered,
both pairs of grandparents
spent many hours reading to me
Yes, the Creswell coots read
from the Bible, but I couldn't hear
most of it anyway, not even when
they AMPLIFIED. And, much to
my amusement, Grandpa Coot also
read James Bond—his "guilty pleasure."

What was truly important, lying
there in the semidarkness,
was the company, and I also found
that with aunts, uncles, cousins,
and friends, many of whom
I'd thought lost to me. Funny
how a near-death experience
brings perspective, both to the guy
who almost died, and also
to those who just about lost him.

Best of All

Abnormal me has a stellar
girlfriend. Alexa is my bedrock,
and as I work on dressing myself
in the clothes Lorelei laid out for
me (color coordination was never
my best thing, but now it's ridiculous),

she's in the living room, waiting
to drive me (in the Ford, which needs
a good romp that I can't give it at
the moment) to Uncle Jessie's wedding.
He and Quin delayed their nuptials
until I could get on my feet again.

> He probably wouldn't have, as anxious
> as he was, but Quin insisted. *It's kind
> of the least we can do, considering
> he got blown up on your behalf,
> don't you think?* Not much he could
> say to that. Weirdly, his heart attack

might very well have saved his life.
What probably salvaged mine
were the first responders who pulled
me from the rubble and stanched
the bleeding. Glad they finished
their doughnuts and got there when they did.

Near As I Can Tell

From the intensity of light through my
window (muted though my traitor
eyes might interpret it), it's a gorgeous
spring day. Perfect for saying "I do"
on an old covered bridge, family

gathered round. I'm including Lorelei
in that description. She has also
been wonderful to me, and though
I still question the way they went
about it, I have come to terms with

Dad's relationship with her. Mom
has forged ahead with her new life,
as I must with mine, whatever the end
product might be. I'll probably never
be a shooting team star, but I will

go to college and hopefully discover
my passion. Who knows? Maybe it
is politics, but until I go looking,
how can I ever find it? I might even
study comparative religion.

I've Thought and Thought

About what happened
in the hospital, and I still
have no clue if my close
encounter was real or imagined.

But it has unlocked my mind
to possibilities. And those
are something I'm eager
to explore. The door opens

and Alexa glides across
the room, at least, that's
how it looks to me. Now
she straightens the buttons

I've managed to get crooked.
Then she lifts up on her toes
to give me a kiss, and it is soft
and warm, filled with promise.

When she breaks away, I pull
her back close, promise, "I love
you." Because if there's one
thing I've learned through all

this, it's to have faith in love.

Author's Note

The idea for *Rumble* germinated a couple of years ago. It was right after the second of two mosque burnings here in the US. As a card-carrying liberal Lutheran whose beliefs run more toward the spiritual than the biblical, I posted on Facebook: *We all serve one Creator*, meaning Christians, Jews, Muslims and, in fact, all human beings. I was prepared for a negative backlash, but not for the comment that came from a sixteen-year-old girl.

It's awfully arrogant of you to think we have to believe in anything, she said. *I happen to be an atheist.*

Her comment struck a chord. In considering it, I kept coming back to the thought that being a teen should be about asking big questions, rather than cutting yourself off from them. Not, "there can't possibly be," but, rather, "what if there is?" Or even, "what if it's completely different than anyone assumes?"

When I'm building stories, my characters spring to life and often tell me things about themselves I didn't know going in. Matt's interest in guns was a surprise, but I went with it, and it completely suits his character. His uncle Jessie and the veteran Gus were unplanned originally, but served to facilitate the climax of the book. I had researched PTSD for *Collateral*, so I understood why war vets sometimes go off. On a personal level, while I enjoy target shooting, I also believe stricter gun regulations are necessary to prevent incidents like the one in this book.

Probably the most interesting piece of information my research for *Rumble* netted was in looking at why some bullied kids commit suicide while the majority of them don't. The common denominator seems to be depression, which is rooted in brain chemistry and can be intensified by external pressures. Antidepressants can be tricky in teens, sometimes even initiating a suicide attempt.

I do research every book heavily. Primary research is best, and I talk to many different people who have experienced the things I write about.

Sometimes they've touched me personally, as is the case with book challenges. Usually my characters share my opinions, but not always, and I have to remain true to who they are. When I said they spring to life, they do.

Some interesting statistics:

- According to the Department of Veteran Affairs (VA), our armed forces face an epidemic of suicide, with a service member committing suicide every 25 hours and a veteran committing suicide every 65 minutes.
- Also according to the VA, "the presence of firearms in households has been linked to increased risk of injury or death for everyone in or around the home, usually as an impulsive act during some disagreement."
- According to the Center for Disease Control and Prevention, suicide is the third leading cause of death among young people, resulting in some 4,400 deaths per year. For every suicide among young people, there are at least 100 suicide attempts.
- Bullying victims are 2 to 9 times more likely to consider suicide than nonvictims, according to studies by Yale University.
- A study in England found that at least half of suicides among young people are related to bullying.

Suicide is a complex issue, exacerbated by depression, feelings of hopelessness, lack of self-esteem, family problems, and other factors. Signs of depression and thoughts of suicide are:

- Dropping grades
- Losing interest in favorite activities
- Withdrawing socially
- Sleeping more or less than normal
- Throwing or giving away treasured items
- Marked changes in personality

If you notice these symptoms in a friend or loved one, take action right away. Help is available. Don't be afraid to ask for it.